MESSSAG[E]
A DEA[D]

"It's a suicide note, Mr. Hawley," said Edward Kane.

"I found the tape on my father's desk this morning . . . sitting right in the middle of the blotter next to the recorder he must have used to make it with. I put it in the machine and turned it on . . . and that's when I heard my father say he was going down to Logan's Town to *kill himself*."

"This isn't a television drama," I said. "It's not normal to suspect things without a reason. Do you have a reason, Mr. Kane?"

"Yes," he said simply. "My father was rich."

"And?"

"And it's not his voice on that tape."

"You're certain?" I asked. "I mean, you're *convinced*?"

"Absolutely." He nodded resolutely. "There's just no way to prove it."

But that's where he was wrong . . .

A BILL HAWLEY UNDERTAKING

BE SURE TO READ *FINAL VIEWING*— BILL HAWLEY'S GRIPPING DEBUT!

MORE MYSTERIES FROM THE BERKLEY PUBLISHING GROUP ...

DOG LOVERS' MYSTERIES STARRING HOLLY WINTER: With her Alaskan malamute Rowdy, Holly dogs the trails of dangerous criminals. "A gifted and original writer." —Carolyn G. Hart

by Susan Conant

A NEW LEASH ON DEATH

A BITE OF DEATH

DEAD AND DOGGONE

PAWS BEFORE DYING

DOG LOVERS' MYSTERIES STARRING JACKIE WALSH: She's starting a new life with her son and an ex–police dog named Jake ... teaching film classes and solving crimes!

by Melissa Cleary

A TAIL OF TWO MURDERS

SKULL AND DOG BONES

DOG COLLAR CRIME

FIRST PEDIGREE MURDER

HOUNDED TO DEATH

CHARLOTTE GRAHAM MYSTERIES: She's an actress with a flare for dramatics—and an eye for detection. "You'll get hooked on Charlotte Graham!"
—*Rave Reviews*

by Stefanie Matteson

MURDER AT THE SPA

MURDER ON THE SILK ROAD

MURDER AT TEATIME

MURDER AT THE FALLS

MURDER ON THE CLIFF

DEWEY JAMES MYSTERIES: America's favorite small-town sleuth! "Highly entertaining!"—*Booklist*

by Kate Morgan

DAYS OF CRIME AND ROSES

WANTED: DUDE OR ALIVE

BILL HAWLEY UNDERTAKINGS: Meet funeral director Bill Hawley—dead bodies are his business, and sleuthing is his passion ...

by Leo Axler

FINAL VIEWING

DOUBLE PLOT

PEACHES DANN MYSTERIES: Peaches has never had a very good memory. But she's learned to cope with it over the years ... Fortunately, though, when it comes to murder, this absentminded amateur sleuth doesn't forgive and forget!

by Elizabeth Daniels Squire

WHO KILLED WHAT'S-HER-NAME?

REMEMBER THE ALIBI

A BILL HAWLEY UNDERTAKING

DOUBLE PLOT

LEO AXLER

BERKLEY PRIME CRIME, NEW YORK

DOUBLE PLOT

A Berkley Prime Crime Book / published by arrangement with the author

PRINTING HISTORY
Berkley Prime Crime edition / October 1994

ISBN: 0-425-14407-0

Berkley Prime Crime Books are published by
The Berkley Publishing Group,
200 Madison Avenue, New York, New York 10016.
The name BERKLEY PRIME CRIME and the BERKLEY PRIME CRIME design are trademarks belonging to Berkley Publishing Corporation.

PRINTED IN THE UNITED STATES OF AMERICA

10   9   8   7   6   5   4   3   2   1

To Sue, my wife.
Love you always.

ONE

■■■■■■■■■

MRS. VICTORIA KANE arrived at exactly eleven-thirty on the morning of Friday, October 23, to make arrangements for the funeral of her husband, Alexander, who had been killed in a car wreck on a lonely country road in Logan's Town, Ohio, just south of Cleveland, early that morning. Mr. Kane's was the first funeral I ever had in my new funeral home, and I wish I could say that everything went smoothly. But the dead man's son, having read about me in the newspaper, decided that the best thing he could do to help his grieving mother through the emotional upheaval surrounding the funeral was to gum up the works in a way that might yet cost me my license, and, by extension, the business upon which I've hung the whole of my future.

My name's Bill Hawley, and at the time of Alexander Kane's death, my funeral home had been open almost exactly six weeks. I'd watched the building rise up from a hole in the ground over a thirteen-month period, costing over half a million dollars that was underwritten by my father, who had used the funeral home that he and his younger brother owned as collateral for my loan. What no one but my dad, my wife, and I knew was that I had "acquired" 375,000 dollars in cash in a rather unusual way six months before we broke ground—which is a story in itself. That money was presently sitting in a safe in my dad's office and would be used to pay the bills during that inevitable dry period during which a fledgling business sits empty. It would also serve as a buffer between me and losing my shirt, which, considering all the Cadillacs and crystal chandeliers a funeral home entails, is no small threat.

I built the place because I hoped that it would give me the sense of independence I'd always yearned for but had never felt prior to that point in my life. I'm thirty-three years old, and from the day I stepped out of college to the moment the new place officially opened, I had worked for my dad. I saw my own business as a chance to prove myself without having to depend on my father for a living. It might sound goofy to someone who's never been there, but being the "and Son" in a sign reading, "So-and-so and Son, Whatever, Inc." is hard. You'd probably think that the "and Son" would have it made. And when viewed one way, you'd be right. But on the flip side is that inevitable, often unspoken implication that, "The kid sure came up the hard way. His father worked his ass off, and now he's gettin' the gravy." My dad calls it, "another American success story," and it's an attitude that gnawed at me for the entire eleven years I worked for him. Eventually, it got so bad that I ended up feeling that every time he handed me a paycheck, he was actually slipping me my allowance. Not that he ever said anything to foster that impression, but by the time I turned thirty, it was about all I ever felt.

So I've got a lot riding on the new place. Not just financially, but psychologically as well. And with that kind of pressure, those first six weeks of goodwilled coffee with any priest or minister who'd hold still, while the phone sat silent and the building sat empty, almost killed me. By the time Mrs. Kane parked her creamy white Lexus in my lot, I was so relieved at finally having something to do that I was virtually trembling with anticipation.

She was about forty-five years old, on the tall side for a woman, trim, with tinted silver-blond hair done in a short, day-at-the-office/drinks-at-seven kind of cut, a unique style of eye shadow that made her otherwise very English/European features look a little Egyptian, and diamonds practically dripping off her. There was some real money in this family, I thought, which meant that they probably wouldn't be spending much of it on a funeral. The successful folks, on average, don't usually "believe in funerals," which translates to not believing in big funeral bills. Not that a person's philosophy is any of my business. My job isn't selling things, it's providing a service. It's just that more often than not it's the people who go the old "pine box" route that feel the need to explain themselves to me, which I find embarrassing.

Introducing myself, I offered her coffee, which she declined, saying as she took a seat with a very ladylike brush of her skirt that she'd wait for her son to arrive. Edward was a twenty-year-old college sophomore, she said, who lived on the east side of town. After half an hour of waiting, she called his apartment, but no one was home. By twelve-thirty it was pretty obvious that he wasn't going to show, and she went ahead and made the arrangements without him, dry-eyed all the way, cool and efficient.

I could tell from her manner that she was a businessperson, and while we were putting together her husband's death notice, she instructed me to mention the "Kane Antique and Collectible Company," which she and her husband jointly owned. I said that my wife, Natalie, was into antiques, and asked her where her shop was located. When she said, "Our main store is in the Tower City Center, downtown," I was duly impressed. Tower City's a ritzy setup, recently built by one of Cleveland's most successful developers, and full of shops that are reputed to be the best and most expensive in town. After the funeral was over, and "things go back to normal," Mrs. Kane invited me to bring my wife down for a tour. "I'm sure she'll find something nice in her price range," she said. And I replied that I doubted it, considering how tight money was for us just then, but I promised we'd stop by anyway.

She decided that one evening viewing, from seven until nine on Sunday, would be sufficient. Funerals were so morbid, she said, and she didn't believe in dragging them out. We'd have a parlor service Monday morning, conducted by a Methodist minister, to whom she had already spoken. The reception would be at a restaurant near the cemetery. She chose a stainless steel casket, a 12-gauge regular steel vault, and a navy-blue, pin-striped suit. "And I don't want any of that horrible, piped-in funeral music during the viewing," she added with a tone of conviction so strong that it made me look up from what I was writing. "There was music playing at my father's wake, and it drove me up the wall."

I made a note in the file, "No Horrible Music," and she rose and shook my hand, saying, "And please, Mr. Hawley, don't think badly of me because I haven't cried. I'm just numb all over . . . from shock, I guess. My husband and I were married for twenty-three years. And I think there's still a pretty big part of me, even after coming here, that doesn't really believe he's gone. I suppose it'll sink in when I actually see him in his coffin, but right now I honestly can't say that any of this feels real. It's more . . . I don't know . . . dreamlike, somehow. You know, as if it were so thin that I could just reach up and put my hand through it. But that doesn't make much sense, does it?"

I said nothing, smiling my most understanding smile and letting her talk.

"Do you think it's possible for a person to hurt so badly that they can't even feel it?" she continued after a moment's thought, her forehead wrinkling with concentration, and her eyes settling on mine. "I've read that people who have limbs cut off in accidents don't feel anything until later when the wound starts to ache as it heals. There's supposed to be a mechanism in the body that protects itself from feeling more pain than it can handle by just shutting off all sensation and leaving a person numb. Do you think that might be what's happened to me? That I've gone numb in self-defense?"

I said that I thought it was entirely possible and assured her that everyone experienced grief in their own unique way, so that analyzing her reactions wasn't really the way to go. I concluded by saying that a funeral's true function is to create an environment where conflicting emotions can work themselves out, and that to that end she should let me know if there was anything at all I could do to make things easier, no matter how silly or trivial the request might sound.

"You'd be amazed at how much difference the littlest things can make," I said. "Tea instead of coffee, pastry for your guests during the viewing, maybe a photograph of your husband on a side table. The next couple of days will probably go by in a blur. But later on you'll start developing a memory, and I think you'll be surprised at the images that will have stuck in your mind. Chances are it won't be the big things, like the casket, or the pallbearers. It'll be the small details that'll linger; and, though I can't make this a pleasant experience, it's my job to make sure that the memory you take away is the one you need to have for your own peace of mind."

She nodded, squeezed my hand again, looked blankly ahead for a moment, and said something about not understanding why her son had stood her up. Then she left, digging for her car keys in her purse as she stepped through the door without giving me so much as another glance. I stood at the window in my office and watched her drive away, experiencing the unsettling sensation that I had just engaged in a business transaction as opposed to arranging a funeral. Funeral arrangements invariably involve some kind of emotional expression. It's just a part of the process. But Mrs. Kane, despite her closing argument about feeling "numb," hadn't given off any vibrations at all. And after almost twelve years in the business, I'm more sensitive to vibrations than anything else. I felt as if the emotional energy level in the room had been perfectly flat, as if instead of settling on the details of her husband's final disposition, I had just sold her a car. Or worse, I felt like I'd just bought one from her.

Frowning, I turned back to my desk and thought about the state I'd be in if it were me making funeral arrangements if my wife had been killed in an accident. There wouldn't be any question of numbness there, I decided; I'd be so whacked out I'd probably need a nurse. Nat's the only woman in the world for me. And it's not a question of marriage vows, or morality, or any of the nebulous intellectual bullshit some people use to justify unwilling monogamy. She's just the only woman I want. Now don't get me wrong, I like women. I like them so much that some of the really beautiful ones can make me go a little weak in the knees. But the reason Nat's my wife is that we just seem to belong together, as if we were made as a set. If something should happen to her, I couldn't even imagine how I'd respond. Also, though I work very hard at hiding it from the people I serve, I'm such an intrinsically emotional person that I've been known to cry after conducting funerals for people I've never even met. Mrs. Kane was apparently one of those remarkable individuals who can keep their feelings locked up inside. And in a way I admired her for it. But at the same time it made me uneasy because I've always wondered if people like her actually have anything to lock away.

I was just starting to dial the vault company when the doorbell rang. Thinking Mrs. Kane had forgotten something, I opened the door to find, instead of her rock-steady gaze, a whisper-thin young man with longish blond hair, eyes red from crying, and a high-pitched, tremulous voice that was filled with so much emotion that it cracked as he exclaimed, "I've been waiting across the street for over an hour. I thought she'd never leave!"

He was dressed in a white V-neck sweater, tan slacks, and brown loafers with no socks. (Why don't kids wear socks anymore?) His entire body radiated irritation, and every time he spoke I received a blast of booze breath— probably gin, I deduced from long, personal experience. I knew he was Edward Kane because his facial resemblance to his mother was almost eerie. And the first question out of his mouth was, "Tell me, please, what did they put down as my father's cause of death?" In return I asked him if he'd spoken to his mother since she left. He flapped his hand dismissively and glowered. "Don't worry about that. Just tell me, what killed my dad?"

"Unspecified internal injuries," I said, quoting what I'd been told over the phone by the Wittmere County Hospital, since Mr. Kane's body had yet to be released.

"Oh my God!" he moaned, flopping himself down on the same chair his mother had occupied for the previous hour and throwing his arm up so that the back of his hand covered his eyes like a lady having a swoon in a

Gothic romance. I thought he was reacting to the tragedy of his father's death after bracing his nerve in a college bar somewhere. But when I tried to express my sympathies, his face snapped up and he reached into his pocket, producing a black plastic audiocassette and saying, "I've read about how you help people in trouble, Mr. Hawley. There were those articles in the *Plain Dealer* . . . and I've seen you on the local TV news. Well, nobody has ever needed your help more than I do now. You can believe me when I say that. And I can pay you whatever you ask."

His words made the back of my neck tingle, and I glanced first at the tape, and then at his face, saying, "I'm not following," with as noncommittal a tone as I could manage, even though the prospect of a "case" had my palms feeling a little damp. I'm known as the "sleuthing undertaker," and even though I think the title's a little silly, it goes a long way toward capturing the essence of who and what I really am.

"It's a suicide note," he explained, rising and laying the tape on the blotter before me. "I found it on my father's desk this morning. I got home after my mother left. I was a little late. I was upset. I must have just missed her. I let myself in with my key, but she was already gone, and the house was just so empty and quiet that this horrible sadness washed right over me. When I was a little boy, my dad used to sit me on his knee when he was working at his desk . . . and, I don't know why, but I wandered into his office and threw myself down in his chair, crying like a baby. That's when I noticed the tape, sitting right in the middle of the blotter next to the recorder he must have used to make it with. I don't know what made me do it, but I put it in the machine and turned it on . . . and that's when I heard my father saying that he was going to Logan's Town to *kill himself*."

He paused as if collecting his thoughts, sighed, and continued with a shrug. "Well, I didn't know what to do. Mom had said that he died in a car wreck. But she obviously hadn't heard the tape. God, could you imagine? I knew she'd be here, so I waited across the street until she left so I could turn it over to you."

When I asked him what he wanted me to do with it, he got very excited and said, "I want you to find out what happened to my dad! This tape says that he was planning to kill himself, but those redneck cops in that jerkwater town say he died in an accident. Something's going on, Mr. Hawley! Don't you see? My father was a very influential man, and he had business dealings all over the world. Coincidences don't happen to men like him. They just don't!"

I picked up the cassette and turned it over, thinking that even if there was something to this, the kid had handled the tape, so any fingerprints on it were already ruined. Looking up, I said, "Okay, so let's say for argument's sake that your father did in fact take his own life, and that for whatever reason, the Logan's Town police got it wrong. Why is that something you'd want to prove?"

He eyed me intently, tears welling and lips pale as he said, "What do you mean?"

"Well," I began, trying to be tactful, "suicide usually cancels life insurance payments, and it's hell on the family. If the coroner ruled your father's death accidental, why don't you just let it go?"

"If it was *your* father," Edward Kane said, his eyes going cold, "would you let it go?"

It was a good question. So good, in fact, that I didn't even try to answer it. Instead I asked, "What kind of insurance did he have?"

"Tons."

"So by asking me to disprove suicide . . ."

Edward Kane stood up, suddenly looking and sounding more like his mother. "I'm not asking you to prove or disprove anything," he announced. "What I want is the truth. That's all. He was my father, and I owe it to him."

"What you want to know is whether or not someone killed him. Isn't that it?" I asked.

"Exactly," he returned.

I examined the tape again, more as a way of moving my eyes from his face than because I expected to find anything

I'd missed before. I didn't like the authoritarian demeanor he'd suddenly assumed. All that people who try to push me around usually succeed in doing is pissing me off.

"This isn't a television drama," I said. "And by nature I'm an extremely skeptical person." I cocked a thumb toward the door, adding, "People come through that door ten times a day,"—I was exaggerating a little, but he didn't know it—"and they almost never talk like you're talking now. It's not normal for someone to suspect things without a reason. Do you have a reason, Mr. Kane?"

"Yes," he said simply.

"Well, what is it?"

"My father was rich."

"And?"

"And it's not his voice on that tape."

"What?"

"It just doesn't sound like him," he exclaimed, wringing his hands and losing that look of determination he'd assumed so briefly in favor of the "little boy lost" expression I suspected was more his natural state. "That's why I waited for my mother to leave. I sat at the desk at home and listened to that tape over and over again . . . and no matter how many times I did, I couldn't get it out of my mind that it was all a load of bullshit! It's not my dad. Don't you see? I don't know who would do such a thing, but that's somebody else imitating him—and doing a pretty fair job of it, too. But they can't fool me. He was my father, after all. I know his voice. And that one's bullshit, Mr. Hawley. Somebody left it for us to find!"

My thoughts were suddenly tangled, and all I could think to say was, "Are you sure?"

He looked at me with exactly the cross expression I deserved.

Finally I said, "Well . . . if you're right, that does . . . uhm . . ."

"Fuck things up?" he asked, with some of his mother's confidence returning to his face.

"Yeah," I agreed.

He had me interested, and I think he knew it. Crossing his arms over his chest, he looked suddenly grim and said, "My proposition is this: I'll pay you to look into it. That's all I'm asking. I'm not suggesting that you go out and chase down any killers or anything like that. I just want you to poke around until you're satisfied that there's enough here for me to go to the police. As it stands, all I've got is my word that my father didn't make that tape. He's dead, so there's no way to prove he did or didn't make it. But if I'm right, and someone did do something to him . . . there"—he closed his eyes and sighed—"I've said it. If someone did do something to him . . . then I want to be able to go to the police with something in my hand that will make them listen to me. Find that something for me, Mr. Hawley. Please. If you don't, I'm sure I'll go crazy knowing what I know."

"You're certain this isn't your father's voice?" I asked, unnecessarily. "I mean, you're *convinced*?"

"Absolutely." He nodded resolutely. "There's just no way to prove it."

But that's where he was wrong.

It was eleven o'clock that night before I figured out how I was going to check the accuracy of Edward Kane's suspicions. Flipping on the prep room's fluorescent lights, I imagined video cameras and microphone stands arrayed around the embalming table, with klieg lights hitting the stainless steel, and me standing over the body, narrating the proceedings. Being an audiovisual junkie, I had everything I'd need to recreate the scene stuffed in my bedroom closet upstairs. But a videotape of what I had decided to do could land me in court. So, appropriately outfitted in a pair of red boxer shorts and a black BATMAN RETURNS T-shirt, I approached the embalming table armed with a portable cassette recorder, convinced that making a dead man "talk" was the only way I was going to settle the nag of worry that had been playing on my mind.

Lying naked beneath a sheet, face serene, eyes closed, his thick brown hair combed straight back, and his mouth set in what was almost a smile, was Mr. Alexander Kane, looking like a different man from the one I'd picked up after making his funeral arrangements with his wife. In the hospital's morgue he had been grimacing, eyes open, his flesh a deep purple-blue, with rivulets of dried blood running every which way from all the incisions inflicted on him by the Wittmere County coroner. It had taken my uncle Joe nearly three hours to make him look presentable, which is something that the general public usually misses about embalmed bodies when they see them in a funeral home. People will glance at a remains and turn up their noses saying, "He doesn't look like himself," as if they were critiquing a painting. "He looks puffy," or, "His skin looks so hard," or, "What did they do to his mouth?" are all things funeral directors hear practically every day.

What people don't realize is that dead bodies start changing at the instant life departs. At the moment a person expires, *E. coli* bacteria in the intestine start digesting the body from the inside out. Gasses form, blood settles, muscles harden, and skin contracts. The longer the interval between death and embalming, the further the process proceeds. And that's not even mentioning the cause of death itself. Every terminal event leaves some evidence to mark its passing, most of which—believe it or not—is erased by embalming. Those serene expressions Americans expect when they view their departed loved ones don't just happen; they're *set* by the embalmer. When a person dies, whatever expression was on his or her face at that instant *stays there*. That's why a funeral director, who sees the before and after of death every day, usually pays more attention to the body at a wake than the family does. In his heart he knows that the image of the deceased he's giving the people he serves is one that is so much more palatable than the reality of death that it's actually a kind of mercy.

Seeing how different Mr. Kane looked now, compared to what he'd looked like when I'd brought him in, I was reminded yet again that the business I was in was based primarily on concealing uncomfortable truths. Maybe that's why I do the other things I do . . . the snooping . . . the risk. Maybe it's because intrinsically I reject deception, even when it's intended as a comfort, that I'm driven to uncover things that other people have tried so hard to hide.

To that end I stepped up to the head of the embalming table and slid my arms under Mr. Kane's cold shoulders so that my hands were threaded under his arms and over his chest. The top of his head rested against my stomach, and the tape recorder's condenser microphone was aimed directly at his mouth. Gently, I slid him toward me a little, braced myself, and squeezed. Nothing happened, so, with a slight readjustment of my position, I braced myself and squeezed again, this time considerably harder, producing a slight gurgling sound in the dead man's throat and forcing up a stream of pink embalming fluid which trickled out of the corner of his mouth. Frustrated, I laid his head back into the hard rubber head block and considered my options.

Dead people groan all the time. Anyone who has ever gone on a body call knows that there's a couple of different levels of air in the lungs, and that even after death there's usually enough deep air left to vibrate the vocal chords if you bend a corpse at the waist when you're pulling it out of bed. It's not even unusual for bodies to groan after they've been embalmed. But the coroner had cut open Mr. Kane's chest and taken his lungs out, along with everything else that was inside him, leaving Uncle Joe with an empty cavity that he had stuffed with cotton wadding. The only way I was going to get any air to come out of there was to first put some back in. So, after wiping the purged fluid off the dead man's chin, I carefully undid the wire Uncle Joe had strung between the screws he had placed in Mr. Kane's upper and lower jaws to keep his mouth shut. Then I stepped into the attached garage off the prep room's delivery door and cut myself about a ten-inch piece of garden hose from a length we had wound on a spool. I took that hose, rubbed a little Vaseline on it to make it slippery, and worked it down Mr. Kane's throat.

Glancing over my shoulder, I checked the embalming room's door, hoping that my wife wouldn't choose this particular moment to come strolling in to see why I wasn't in bed. Then, taking a deep breath and mentally trying to convince myself that I wasn't off my nut, I blew into the hose, hard, hearing a gurgle deep inside Mr. Kane and seeing his abdomen swell ever so slightly. Putting my thumb over the end of the hose, I withdrew it and clamped my hand over the dead man's mouth, maneuvering myself back to the head of the table and picking up my tape recorder as I worked my arms over his chest again. This time, when I squeezed, instead of a feeble, almost inaudible gurgle, I got a solid groan, about three seconds long that, when replayed on my cassette, sounded like anything but the voice of a dead man.

Satisfied that I had what I needed, I left Nat a note, got dressed, and headed downtown, pulling into the county morgue's parking lot at just after midnight. The top was down on my Miata, and the late October air was unseasonably warm. They call Cleveland the "North Coast" because it's located on the southern shore of Lake Erie, one of the Great Lakes that separates the continental U.S. from Canada. All that water does a number on our weather, and it's not unusual for our temperature to rise or fall twenty degrees in a single day, particularly in the spring or autumn. My Miata—which technically belongs to my wife—is a little two-seater Mazda sports car that's red, way cool, and that a friend of mine juiced up by dropping in a Ford V-8 with a four-barrel carb. When you own a convertible in Cleveland, you learn to use it every chance you get, because once the nasty weather sets in, your top might stay up for three or four months.

Rusty Simmons was waiting behind the reception desk, his eyes gleaming with amusement and his mouth stretched into a grin. Rusty's my best buddy downtown, and our friendship goes back to when I was fifteen, which is almost twenty years now, God help me. They used to call me "Wild Bill" because me and a guy named Walter did all the morgue runs for North Coast Medical Services, a private ambulance company just starting out. We had one old station wagon, a broken-down Chevy van, a hearse, and no business doing half the shit we did. The owner had decided to try making a go of it over boilermakers in my grandparents' bar, and my only qualification for even riding in the back of an ambulance was that my father was a fireman. The morgue contract was lucrative but a pain in the ass for the grunts actually doing the work: five bucks a body, anytime, day or night. They didn't call me Wild Bill for nothing.

Rusty led me up to the second floor, speaking pleasantries and shaking his head a lot. He's a big man, weighing in at about 280, which he carries mostly around his waist. He's about six foot three, with very dark skin. At one time his hair had been red, thus his nickname, but at sixty-four he's almost completely grey now, and has gone bald on top. He has the biggest hands I've ever seen on a man, and the story goes that in his younger days he was a prizefighter, which he denies. But what he's really known for is his book, a carefully indexed collection of police and coroner's reports he keeps of all the murders that go through the morgue. At first the higher-ups frowned on his penchant for collecting the details of violent crime, but recently his book, which is the most thorough and well-organized record anyone has ever seen, has come to be regarded as a kind of natural resource, and cops who had been clandestinely slipping him information for years have started openly contributing material, knowing they've got the wink from upstairs.

At the end of the hall on the morgue's second floor is a room where the coroner's investigators store some of the hocus-pocus shit they've been able to persuade the disbursements officer to let them buy. Morgue investigators mostly check addresses on people who are found dead without relatives, interview neighbors, run down bankbooks, and verify social security numbers. They don't really need a lie detector, or a microscopic camera designed to photograph clothing fibers—that kind of work is done at the police lab down the street—but the morgue guys have them anyway, and there they sit, in room 247, locked up like a museum. Included in this collection is a voice spectrograph, an unusual device that came into vogue during the 1970's when it was thought that suspects could be "fingerprinted" with recordings of their voices. The reliability of voice spectrograph evidence is so debatable that it's still not admissible in court.

"And this voice you got's from the dead guy?" Rusty asked, turning on the lights.

"Yeah," I said, pulling out the two cassettes I'd brought.

"What's his name?"

I couldn't resist pulling his chain a little as I replied, "What difference does it make? He ain't your case."

"Where'd he come from?"

"Logan's Town."

"Shit."

"The Wittmere County coroner ruled it accidental, man."

"Nitwit County don't *rule* on nothin'; best they can do is guess, and you know it."

"Regardless. It's out of your jurisdiction."

"I wanna keep track anyway."

"Why?"

"Why you bein' obstinate, Bill? Every time you come lookin' for a favor, some kinda shit end up hittin' the fan. You like a shit magnet."

"You know, I'm not really sure how I should take that." I frowned, feigning deep thought. Then I handed over a paper detailing Alexander Kane's particulars as I knew them, saying, "Okay?"

Rusty looked it over, nodded, and said, "Okay. Now tell me 'bout it."

He listened carefully as I went through it, nodding his head a couple of times, and saying when I was finished, "Okay, so what's the plan?"

"The plan," I replied, looking at the voice spectrograph machine, "is to find out exactly what's on this tape. Now, how does this beast work?"

Rusty, who had never finished high school, loves to watch the investigators and doctors in the coroner's office do their jobs. As a result, he knows how to work most of the equipment in the place, and confident that he wouldn't let me down, I sat back and watched him go to it. He chortled and shook his head, saying things like, "I ain't never seen the match to it," under his breath, and in about twenty minutes he had things ready to run.

What he did was to first take the tape I had made in the embalming room, snap on the power to an old reel-to-reel recorder, hook up some wires, and copy the cassette onto the reel. Then he hit something called, "Loop Record," letting the machine run for a couple of minutes before he rewound it and let it play. What he had done was to repeatedly record the "huh" sound I had been able to get Alexander Kane to make so that the tape he now played sounded like, "huh huh huh," over and over again.

"Now for the tricky part," he said, putting the suicide cassette into a player and transferring it onto a reel-to-reel tape while listening to what it said. At one point his eyes lit up, and he hit a counter switch on the reel-to-reel, marking a spot. Then he isolated that spot, which was the first sound in the word, "hundred," recording it in the same way as he had the "huh" sound from my embalming room tape, and saying, "Okay, let's see what we got."

A voice spectrograph machine reads the magnetic markings on a tape and produces an ink representation of them using very sensitive graph etchings similar to the ones on a lie detector. First Rusty ran the suicide tape sound through the machine, getting a graph of something that resembled a pen and ink drawing of flowing water. Then he did the same with the tape of the sound I'd gotten in the embalming room, producing another graph that, just viewed side by side, looked very similar to the first. But when he ran the two graphs through a machine that copied them onto transparency film, laid them one atop the other, and stuck them up on a backlit board like the ones doctors use to read X rays, we were able to make a careful and detailed comparison.

Finally, after about five minutes' study, I straightened up from where I had been leaning over the desk, and said, "Well, we know one thing: they're the same."

"Yup," Rusty agreed. "Not that nobody would pay it any mind in court."

"No." I nodded. "But that's not why I did it. I just wanted to see if the kid was straight."

"Meaning?"

"I don't know. The way it was before, with the old man leaving a tape and going off, it was strange. But now . . ."

"It's weird," Rusty cut in. "Since you know the voice you got outta that body is right, then it looks like the suicide tape really was made by that same guy before he died."

"Yeah," I mused, "in a car accident, on the way to kill himself. That's quite a coincidence."

"Unless driving into a ditch is the way he intended to do it," Rusty offered.

And I said, "Right. Foolproof and painless. And then there's the guy's son . . . flaky as hell and convinced that it's not his dad talking on that tape. So what the fuck is that all about?"

"You're thinkin', ain't you, Bill?" Rusty asked.

I nodded.

"You know, that ain't always a good idea with you."

"Don't worry, man," I said. "I'm just a little interested is all."

"I ain't worried," Rusty said, snapping off the light board and sitting down. "I gave up worryin' about you a long time ago. Now, whenever you show up, I just make sure there's a clean page ready in my book."

TWO

■■■■■■■■■

SINCE ALEXANDER KANE wasn't scheduled to be viewed until Sunday evening, I convinced Nat to drive down to Logan's Town with me on Saturday morning, just to have a "quick look around." The sky was an eggshell blue, washed with watercolor traces of clouds so white as to appear slightly unreal. The temperature had dropped to just below fifty degrees, which meant that after we put the Miata's top down we had to turn on the heat inside the car so that warm air would rise up from around our feet as the cold outside breeze tousled our hair. Logan's Town is about an hour south of where we live, and it wasn't until the city streets gave way to the winding meander of Route 31 that I brought Nat up to speed on Mr. Kane and the suspicions his son had raised about his death . . . for whatever they were worth.

Nat wore dark sunglasses and a black baseball cap with the word MIATA stitched across the front in shiny red letters. She had one hand on her knee and the other on the top of the side window so that the rushing air billowed the sleeve of her forest-green windbreaker and whipped her long black hair into twirling gyrations that seemed almost magically coordinated. In profile, her lovely face looked long, her high cheekbones hinting at the American Indian who was her great-grandmother, her sharp nose descending to a point—which she still teasingly threatened to have surgically altered—and her skin aglow with a pink radiance brought on by the air's stinging cold. We had met in college when I was a junior and she a freshman, and we had been together ever since. I asked her to marry me on our first and only real date—an Ozzy Osbourne concert during which she fell asleep, scaring me half to death because I thought she'd died. She turned me down but told me to try again, which I did periodically for the next three years. The upcoming November fifth was our ninth anniversary, and to celebrate it we were planning a trip to New York City. Nat's only objection to what I was saying about Mr. Kane came when she warned me to be careful about not messing up that trip. And I promised—a bit prematurely, as events would soon demonstrate—that nothing would get in the way of our vacation.

I ran through things chronologically, speaking loudly and squinting against the sunshine that snapped so brightly off the blacktop as to make the road ahead look wet. When I was through, she pursed her lips but kept her opinion to herself.

"If it was just the tape," I shouted, navigating the car over the gently rolling hills that were alive with the fiery blaze of falling leaves, "I think it would almost be enough to get me interested. But it's not. It's Mr. Kane's body, too."

Pulling the cassette of the suicide note out of my jacket pocket, I popped it into the tape player. But before I turned it on, I told her what my uncle Joe had said just before we left for our ride.

Nobody knows a dead body better than an embalmer, and I include coroners in that list when I say it. A coroner will chop up a body and run tests until he or she knows what killed the person who used to call that body home. But an embalmer understands the body itself; he has to, because it's his job to make that body look good. He knows what it's going to do before it does it, and he understands things about the way a person died that bear on what kind of fluid he's going to use to mimic the blush of life.

My uncle Joe Hawlinski, who never legally Americanized the spelling of our Ukrainian name, spent two years as an Army embalmer in Vietnam, sewing body parts back together under slop-house conditions in a morgue in Da Nang. He once told me that before going overseas all the embalmers in his unit were placed together in a room where an officer pronounced the words, Saigon and Da Nang, instructing them to each pick one of the two. Neither meant a thing to Uncle Joe, so he chose Da Nang, which he later learned was a mistake. Saigon was the big city, where Army embalmers worked regular shifts and slept in real beds. Da Nang made the conditions depicted in the old "M.A.S.H." TV show look sophisticated. There, Uncle Joe worked twelve- to sixteen-hour days, often embalming body parts that were so badly mangled that he wasn't sure what they were. You can't buy experience like that, even if you'd want to. Consequently, in the civilian world, he was the hands-down best embalmer in town. And when he said something about a body he'd embalmed, he knew about what he spoke.

When I told him that the Wittmere County coroner had ruled Alexander Kane a "pending—accidental auto" and asked if what he saw of the body went along with that or not, he laughed into the phone, saying, "Who knows?" Uncle Joe explained that the body he had embalmed had been so mutilated that it was impossible for him to say much about it. The coroner down in Logan's Town was eighty-two years old and had a reputation as a real, four-point, G.I., military-style cutter—meaning that when he did an autopsy, he didn't mess around.

"He chopped that guy up one side and down the other," Uncle Joe said, speaking in that clipped, closed-lip way of his. He's my father's younger brother, and people say that over the phone his voice and mine sound alike. "Since that goof a few years ago," he continued with a chuckle, "he's been overcompensating. What he did to . . . what was his name? Kane? What he did to Mr. Kane was a sin. Really, Bill. I'm not exaggerating. There were incisions in that body like I've never seen."

The "goof" to which my uncle referred involved an incident that had happened about five years back when a Logan's Town resident dug up some bones from a field behind his house and took them to the local coroner in hopes of having them identified. After examining the bones, the coroner announced that they were human, and an investigation was begun, complete with rumors of backwoods Satan worshipers sacrificing children during secret ceremonies. Logan's Town got a lot of attention in the local news, until the Cleveland coroner, after having looked over the bones at the request of the Wittmere County Sheriff's Office, revealed that they belonged not to a satanically sacrificed child, but to a sheep. Okay, the reporters wrote, trying to milk a good thing, the Satanists were sacrificing sheep instead of kids. But despite their best efforts the story faded away, leaving an embarrassed coroner determined to protect what was left of his reputation by aggressively posting every body he got near.

"What do you mean, incisions like you've never seen?" I asked. "Are you saying they were suspicious?"

"No, not suspicious, exactly," Uncle Joe responded. "Just excessive. That body could have been hit by a train and I wouldn't have been able to tell. Hell, Bill, they even took vertebrae . . . every internal organ, two ribs, about four vertebrae, and his eyes. And they didn't return the viscera."

Normally the internal organs removed during an autopsy, called the viscera, are returned with the body in a garbage bag that we have to put under the casket's mattress since trying to fit it in the abdominal cavity would be like trying to get toothpaste back in a tube. Not having the viscera returned with Mr. Kane was unusual, and I said so. To which Uncle Joe responded, "Nothing they do in Wittmere County surprises me anymore. When I get a body from out there, I'm happy when it's got both its arms."

When I finished describing my conversation with Uncle Joe, I hit PLAY on the Miata's cassette machine, making the alleged voice of the dead Alexander Kane speak its farewell litany.

"There are a hundred reasons for me to take the coward's way out, and only two reasons not to . . . and they are my wife and son. I'm afraid the numbers just don't add up. So this life of mine is over. That's it. Good-bye."

"That's all?" Nat asked, glancing my way.

"That's all." I nodded, rewinding the tape.

"Not exactly a dramatic farewell."

"And did you notice that he didn't tell his only two reasons to live that he loved them?" I asked. "I've seen a few suicide notes in my time, and apart from the ones left by people suffering from painful diseases that they can't stand anymore, they've all broken down to one of two motivations: love, or hate. You either hate somebody so much that you're getting back at them by taking your own life, or you love them so much that you can't bear either living without them or screwing up their lives with your miserable existence."

"So where's this one fit in?" Nat asked.

I shrugged, watching the road as a big green sign that said, WELCOME TO LOGAN'S TOWN, HOME OF THE MUS-TANGS, flashed past.

"I don't know," I said, after pondering for a moment. "But you'd think that if all he had to say was two or three sentences, he'd have left a note. Dictating a suicide letter into a tape machine seems a little . . . overproduced."

"What do you mean?" Nat asked, turning to face me in her seat.

"If you had two sentences to leave," I asked in return, "wouldn't you just write them down?"

"So you'd be happier with more, huh?"

"Not exactly. I'm just trying to put myself in his place. Okay? I'm Alexander Kane, and I'm about to die. For some reason, I've settled on kicking the big one, and I'm saying farewell to my wife and son, who, theoretically at least, are going to be bummed when they find out what I did. I'm at my desk at home, where, according to Edward Kane, I conduct a good part of my business, including, presumably, some of the correspondence I have with people all over the world. I've got pencils, paper, a computer, a typewriter, and a tape recorder, all sitting right there in front of me. For some reason I choose the tape recorder, maybe because it's more personal, or maybe because it's easier for me to talk than it is to write or type. But whatever my reasoning, I settle on the tape recorder, clear my throat, and produce . . . that." I indicated the Miata's dashboard tape machine with a jerk of my hand. "Kind of feeble, don't you think?"

"Maybe he couldn't think of anything else," Nat offered. "He did have a lot on his mind."

"Maybe. But then why didn't he say so? You know, something like, 'Sorry, honey, I wish I could explain all this to you, but I just can't find the words.' Or, 'I thought I could make you understand, but now I know it's impossible.' A reference, a stumble, an attempt for God's sake. It would have taken him an extra ten seconds tops and left his wife knowing that she was at least in his mind at the end. Instead, he's talking about numbers not adding up and hundreds of reasons for suicide that he never bothers to explain. Unless he was one cold son of a bitch, and even if he was, that's still a pretty lame farewell."

"Maybe that's the reason his son didn't believe it was really his father's voice," Nat offered.

"What do you mean?"

"Maybe he wasn't talking about the timbre of the voice," she explained, "but the way his father expressed himself."

"Meaning what?"

"Meaning that his father was upset and not thinking clearly. Or at least not thinking the way he normally did. So he may not have sounded the way his son was used to hearing him sound."

"So then you don't think there's anything suspicious about that tape at all?"

"I didn't say that. I'm just pointing out that before you accept the word of a drunken, emotional college student whose father just died, maybe you should kind of turn things over a little and see how they look from a couple of different angles."

"But to leave a suicide tape, and then to die in a car wreck the very same night?" I protested.

Nat lifted one hand, saying, "The wreck is a separate issue. Maybe they're not related."

"You really think so?"

"Don't you?"

"No."

"Me neither."

"But you just said . . ." I began, stopping in mid-sentence when I saw the smile spreading over her face. "You make me crazy sometimes, you know that?" I added.

She nodded. "That's my job."

When we got into Logan's Town proper we drove through a central area of about ten streets lined with touristy shops that included an inordinately large number of antique stores. Outside of town the streets spread out, and the houses thinned until we found ourselves amid honest-to-God farms. We turned around and drove through town again, allowing the shape of the place to settle on our minds. The town was laid out like a wheel, with all the streets running into a central square where a gazebo was set up for band concerts. We picked a "family-style" restaurant where we intended to have lunch later that afternoon and, after getting directions at a gas station, headed out to where State Route 16 bisected Lincoln Street, which was supposedly where Mr. Kane had met his death.

It didn't take us long to find the spot. The land was perfectly flat, and there wasn't a house for a hundred yards in any direction. Lincoln Street was a narrow rut of a road that ran across the ribbon of asphalt that was State Route 16. Along it was cut a drainage ditch, and on the southwest side of the intersection two ruts were gouged into that ditch where Mr. Kane's car had come to rest. Apparently what had happened was that Kane, speeding down the state route in the dark, had somehow gotten disoriented and veered off the road, hitting the drainage ditch, which ran across his path on either side of the intersection. His front tires dropped into the ditch, throwing him into the steering wheel, which ruptured his internal organs and killed him.

I parked the Miata on the state route's gravel shoulder, and Nat and I got out to look at the ruts.

"Well," she said, her hair blowing in the stiff wind whipping in off the surrounding fields, "they're ruts, all right."

"At night nobody would have seen a thing from those houses," I said, pointing at the homes visible from where we stood, one to the west, the other to the north. They were both so far away that I couldn't even tell what color they were. "With the headlights pointed down, they might not even notice the car sitting here in the dark. I wonder who lives up there."

While Nat waited, I tried to make sense of the jumble of skid marks burned into the pavement. From what I could tell, it looked as if at least three cars had come to a screeching halt there recently. In the bottom of the ditch was a trickle of brackish water, and it was while I was looking at the muddy flow that I noticed the silver paint sprayed on one of the ditch's walls. It was in the shape of a man, lying with his shoulders down near the water so that his head would have been submerged. Apparently, Mr. Kane had not died in his car, but had gotten out after the accident, only to stumble into the ditch.

"Where's his car now?" Nat asked from where she had placed herself in the Miata's driver's seat.

"Let's find out," I said, slamming my door as she turned us around and headed back to town.

Sheriff Cornell Paulson burst every preconception I had about what a small-town sheriff was going to be like. He was probably my father's age—between fifty-five and sixty—lean, articulate, and friendly. He had dark hair, greying at the temples, styled and blown dry, a nicely trimmed moustache that ended exactly at the edges of his mouth, and a warm handshake accompanied by steady green eyes that looked right at me when he spoke. He didn't give me a hard time at all when I introduced myself, but very politely asked why I wanted to see Mr. Kane's car. When I showed him my private investigator's card—a blue one signifying that I was serving an apprenticeship under a "master investigator"—he smiled wide and slapped me on the back, saying that he had never heard of a funeral director/investigator before, except for "that fella up in Cleveland who's in the paper every now and again."

"That's me," I said, and the expression on his face told me that I had just made a friend.

He walked us around to the back of his office where there was a dirt yard surrounded by an eight-foot cyclone

fence topped with razor wire. Alexander Kane's car sat
off to one side amid a bunch of other cars, mostly junk,
that the sheriff explained were evidence in other cases or
waiting to be claimed by local drunks from whom they had
been impounded, mostly the latter since, "We don't get a
call to do all that much investigating down here." I was
just reaching for the gate when the sound of barking made
me pull back, and a great, flea-bitten dog that looked like
a cross between a Doberman pinscher and a bloodhound
bound out from between two cars, jumped up on the fence,
and snapped its jaws.

"It ain't a real good idea goin' back there," the sheriff
said, smiling at the dog. " 'Cause old Nicholas here takes
his job real serious. Junkyard dog and all." From the fuss
old Nicholas was making, I could see that he certainly did
take his job "real serious." And I could also see, even from
where I stood, that there was no sense pressing my luck.
A closer examination of Mr. Kane's car wouldn't yield me
anything, because its entire front end was gone. It was a
fairly new BMW 325i, gunmetal-blue with a thin silver
accent stripe. Its front tires, bumper, grill, and fenders had
all been removed. "For police purposes, don't you know,"
said Sheriff Paulson, who, I noticed at that moment, with
old Nicholas still barking behind the fence, had not stopped
smiling since I first shook his hand. The driver's side door
on the car was gone, too, and I looked at that gaping hole
for quite a while.

Returning to the office, we found Deputy Churchill King,
or Church, for short, standing by a desk with a coffee mug
in one hand and a cigarette in the other. He was a good six
feet tall, maybe thirty years old, wiry, tanned, and quiet.
To me he looked like maybe he'd seen *Dirty Harry* one
too many times. I disliked him instantly, and the comment
he made about his not "having much truck" with private
investigators as we shook hands after the sheriff's intro-
ductions didn't improve my opinion. We left him to "watch
the shop" while the sheriff treated Nat and me to lunch.
The food was lousy—with Nat and me being vegetarians,
it's hard eating in restaurants anyway—but Nat had a ball

at the antique stores, which, it turned out, are Logan Town's claim to fame.

"Folks out this way know 'bout old stuff," the sheriff explained, strolling along the sidewalk with his thumbs stuck in his belt and a toothpick in his mouth. "We got six shops that sell antiques, and folks come from all over for our Labor Day Fair, when there's stuff spread out on the commons."

I observed that antiques was a rather unusual thing for a small, apparently farm-oriented Ohio community to base its economy on. And the sheriff explained that it was all more or less Alexander Kane's doing.

"He pretty much started it. And his wife, too, of course," he added, tipping his flat-brimmed hat Nat's way. "His father, Ochre . . . we used to call him Okie—old Okie Kane, one glass eye and a stutter—he had a shop that sold the furniture he made by hand. It's the one over yonder with the sign that says, COUNTRY NOTIONS. Alex was raised in that shop, turnin' chair legs on a lathe by the time he was nine. Okie'd sell stuff secondhand, too. Lotta farmers die leavin' their wives needin' cash so bad they have to sell the fixtures. Estate sales in the country can be quite embarrassin'—all your neighbors rootin' through your belongings, bedroom stuff right out there in the bright light of day. So as a courtesy, Okie'd sell the nicer stuff in his shop on consignment. But he was never what you'd call ambitious. Alex was, though. When his mom and dad took an early retirement down in Florida, Alex married a city gal and started cartin' stuff up to Cleveland and bringin' other stuff back. Time went by, and he got so prosperous he backed other folks in the business, set 'em up, and supplied 'em with stuff to sell, takin' his cut off the top.

"It's a shame how he died, young man and all. I been pushin' for more lights out Lincoln Street way. Maybe now folks'll listen."

As we walked, I couldn't help noticing that the silhouette of Deputy Churchill King standing in the sheriff's office window was as motionless as if the man were made of wood.

"I told him to slow down," the sheriff continued, shaking his head as he pitched away his toothpick. "He was always tearin' round in that damn foreign car like he was crazy. Him and his son . . . but mostly him. Me and Church wrote him tickets every now and then, more for appearances than anything else. But we couldn't really say much. I mean, with all the income he brought into town it woulda been ungracious not to cut him a little slack. But I told him, 'Al, you're gonna kill somebody else or yourself, if you don't ease up. Ya gotta slow down for your own good.' But he wouldn't listen. Successful folks is like that, think they know everything.

"And by the way . . ."

We had arrived back at where the Miata was parked. The figure of Deputy King was conspicuously absent from the office window.

"I'm gonna give y'all a little advice," the sheriff said, sounding more serious than I had so far heard him, despite his smile, which I had decided was a more or less permanent fixture on his face.

"Actually," he continued, correcting himself, "it's more like a favor. What I'd like you to do, is not to get yourself too involved in what happened to ol' Alex Kane. See, we've got our own investigation goin' on down here, and I take it kinda personal when outside parties try to help. Gets in the way. Makes for sloppy procedure. What I'm tryin' to get across, I guess, is that despite what you mighta heard 'bout sheep bones and all, and not withstandin' your intentions, as good as I'm sure they are, we've got everything under control."

"But if Mr. Kane's death was ruled accidental, what's there to investigate?" I asked.

"Now, see, that's what I mean," he returned. "Dr. Webster, our coroner, he specifically put the word, pendin', in his original report. That means that at the time the report was written all the evidence we had pointed to Al's death bein' accidental. But after lookin' things over more careful like, we've decided to amend the rulin'."

"To what?" I asked.

"Possible homicide." The sheriff smiled. "Now, y'all have a good day."

On the way home Nat drove, baseball cap off, sunglasses on, scowling. She hadn't said six words all afternoon, and I left her alone, just enjoying the ride while I waited. She's no shrinking violet, my Nat. She says what's on her mind. But we were almost home, off the freeway and cruising slowly through a tree-lined section of the parkway, before she finally spoke. "I think you ought to drop it," she said, making me turn in my seat, waiting for more. She glanced at me to see if I was listening. When I nodded for her to proceed, she said simply, "If the sheriff's investigating, then what's there for you to do?"

She pulled into the funeral home's driveway, hit the automatic garage door opener, backed in, and turned off the engine. Looking over at me she took off her sunglasses and revealed a very concerned pair of deep blue eyes.

"You ever see those experiments they do in high school," she asked, "where you take two electrodes and move them closer and closer together until you get a spark that jumps from one to the other?"

"The power arcs," I said.

And she nodded, saying, "Well, that's you. You've got two sides: the Bill Hawley who's the normal, everyday businessman guy and the compulsive Bill who spends his time 'not drinking' and 'not smoking.' When you first gave up the booze after Jerry's accident, you spent so much time *not* drinking, that you hardly had the energy for anything else. But every now and then, despite yourself, your two sides get so close together that the spark jumps, and there's an arc."

"What's this got to do with Alex Kane?" I asked.

She shook her head as she replied, "Just listen. Now, in addition to the flash, which can really light things up sometimes, when the spark jumps, the energy you've got pent up inside you is released, which means that things can then go back to normal. You used to drink as a way of blowing off steam; now you try to kill yourself every evening on the stair machine. But it's not the same. So we have the other Bill Hawley looking for opportunities, the unlikely detective, the guy who seems to feel that taking on someone else's problems adds just enough pressure to his own life to burn off the pent-up energy he's accumulated over time.

"But face it, Bill, they don't need you on this one. There's a sheriff and a coroner taking care of things. You'd just end up being in the way."

"So what's the point?" I asked, feeling myself getting defensive.

Nat took my hand and said, "I know you want to run with it. I saw it in your face all day. You want to be the Bill Hawley whose name is on that little blue card you've got stuck in your wallet. But all you've got is some flaky kid's notion that his father died under murky circumstances and a 'questionable' tape recording, which you probably should have turned over to the sheriff this afternoon."

"You noticed that, huh?" I asked.

She nodded. "And I don't want to see Mrs. Kane's downtown store anymore. I saw a couple of things in their shops that I think were phony, so I'm not interested in anything they've got for sale, even if I'm sure it's genuine."

"Phony? But can't they get in trouble, pulling something like that?"

"Let the buyer beware. With antiques and collectibles, it's up to you to decide which is which. You choose wrong, you lose."

"Wow."

She smiled, got out of the car, and led me into the service area off the garage. We were nearly to the stairs to our apartment when my brother Jerry's voice stopped us short.

"I'm glad you guys are home. We got one down at the clinic."

With a thump Jerry maneuvered the front of his wheelchair through his door and into the alcove. He's younger than me by three years, and was paralyzed from the waist down in a traffic accident I still blame myself for. We designed the new Hawley Funeral Home partially with him in mind. He lives in a first-floor apartment next to the office and receives a salary from the company for his services as "Executive Assistant." With a grin he handed me a scrap of paper with a name written on it, saying, "They're just dying to get in. Hi, Nat."

I took it gratefully, looking at Nat, who said, "See? You're going to have enough to do with just being a successful funeral director."

Nat went upstairs to start dinner, and I threw the cot in the van and headed over to the clinic, which is located downtown, about a forty-five minute ride from the funeral home. I was actually whistling as I drove, feeling like a million bucks. Things were definitely turning around. Two calls in as many days, and no worries about what I should do regarding Mr. Kane. As much as I hated to admit it, Nat was right on that score. I had no business sticking my nose into something that the proper authorities were already handling. It was like a weight had been lifted off my shoulders.

But that weight came crashing back down when I walked up to the security desk at the clinic and was informed that there was no deceased by the name I had written on my form. "Are you sure?" I asked. The black lady in the security guard's uniform turned the death book around and showed me the list. I ran my finger down the page, comparing names and finally asking if I could use her phone. She said, "Sure," handed me the receiver, and watched my face as I dialed the funeral home.

"That's funny," I said. "No one's answering."

I dialed again, making sure I'd gotten the number right, but still no one answered.

I drove back worried, speeding down the freeway, feeling an unsettling sensation churning in my stomach. The first bad sign was that the funeral home's side door was open. Not just unlocked, but yawning open. I screeched to a halt, hopped out, and raced toward the building. My heart was pounding in my chest by now, although I had no idea why I was so worked up. It was just a feeling I had. A sense of impending trouble . . .

No. That's not right.

Not *impending* trouble.

I knew I was too late.

Nat was lying on the floor at the bottom of the stairs. Jerry's wheelchair was overturned nearby, wedged in the doorway to his apartment. He was on the ground, his useless legs twisted at goofy, rag doll angles, and an ugly swelling under his left eye as he lay propped up on one arm, stroking Nat's hair. Nat's eyes were closed. Jerry's were red with tears. As I filled the door frame over him with my body, he looked up at me with more anger, frustration, and fear on his face than I had ever seen in any human being, putting every ounce of that emotion into his voice as he shouted, "HAW 9834! Quick, write it down!"

But I hardly heard him. My attention was consumed by the blood, shining red against the white tile beneath my wife's face, and the strange, unnatural way her arm was bent where it folded itself beneath her body. That's all I was seeing . . . that, and the face of Sheriff Cornell Paulson, grinning in my mind as he spoke around the toothpick sticking out of the corner of his mouth: "I told you everything's under control. We're pretty good at what we do down here, especially when we put our minds to it."

Then everything suddenly looked as if I were viewing it through water, waving precariously and making my legs wobble as I stumbled once, grabbed the door frame with my hands, and went running for the phone.

THREE
∎∎∎∎∎∎∎∎∎∎∎

"HE RANG THE bell, and when Nat answered, the redneck son of a bitch told her to run," Jerry said, the words coming in a torrent, his entire body trembling with rage. "After it was over I could see his car through the open door as he ran back to it, and I memorized the license plate. HAW 9834. I don't think I'll ever forget it."

Jerry's fear was gone. For him, fear never lasts long. But the rage that seethed up from inside him, the unbridled temper that made him such a hellion before his accident, was like a fault in the earth giving way and making his entire body quake. He was sitting in his wheelchair, holding an ice bag on his lap, apparently oblivious to the bustle of the emergency room waiting area around us. I was kneeling next to him, listening as best I could, which wasn't very well because Nat was in there, somewhere, hidden behind a striped curtain on a gurney where they wouldn't let me see her. My hands were clammy with sweat, my breathing was rapid enough to make me feel light-headed, and my heart was pounding.

At that moment, Jerry was my lifeline, my anchor to the world. His voice, his passion, his rage . . . they were drawing me to him from the disoriented sensation that swirled in my head, my chest, my hands. Nothing seemed real but Jerry just then. Not the cops with their creaky leather belts, not the ambulance attendants with their back board and leather straps, not the brown-skinned Pakistani doctor with his tiny hands and big promises. None of it was real but Jerry. And I clung to him because he was all I had separating me from the panic I could feel building with every one of my heart's jackhammer thumps. It was in there, that blackness. It was inside me. And it was waiting.

He had gone back into his apartment and closed the door, he said. He had rolled himself in his wheelchair up to the window and watched me leave the parking lot in the van. And he had watched as, barely a minute after I had gone, a car pulled in and a man got out.

"When I saw him, I thought, now who? So I rolled over to my door and heard Nat skip down the stairs. She says, 'Can I help you?' And the fucker says, 'Run lady. I'm supposed to hurt ya and I like it when ya run.' I don't think Nat believed him 'cause she said, 'Whoever you are, that's not funny.' And I hit the button that swung my door open so the guy would see that Nat wasn't by herself. Sometimes a prick will deflate when he sees that he's not just dealing with a woman."

Then the guy reached for her, Jerry continued, which made him shout, "Run, Nat!" Apparently that was not what he should have done, because Nat immediately turned and headed back up the stairs, with the guy in the doorway right on her heels, wearing a grin that made Jerry feel sick to his stomach.

"He caught her at the top and just pitched her back down," he said, his voice shaking. "She landed hard, Bill. Real hard, once. And then her head went under and her legs came over, and she rolled, and I saw her, and I couldn't . . . my legs . . . and . . . I tried to catch her. I mean, I fell forward out of my chair as she got to the bottom so that she'd land on top of me. And the guy who did it came down and said, 'So from now on, you'll mind your own bizness.' And I'm lying there, looking up at him . . . and that's when he kicked me."

I was kneeling against his wheelchair, so that Jerry's battered face hovered over me by about a foot. Looking up at him as I was, my attention was focused on the imprint of bruise that swelled the flesh beneath his left eye and distorted his features. There were no thoughts in my head, just images. Pictures, without the imposition of perspective.

Truncated, free-floating, disassociated glimpses of what my little brother had just described. I almost reached my hand out to touch him. But I didn't. Instead I just knelt there. . . .

"Six foot, maybe a little more," Jerry said, describing the man to me with a steady eye and a slow, deliberate tone of voice. "Jeans, red flannel shirt, pointy-toed cowboy boots. Dark brown hair, hazel eyes set wide apart. Wide mouth. Thin lips. Long nose. No scars . . .

"Hey! Where you going? Bill?"

Two nurses and an orderly were taking Nat out of her cubicle, and the little doctor was standing by the curtain looking at a clipboard. I was walking toward the doctor, focusing my mind on him. Nat didn't move on the cart. She had been unconscious when they loaded her into the ambulance, and she was unconscious now. A police officer materialized out of the periphery of my vision, touching my arm. But I pulled away, making the doctor look up from his work as if I had startled him.

Two fractured ribs, a concussion, and a broken arm, he said. She'd lost two teeth. They were taking her to X ray again because a third rib looked questionable. I wouldn't be allowed to see her until tomorrow. She wouldn't be awake before then. No, I couldn't sit by her bed. No, I couldn't hold her hand. No, she wasn't going to die.

She wasn't going to die.

The words came at me like bullets.

I couldn't see her . . . and she wasn't going to die.

Then the cop was at my arm again, and this time I pulled away violently, snapping heads our way with my anger and pointing at my brother as I shouted, "Talk to him! He saw it! I didn't! I didn't see a thing!"

Then I forced my way out of the hospital and got in the van. My father could take Jerry home. Dad had been fluttering around for almost two hours, talking to all his old buddies in the E.R.—he's a retired fireman and always seems to know everybody. So let him take Jerry home. Let him take care of Jerry. Let him take care of everything. I had to think. I had to get away. I needed someplace quiet. I needed a drink.

• • •

Every drunk in the world drinks for his own reason. Mine was punctuation. Getting drunk was a way of slowing things down so I could catch my breath. Or at least that's what I used to think. I never tried to explain it to anyone, at least never in those terms. But what I eventually realized was that because it's impossible for anyone to master every aspect of his life, I periodically gave up, got drunk, and became like a leaf on a stream, content to go wherever the current took me, which was straight to a hangover, which, since I was raised Catholic, was perfect. In a strictly theological sense, hangovers were like penance that washed away my sins and left me free to sin again. The whole system operated on some subconscious level, and all I had to do was lay dollar bills on the bar. Nat was the one who had finally helped me to lift myself out of that hellish cycle, and now it was Nat who, indirectly, was sending me back into it.

I don't really remember anything about the time between when I left the hospital and when I crawled up on a bar stool, ordered a mug of beer, and fed quarters into a cigarette machine. The bartender wanted to be friendly, but I grunted and he left me alone. As I sat there in the dark, sucking in smoke and staring at my drink, my mind went blank and an unfamiliar sensation of heat started radiating out from inside me like the coil inside a toaster beginning to glow. My hands performed all the old tasks: the matches, the ashtray, the glass, but it wasn't the same. I was only there a little while before I realized that during the past three dry years something fundamental had changed inside me. Or maybe the change had come more recently, and this was just the first time I'd noticed.

"Hey, how ya doin'?" a voice came after a time, accompanied by the sound of a bar stool scraping into place nearby.

When I turned, I found Larry Fizner motioning for a round on him as he pulled off a wet overcoat and said, "It's raining like a bitch out there. So, this is the joint your grandparents owned? Your brother said I'd find you here. Said you'd be shit-faced. Are you?"

"Would you be surprised if I said no?"

"No. But I think your brother would. He said that I'd have to scrape you off the floor with a spatula."

"Yeah, well, sometimes Jerry gets excited."

The bartender brought the drinks Larry had ordered, and in the wall mirror over the bottles around the cash register I watched him pay. He'd been retired from his job as an investigator for the county tax department for nearly five years, doing his own investigative work and trying his best to stay young. I first met him when I got involved in the "Scholtz case" about a year before, and I hadn't really seen him since. Truth be told, I was avoiding him. He was the "master investigator" under whom I was theoretically serving my apprenticeship, and he kept bugging me to go on "stakeouts" with him. He was a small, wiry man, about five seven, maybe 130, with grey hair that he combed over his bald head from the sides in long, oily tendrils and a pair of steel grey eyes that never seemed to blink. He wore thick glasses with black plastic frames, and his taste in clothes ran to loud sport coats, white belts with matching shoes, plaid Polyester pants, and a pinky ring with a black stone set in its middle that I had never seen him without. He carried an old .38 caliber policeman's special in a holster that he clipped onto his belt in the middle of his back where his jacket would keep it covered. And he had a gruff, rumbly, cigarette-voice that tended to wheeze between words.

"Well, here's to it," he said, draining his shot glass and hoisting his beer mug high. He drank the chaser, smacked the mug down, and said, "So, where you at?"

Ignoring the shot and beer he'd ordered for me, and my own untouched drink, I slid off my bar stool, shrugged, and moved away from the bar with Larry following behind. "I don't really know. But it's someplace I've never been before. That's for goddamn sure."

The Lakefront Tavern, which was where my father and uncle were raised, was purchased by a Hungarian guy after my grandparents died. I still drive by every once in a while, remembering the Christmasses I spent there as a kid, playing the bowling machine with dimes marked with red nail polish that the company man would return when he opened the cash box once a week, hiding in the old-fashioned phone booth in the corner with its accordion door, watching my grandmother cooking holiday meals in pots designed for feeding an army. The place had a pressed tin ceiling, a thirty-foot hardwood bar scarred with forty years' worth of cigarette burns, and two huge windows that faced Scranton Road.

Stepping up to one of them, I said, "You know, one night a drunk drove his car right through this window. He was so trashed that he got out and ran away. Just left his car sitting right next to the pool table. My dad told me about it one time. It happened before I was born."

"Cops ran down the license plate number your brother got off the guy's car," Larry said. "Plates were stolen. Guy who'd lost 'em didn't even realize they were gone until a cop showed up at his house. He lives in a city that's located almost exactly halfway between Logan's Town and Cleveland."

"You know what's funny, Mr. Fizner?" I asked, turning to look at him. "Jerry was right. I was going to get drunk. That was the plan. But it didn't happen. After I ordered that drink, I spent the next hour staring at it. But I didn't touch it. How about that?"

"Why you been avoidin' me, Bill?" Larry asked.

And I shrugged, saying, "I didn't want to be like you. Or maybe Nat didn't want me to be like you . . . I'm not sure which."

"And now?"

I turned and indicated the area around us with a quick movement of my hand, saying, "One night a guy came in to rob the place. He had a gun, and there were maybe a dozen customers sitting around, plus my grandparents, and my dad, who was working behind the bar. The guy made everybody go into the ladies' room and lie on the floor while he emptied the cash register. Then he told the guy who had been playing the piano up on that little stage to play a song, saying that nobody was supposed to move until the song was over. He did that so anybody walking by outside wouldn't think anything suspicious was going on.

"You get that? Nobody walking by outside was supposed to look in the window and think that one guy sitting alone on a stage and playing the piano at a hundred miles an hour to an empty bar was suspicious. That happened before I was born, too. My dad was sixteen."

"Your brother told me about your trip to Logan's Town," Larry said.

"Yeah?" I returned. "So?"

"So, hearing of your misfortune, I made a coupla quick phone calls, boarded my parakeet, and headed down to offer my support, because that's the kind of guy I am— compassionate. You know, one of life's bleedin' hearts. Also, I know shit."

"What kind of shit?"

"Ah, listen and learn."

Leading me over to a corner table where a man sat in the shadows, he explained, "This gentleman's name is Uri, Bill. He doesn't have a last name, or a green card, but for a former godless commie he's remarkably accommodating. I asked him to meet me here because he's got something to say that I thought you might find interesting."

The man to whom Larry Fizner referred hardly acknowledged us, but instead sat hunched over a cigarette that burned in an ashtray near a hard pack of Marlboros. He was a big man, maybe forty years old, with thick dark hair and very bushy eyebrows. Larry and I sat down and faced him over the tiny round table, and glancing up resentfully, he pulled a face that indicated that he was cooperating under duress.

"Uri is a merchant," Larry explained, helping himself to one of the man's cigarettes. "He came here from Europe about five years ago and specializes in imported goods. Isn't that right, Uri? You're what they'd call a 'cultural entrepreneur.' "

The man named Uri glowered and stubbed out his cigarette without so much as looking at either Larry or myself.

"Uri's treasures come from Eastern Europe," Larry explained, addressing Uri but speaking to me. "Under the

Soviets it was illegal to export anything that was worth money. Religious icons, paintings, carvings, furs ... all that kinda stuff was strictly off-limits, which is why Uri did so well. Scarcity drives up prices. But when the wall came down and it looked like democracy would put him out of business, he found a way around it. So come on, Uri, explain to Mr. Hawlinski how the world works."

Uri sighed and lit a cigarette. His fingers were as thick as sausages, and his voice, when he finally spoke, was deep and heavily accented.

"After Yeltsin," he said stubbornly, "certain special objects became available."

"For available, read, stolen," Larry offered helpfully. "What Uri is trying to say is that once the old guard saw that there was nothing they could do to stop democracy from coming, they realized that pretty soon they'd be standing in line for their soup like everybody else. So they started selling off the family jewels, so to speak. Huh, Uri?"

I hadn't said a single word so far, but for some reason it was to me that Uri directed his remarks.

"After the war with Germany there was much confusion," he said, twirling his hand slowly as he searched for words. "The Germans stole many things, which were later found."

"Found?" I asked. "Found by whom?"

Uri twirled his hand again, as if indicating the population at large, including, presumably, people present in the bar at that moment.

"Many people," he said.

"And these many people took the things they found, where?" Larry asked.

As an answer, Uri merely shrugged.

"Translation." Larry smiled. "During World War Two, the Nazis stole everything they could carry from every country they invaded. Art, gold, furniture, you name it, they boxed it all up and carted it off. At the end of the war, whenever the Russians got to a German city before the Americans, they boxed up all the stolen shit they could find and stole it again. Later, when the people who had lost shit to the Germans said, 'By the way, did any of you guys ever find my stuff?' the Russians said, 'Nyet. We find nothing.' Meanwhile, all this precious junk was on display. Where, Uri?"

"Uhm, private areas of high security."

"Right. So, for the last fifty years," Larry explained, "the leaders of Russia have been sitting on a stolen art collection they denied they had. No one will ever know its exact catalogue because it was such a big secret, but we know it exists for two reasons. The first is that as a good faith gesture, Boris Yeltsin admitted to some of it not long ago. And the second is what, Uri?"

"Uhm, certain objects have reappeared."

Stubbing out his cigarette and smacking the Russian on the shoulder, Larry beamed as he said, "For the last couple of years, big shot communists have been using people like Uri here to secretly sell off their collections for cash. Just like when they rolled into Berlin and took whatever they could carry home in gunnysacks, the generals in the politburo ran off with the silverware while Yeltsin was fending off the tanks in Red Square, or wherever it was he fended them off."

"Many hundreds of millions of dollars worth of objects were removed," Uri offered, his eyes sparkling a little as he spoke. "Many things . . . beautiful things . . . gone." He fanned his fingers as if scattering flower petals.

"And through various twisted avenues," Larry said, "some of these beautiful things have ended up here, in this country."

With a sudden burst of economy, Larry then leaned forward and explained it to me with precision. Some of the Russian hierarchy had seen the change in their political and social positions coming and had started making arrangements for their economic futures as much as five years ago, he said. So the world had gotten its first taste of what was to come as a trickle of goodies emerging from the East. But since these goodies had been stolen in the first place, meaning that there were people, and governments, with legitimate claims to them, great care had to be exercised when they were sold. And that's where Uri, and his like-minded associates came in.

"An entire cottage industry sprang up," Larry said, "designed to match the people who wanted certain things with the things they wanted, making sure that the people who originally owned them never find out where they're at. Get it?"

I was about to say, "Yes, but what's this got to do with the guy who tried to kill my wife?" when Larry, apparently reading the question in my eyes, held up his hand and said, "Now that you know the background, listen while Uri tells you the story I asked him to come here to tell."

I looked at Uri, who, frowning and twirling his cigarette lighter on the table, said, "Hawlinski? This is Polish?"

"Ukrainian," I said.

And he nodded thoughtfully, as if this distinction had explained something significant. Then, with a resigned sigh, he began his story . . . in Ukrainian.

I stopped him by saying that I didn't speak the language.

"What languages do you speak?" he asked.

When I said that I only spoke English, he shook his head in the same disgusted way my grandfather used to. My grandfather, with his third-grade education, spoke Ukrainian, Russian, Polish, Slovak, English, and enough German to get by. He considered anyone who wasn't at least bilingual mentally deficient to the point of probably being slightly retarded. Uri obviously shared that opinion.

The thrust of his story was that, while they were fairly competent in detecting smuggled drugs, the customs agents on the Great Lakes were generally not qualified to accurately identify stolen Russian art objects. Consequently, it wasn't unusual for the precious wood carvings, priceless gold pieces, and even jewelry that Uri had labeled "collectibles" to be waved through without incident.

"Is unbelievable," he said proudly. "We say, 'Is junk come from Poland,' and police nod and stamp box like is full of potatoes. Most popular item lately is anything from church. Sometimes this not so easy. Icons heavy and hard to explain. But we get them anyway."

"And who buys this stuff?" I asked, because the notion of someone purchasing religious objects from a burly, Marlboro-smoking, expatriate Russian didn't sit right with me. "A priest isn't going to meet you on a freight dock to buy icons he knows are stolen, is he?"

"Maybe." Uri shrugged, eyeing me as if seeing something in my face he might have missed before. "To tell a lie, is first important to find story person hearing lie wants to believe. To sell picture, is first important to find person who looks like he should be selling picture."

"So who's your respectable middleman?" I asked, although I had a feeling I already knew.

Uri clenched his fists and stared at Larry, his eyes narrow and his expression radiating distaste. Finally, he said, "Right now, is new guy. None of your business. But before, was Alex Kane. Alex Kane best dealer ever; never no trouble. Not like now."

"So, Mr. Kane's death must have come as quite a blow to your profit margin," I observed, thinking that this was what Larry had wanted me to hear.

But to my surprise, Uri shook his head as he said, "Kane not buy anything from Uri for almost two years."

"But you just said that he was your best dealer."

Uri said, "Two years ago I spend much trouble to bring beautiful icon from church in Siberia. Is perfect . . . beautiful, much gold. I say, 'Is special, for you.' But he say, 'No, Uri. I not need this.' I say, 'Is beautiful. Is worth many thousands of dollars.' And he say, 'So you have no trouble to sell it somewhere else.' I say, 'What I do? You mad with me?' He laugh and say, 'No. But this thing you have, I not need. Thank you. Good-bye.' He buy nothing since. And then"—he lifted one finger to his temple as he squinted his eyes and looked at me conspiratorially—"comes great mystery. Uri hear, uhm . . . how you say, story somebody say is true but maybe not?"

"Rumor," Larry offered.

Uri nodded. "Uri hear rumor that say man from Canada buy very beautiful, very secret thing from Alex Kane.

Where Alex Kane get this beautiful thing, no one know. Not from Uri, that for damn sure. Uri ask Alex Kane, 'Is true about this secret thing you sell?' Alex Kane say, 'No, Uri. Is not true.' But the way he say this, Uri know it is lie."

With that, Uri lapsed into silence.

"Very good." Larry smiled. "Now get out of here."

Wordlessly, and without so much as glancing my way again, the big man rose and left the bar.

Larry got up, went to where I had left the drinks he'd bought for me, and returned with them, saying, "It's a sin to waste good food." Downing the shot, he grimaced a little, took a long pull of beer, wiped his lip, and asked, "So, what do ya think?"

I replied, "What am I supposed to think?"

"Okay," he said, ticking off the points on his fingers, "Alexander Kane owned a very successful string of antique stores, with outlets in a couple of cities locally. He also dabbled in foreign collectibles, privately and on the sly. After he dies in a car wreck, his son shows up with a tape of his father threatening suicide that he thinks is bogus." He paused, commandeering my pack of Camels because, "They're making you turn green anyway." Lighting one, he continued, "So, off you and Nat go to the scene of Kane's fatal accident, where the local sheriff tells you that Kane's death has been upgraded to a 'possible homicide.' You come home, get a bullshit body call, and while you're gone somebody bounces your wife down the stairs and boots your crippled brother in the kisser."

I bristled at his description, but when I looked at him, he shrugged and said, "Reality, Bill. It's a bitch. Okay, now let's examine it:

"If Uri's to be believed—which he is, because if he had on me what I have on him, I'd tell anybody anything they wanted to know—Alexander Kane was moving smuggled Soviet artworks through his shop. But two years ago he decided to stop buying from Uri, who later heard that Kane was still moving hot merchandise on the sly. Now, what's that tell you?"

"That Kane found a new supplier," I answered, getting wrapped up in Larry's scenario despite myself.

"Right," Larry agreed. "But what if I told you that, even after trying to find out who that supplier was for six months, I haven't been able to come up with a name?"

"I'd say you haven't looked hard enough. And what's this got to do with you anyway?"

"Deep waters, Bill, my boy. Muddy pools. Anyway, the most important point to you is that somebody hurt your wife. Right?"

"He nearly killed her," I hissed.

"And I assume you want to find out who that somebody is. Right?"

I nodded, not trusting my voice at the moment.

"Do you see a connection between Uri's story and what happened to Natalie this afternoon?"

I frowned as I said, "Apparently, somebody didn't like us poking around in Logan's Town and decided that hurting Nat was the simplest way to make us back off."

"Uh-huh." Larry nodded. "Meaning what?"

"Meaning," I began, concentrating, and for the first time since the assault, succeeding in pushing the image of Nat's crumpled body from my mind, "that there must be something going on down there that's worth almost killing somebody over, just because they asked a couple of questions."

"So," Larry said, "if we find out what's going on in Logan's Town . . ."

"We'll find out who hurt Nat."

He smiled as he raised his beer mug in a toast and said, "Bravo, Bill. And what are you gonna do to the guy who bounced your wife, once you've found him?"

"I'm going to kill him," I said, more calmly than I thought I could. I'd been turning it over in my mind, but now that I'd come right out and said it, it sounded dumb, overly dramatic, and somehow unreal. But I also understood that it was very much what I wanted to do. No, not even that so much. It was what I needed to do. It was like a physical drive that I had known was there, lurking in that darkness I had first felt in the pit of myself in the emergency room. And now that I had identified it, I was shaken.

"Then you'll find him by yourself," Larry said, rising in apparent preparation to go.

I jumped to my feet, exclaiming, "Oh don't give me that righteous, protector of the law crap! If that was your wife lying in that hospital, you'd do the same goddamn thing! I know you, Larry Fizner. The fucker wouldn't stand a chance!"

"Maybe," he agreed. "But you're not me. You'll get caught. And I don't want to have anything to do with a murder charge, not at my age. I'm not gonna die in jail. Not for you, or anybody else."

The calculated coolness of this statement disarmed me, making me realize that Larry, in his lemon-yellow sport coat that looked like he'd paid fifty cents for it at a Goodwill bin, was at least two steps ahead of me again. He was right, I understood. Absolutely right. I'd never get away with it. I might be able to actually do the deed . . . although even that remained to be seen. I mean, after all . . . it was murder we were talking about. But even if I got through the moment and actually ended up with the guy's blood on my hands, they'd catch me and put me in jail. I might even get the gas chamber. It would be flat-out, undeniable, premeditated murder. And Nat would be hurt again.

"So show me how to do it right," I said, my voice low, my hands shaking.

"I thought you didn't want to be like me," Larry said, looking me in the eye.

"It's too late," I said, tapping my chest with two fingers and adding, "I'm already like you. In here. I just don't know enough"—I tapped my forehead—"up here."

Larry looked at me for a moment longer, then said, "Okay. Lesson one is that you can't kill him, and you know it. You know it here." He tapped my chest as I had done, and then pushed my head back with his palm, adding, "And you know it here, too. You want to do it . . . but you know that, with your motive, there's no way you'd ever get away with it. You'd be the first person the cops questioned. You can't kill him, but . . ."

"But what?" I asked eagerly.

"You can make him wish you had. He's already showed you his weak spot when he went after Nat. Whatever's going on down in Logan's Town is mighty important to this guy. If you fuck it up, you fuck him up. Capish?"

I nodded, the logic of it all working its way into my mind.

"Now sit down," Larry said, smiling, "and let's talk."

He spent the next half hour or so trying to convince me that I was pissing away a good opportunity by not letting him "school me in the art of investigation" more. I drank a cup of coffee and got a headache. He drank a couple more beers and got looped. It was just going on eight-thirty when he finally climbed into his ratty yellow conversion van and drove off, leaving me on the sidewalk under the awning over the Lakefront Tavern's front door, watching his taillights fade into the rain and realizing that I didn't even know where he lived.

In exchange for my promise that we would approach the "Kane case" together, "like in the old days," he had said that he would eventually explain to me how it just so happened that he knew someone who had been involved in an illegal smuggling operation with Alexander Kane. "I know a lot of shit," he'd said. "You should hang around with me more." I had nodded in a noncommittal way, remembering that the last person who had hung around with Larry Fizner, a young woman named Judy Newhardt, was presently serving a life sentence for murder.

From the bar's phone booth I called my brother, who answered on the first ring. Growing immediately hostile when he heard my voice, he started in about how pissed he was that I would go off and get drunk when Nat needed me, until I convinced him that I was sober, which shut him up. No, he said in response to my next question, Nat wasn't awake yet. He'd been calling the hospital every couple of hours to check on her condition, and all he knew was that the X rays had come back showing that her third rib wasn't fractured, and that, though painful, her injuries weren't life-threatening.

"They're going to pretty much keep her under until tomorrow morning," he said. "They set her arm, and wrapped her ribs, but when she comes to she'll hurt like hell, so they're giving her a good night's sleep tonight."

"Did they say what time in the morning she'd be awake?" I asked.

"No," he replied.

"Okay," I said, looking through the folding glass door of the phone booth at three guys hunched on their stools in front of the bar. "This is what I'm going to do. Larry Fizner just left . . ."

"So he found you, huh?" Jerry interrupted.

And I nodded as I replied, "Yeah. But you didn't really need to call him."

"It was either him or Dad, and I figured Larry wouldn't rough you up too bad. If Dad found you drunk, he'd kick your ass."

"I know," I agreed. "But I wasn't drunk."

"I didn't know that. You've got a record, Bill."

"Okay, forget it already. Anyway, Larry gave me a lead . . ."

"A lead?" Jerry said with enthusiasm. "So you're going to do it, huh? You're going to find the son of a bitch?"

"Yeah," I said. "I'm going to try."

"I want to be there when you do," Jerry insisted, his voice dropping a register. "Even if I can only watch."

"Now listen," I cut in. "I might not be home until late. Larry gave me a lead, but it's only a beginning. I've got a lot of ground to cover, so I want to get started. Now I'll tell you what I want you to do. I know it's a Saturday night, but while everything's still fresh in your mind, call Dad's buddy, Mike Agnello; you might have to get Dad to give you the number . . ."

"You mean, 'Michelangelo'?"

"Yeah. Ask him to bring his kit over and go through the routine with you. Maybe it'll help later."

"I only saw the guy for a couple of seconds, Bill," Jerry protested. "And besides, I already did all that with the local cops."

"Let's just give it a shot with Mike anyway, okay?" I returned. "I should be home by . . . what time is it now? Eight-thirty? I should be home by midnight or so. We'll see what you guys come up with then, okay?"

"Okay. I'll try. So you're really going to do it, huh, Bill?"

"Yeah," I said. "I really am."

"So, like, watch your ass. Okay?"

"No sweat. Keep checking on Nat. Okay?"

"You got it."

I hung up, wishing Larry hadn't taken my cigarettes, but resisting the temptation to buy another pack. That was one habit I didn't need to rekindle. Instead, I bought another cup of coffee to go, and turning up the collar on my long black undertaker's coat, scuffled through the rain to my van. I got in, put my Styrofoam cup in the holder on the dashboard, and wiped the steam off my glasses with the wide end of my necktie. Deciding that I had enough gasoline for the trip, I U-turned up the cobblestone side street, made a left onto Scranton Road, and jumped on Interstate 71 South, figuring that I'd be in Logan's Town by a little after nine-thirty. On the way, I tried to settle on a course of action.

I'm a big fan of linear thought: one point leading to another, with what goes before determining what follows after. The problem with my present situation was that I'd picked it up in the middle—or from Mr. Kane's point of view, the end. Larry's information about smuggled Russian art opened up all sorts of possibilities. But there were two things that bothered me. One was the suicide tape, because I was convinced—on slim evidence, to be sure— that by showing up at the funeral home and expressing his doubts about its authenticity, the dead man's son had placed himself in the picture. And the second was the recklessness of the attack on my wife. It was a stupid overreaction at best, specifically aimed at her since whoever had done it had gone to the trouble of decoying me out of the way with that phony body call.

In Logan's Town we had asked no pointed questions, raised no specific suspicions, and made no definitive statements. As a matter of fact, the only person we'd even spoken to was the fucking sheriff, and despite all my stereotypical images of corrupt, small-town authorities, there was no way I could honestly entertain the notion that Sheriff Paulson had been involved in an assault. Deputy King . . . now he was another story—and his description more or less matched the one of the man Jerry had seen. But in his case I was probably just letting my own personal distaste color my judgment. Right now, the most important thing for me to do was nail down some facts. There was only one place I could think of where I could find out what went on in Logan's Town without prejudice . . . and that's where I was heading.

FOUR
■■■■■■■■■

THE WITTMERE COUNTY Hospital is located across from the Logan's Town freeway exit. If you want to know what goes on in a city, the place to find out isn't in a beer joint like you see in the movies. It's in the local emergency room, because that's where the cops hang out, and the combatants end up once the dust has settled. The place was quiet except for a guy groaning from behind a pink curtain. The nurse at the receiving desk looked up as I stepped in and narrowed her eyes when she saw me. Though I hate to admit it, at thirty-three years old, after having been in the business for over eleven years, I now look like a funeral director. I'm five feet eleven inches tall, weigh 210 pounds, have a thick chest and middle, short, sandy brown hair, a fairly round face, blue eyes, and a certain amount of dignity—meaning that I dress nice. I was wearing dark trousers, a white shirt, a dark tie, and my black, knee-length, cashmere overcoat. The nurse glanced at her book as soon as she saw me, only to look back up, saying, "Did somebody die that I don't know about?"

I smiled my most winning smile, despite my throbbing head, and asked to see the nursing supervisor, who appeared about ten minutes later, holding a Garfield coffee mug, and led me to her office with an expression of curiosity on her face. She was a small, compact woman, about fifty years old, with greying hair pulled tightly back on her head. She had a poster on her office wall depicting, "The Truth About Evolution," which showed a series of footprints, starting from the poster's lower left-hand side as something that looked like they might have been made by a frog, moving on to the prints of an ape, then to a man's bare foot, then to a man's shoe print, leading finally to the prints left by a woman's high heels. She sat down behind her desk, and I started my pitch by saying that, as the funeral director taking care of Mr. Kane, I found myself in a rather awkward position.

"The problem is," I said, making sure my voice implied that I was looking to this fine lady for help, "that the family insists that Mr. Kane was wearing a Rolex wristwatch when he died. And I'm afraid that no such watch was included in the personal effects I received when I picked him up. Now I know that in some accident cases the sheriff's office holds back property, so before I talk to them, I thought maybe you'd check your property book and see what you've got Mr. Kane recorded as wearing when they brought him here."

"No problem," she said. She got up and returned in a couple of minutes with a pair of vinyl-covered notebooks which she opened on her desk as she put on a pair of reading glasses and started turning pages. "I was here the night he died," she commented distractedly. "What a mess."

"He was pretty wracked up, huh?" I asked.

The woman shook her head as she explained, "I'm not talking about the body. I'm talking about John Gilbert. The man was a basket case. And I can't imagine what this has done to the immigrants."

"Immigrants?" I asked.

And she looked up at me quizzically, saying, "You really don't know, do you?"

"No," I said. "I'm from out of town. All I got is a pending burial permit from your coroner."

With what I can only describe as a mischievous smile, the nurse seemed to think something over for about ten seconds before she said, "You want some coffee?"

"Do I?" I asked with a knowing tone.

She looked at me for another couple of seconds, then said, "Yeah, I think you do."

• • •

An hour later I was standing on the gravel shoulder of State Route 16, looking at the drainage ditch that ran parallel to Lincoln Street, with the rain thrumming on my black umbrella and my mind ringing with her words. The silver spray-painted outline of Mr. Kane's prone body that had been on the side of the ditch was washed away, and the trickle of water in the ditch's bottom, which had been no more than four inches deep that morning, had swelled, running blackly beneath the rain-patterned beams thrown by my idling van's headlights. Directly ahead of me, on the opposite side of about a hundred yards of empty field, loomed the house Nurse Marge Hoke had described as, "the place where the immigrants live. I can just imagine how they must have carried on when they heard the news."

According to her, Alexander Kane was brought in D.O.A. at one A.M., Friday morning. After running through a C.P.R. routine for the sake of form and finding water in his lungs, the E.R. doctor pronounced him dead, and someone called the coroner. They were just taking his body down to the cooler—this was at nearly two in the morning—when a man named John Gilbert burst into the E.R., shaking like a leaf and wanting to know if it was absolutely certain that Alex Kane was positively dead.

"It was weird how he phrased it," were the nurse's exact words. "He came roaring in demanding to know if we were one hundred percent positive that Mr. Kane was beyond hope. It was like he wanted a guarantee. Not like he was asking about Mr. Kane's welfare, but more like he didn't want there to be any question of a mistake about his condition. When I told him that there was absolutely no doubt in the world, and not a single thing that anyone could do on Mr. Kane's behalf, he just ran back out into the night, like he had something to do that couldn't wait another minute."

"Who is he, exactly, this Mr. Gilbert?" I had asked.

Nurse Hoke replied, "Why, John Gilbert's Mr. Kane's business partner. They were very close. Actually, maybe partner isn't even the right word. We call him the 'overseer' around here. It's a joke, really. But it's not, too, if you get my drift."

The scenario the nurse finally constructed depicted a rather unusual situation, "out at the old Maynord place." Alexander Kane had apparently sponsored a Russian family, guaranteeing them employment as a condition of their immigration from their home country. There were three people in total who had come: two men and a woman. The woman and the younger of the two men were either brother and sister, or husband and wife. The older man was thought to be the girl's father. But no one really knew for sure because they spoke no English and never left the property surrounding the house off Lincoln Street where they lived outside of town. The only town resident who had any contact with them was the "overseer," John Gilbert, who worked for Alexander Kane, and whose responsibility it was to see that the immigrants' needs were met. He carted groceries and such up to the house every week, and brought back what the immigrants made for Mr. Kane.

"Made?" I asked. "What do you mean, made?"

"They were artists, we think," Nurse Hoke replied. "Or at least the girl was."

"But if no one ever spoke to them, how did anyone know what they were doing up in that house?" I asked.

Nurse Hoke explained that, shortly after the house was occupied, beautiful little pictures started appearing in one of Kane's shops on the circle downtown.

"Oh, they were lovely little things." She smiled somewhat dreamily. "So delicate, and foreign-looking. Mr. Gilbert said that the artist was a sensitive girl who was nervous because she was in a new country and didn't feel like she fit in yet. Mr. Kane had sponsored her because her talent was being stifled at home. And wasn't it amazing what a little freedom could do? Could you imagine, looking at these little paintings, what beautiful things she'd make once she settled in?"

But if Mr. Kane was such a generous sponsor, paying to bring an artist and her family over from Russia and setting them up in a house all their own where she had all the time and freedom she could ever want, then why'd the townspeople call the man who took care of them the overseer? I asked.

Nurse Hoke's reaction was a slight blush as she explained that his nickname was just a joke. "You know," she said, smiling and waving her hand dismissively, "like he was takin' care of the servants. It was a josh. We was cuttin' up like Mr. Kane had bought these people like slaves in Europe and shipped 'em over so this girl could make him pictures to sell and get rich on.

"I just hope," she concluded, "that wherever they settle next, it's as nice for them there as it was here."

When I asked her what she meant, she explained that the day after Mr. Kane died, the immigrants had moved away.

How did she know that?

Why, John Gilbert had said so.

Had anybody actually seen them go?

Well, no. But why would Mr. Gilbert lie?

Did he say where they went?

"To Cleveland." Nurse Hoke had smiled wistfully. "They're probably on their way to a fairy-tale life, considering what they must have come from in Russia. Art galleries, parties, interviews, money . . . Oh, I think that girl's going to feel like she died and went to heaven."

As the rain dribbled off my umbrella, the words "overseer" and "died and went to heaven" reverberated in my mind. Around the ground at my feet curled a soft blanket of misty exhaust from my van's idling engine, and straight ahead, over the featureless dark of a bare, country field, was the hard-edged silhouette of the immigrants' empty house.

But why was it empty now? I wondered.

And where had the immigrants gone?

Closing my umbrella, I climbed back into my van, then drove slowly up the road, turned into the driveway, and crunched along the gravel with my headlights out. I parked around back, figuring that the house would block my van from view should someone be watching from the only other house in the area, which was a solid two hundred yards away.

I opened the driver's door a crack and called, "Hello?" I called two more times, louder, hearing my voice swallowed by the hissing rain. All the windows on the house were dark, and my greeting didn't stir up any barking, which was what I was leery of out in the country like I was. Dogs scare the shit out of me. I was ripped up pretty good at the age of eleven when I stepped around the back of a gas station looking for a men's room. The owner had a German shepherd tied up back there, and before I could get away it did sixty stitches worth of damage. If it hadn't been on a chain it would probably have killed me. As it was, it just left me with a bunch of scars on my arms and legs, and a phobia about being bitten that has pretty much remained intact to this day.

I carry a flashlight in the drawer beneath the passenger's seat in my Dodge Grand Caravan, and I pulled it out. I considered retrieving the tire iron from the back as protection but decided against it. Closing my door gently, I snapped on the flashlight and moved quickly in close to the house where the rain didn't reach me, carrying my umbrella folded up under one arm and pulling on a pair of black leather gloves.

Stopping to listen, I cupped one hand over a window, saw nothing, and walked along the bushes lining the porch until I reached the stairs. The house was one of those three-story, Victorian-looking things, with a turret on one side surmounted by a lightning rod, a long front porch that stretched the length of the house, and a lot of windows. To my amazement the front door wasn't even pulled all the way shut, let alone locked. As I watched it swing open after I'd given it a little push, I wondered if Mr. Gilbert could have been in such a hurry to move the immigrants that he'd forgotten to lock up after they left, or if this was one of those mythical, middle-American towns where people felt so safe that they left their doors open even when they weren't home.

"Hello?" I called, playing my flashlight's beam over the foyer as I stepped inside and considered whether it would be wise to turn on a lamp. I decided that it wouldn't and resigned myself to looking the place over in the atmosphere of exaggerated tension created by the knife of white thrown by my flashlight. Twisted shadows undulated on the floor and walls as I closed the door and turned to find what looked like a complete complement of furniture, right down to a coffee table upon which was piled the rubble of a meal eaten in front of the TV. There were clothes thrown everywhere, and at least one overturned chair. For the hell of it I announced myself again, asking if there was anybody home but knowing in my bones that the place was empty. In the dining room there were cardboard boxes crumpled on the floor, sheets of newspaper scattered everywhere, and, on the table, a cookie sheet upon which was piled a pyramid of black ash, which I didn't touch, but puzzled over for a long time. Something had been burned here, and then the ashes had been chopped up fine with a fork, which lay next to the cookie sheet, staining the white tablecloth with smudged black patches.

Turning to the kitchen, I found that it looked as if it had been hit by an earthquake, with the sour smell of spoiled food tainting the air, and practically every cupboard open. It was so cold that my breath made steam, and when I aimed my flashlight's beam at a thermostat I found that the heat had been turned off. Somehow, seeing that the furnace wasn't on relaxed me because it erased even the slightest question of occupancy, leaving me able to concentrate on what I saw without distraction.

The upper floors contained four bedrooms, three of which looked used, the last empty. In one of the used rooms I found drawers full of a man's clothes. Holding them up to myself in the mirror, I determined that their owner was roughly my size, if a little shorter. In the second room I entered I found another man's clothes, these belonging to someone taller and slimmer than me. And in the last occupied room I found the remnants of a woman, verifying to me that the two young people of whom the nurse had spoken were in fact brother and sister, and not husband and wife. The double bed in the girl's room was unmade, and a bunch of her undergarments were tangled in a ball on the floor. Dangling from a clothesline stretched across the inside of one closet were two bras and a pair of panties. And scattered around the room were all sorts of other odds and ends: bobby pins on the dresser, a hairbrush, hand mirror, coffee cup, clock radio, shoes, socks, a plastic belt, a bag of cough drops, and on a night table next to the bed, a framed color photograph lying on its back. Sitting down on the mattress I lifted the picture and angled my light on it so that the beam didn't glare, seeing the "immigrants" for the first time.

My throat constricted as I realized that I knew them . . . maybe not as individuals, but as a kind of person with whom I was intimately familiar. I had seen old photographs of my grandparents, taken in Europe when they were young, and in this country soon after they had arrived, and they were the same. There was the identical stiffness in the way they stood, indicating that they considered the taking of a photograph a momentous event; the same, rough features, the thick lips and noses, heavy hands, and gentle eyes that marked them as Eastern Europeans, people of the earth, and the products of hard lives; and there was the implied closeness, the affection, the sense that they belonged together, like the rain and soil. But there was also something sad about the picture—three people, a single family, without a mother, the men standing behind, the woman seated in front—because, for some inexplicable reason, it felt like history.

I put it back where I found it and continued my search, looking now for the traces of three specific human beings, not three strangers. What's more, I was looking for something I had yet failed to see: some evidence that they had moved voluntarily. Because so far it looked to me as if the only thing not at home in this house were the immigrants themselves.

In the turret room on the house's third floor I found the first evidence that the girl was the artist Nurse Hoke had claimed her to be. The room was round, with tall curtainless windows on three sides and an easel positioned in the room's center so that the artist could stand with the light falling over her shoulders and onto her work. There were no finished paintings leaning against the wall, no works in progress, sketches, notepads, photographs, or anything else touched by the artist anywhere in the room. But there were art supplies: paints, brushes, charcoal, rags, thinner, and . . .

I leaned in close to a table set near the easel as my flashlight illuminated something that sparkled in a peculiar way. There, in a little black pot, was something into which I inserted the index finger of my right hand, pulling it back and turning it before my eyes. Gold dust. Or something that looked very much like it.

I looked the rest of the place over more carefully but found nothing that rang any bells in my mind. The gold dust on my finger seemed to tingle, and as I headed back down the stairs to the first floor I wiped it off on the inside of my overcoat pocket. There was a stairway that ran down to the basement at the back of the kitchen. When I descended it, I found a large, musty room that I examined by running my flashlight ahead of me without letting go of the rickety wooden bannister. There were cobwebs everywhere and a thick coating of dust undisturbed on the concrete floor. Obviously, no one had been down there in a long time, so I turned and returned to the kitchen.

I was just about to head for the front door and my van, when the smell of sour milk in the air made me pause and look around. The refrigerator was closed, and there wasn't a milk carton or any glasses or plates of rotten food lying anywhere I could see. Stepping into the middle of the room, I closed my eyes and took a deep breath, licked my lips, and got scared. What I had mistaken for sour milk at first I now understood was something more. With a renewed sense of caution, I began my search afresh, running my flashlight beam under the kitchen table, along the floor in the corners, and finally over the door of what I took to be a pantry near the sink. Gritting my teeth, I swung the door open and sighed deeply, not really surprised by what I had found, but saddened beyond words.

There was a telephone on the wall next to the pantry door, and I almost used it to call the sheriff. But after a moment during which I stood staring at the body with my heart thumping and my mouth going dry, I got a better idea, and leaning down, I took a closer look at what I'd found.

She was crumpled in the corner of the pantry with the right side of her face pressed to the wall. Around her neck was tied what looked like a length of decorative curtain cord; her legs were curled beneath her; and the smell of her voided bowels hung thickly in the air around her. She was wearing a rust-colored leather coat, knee-high suede boots, and new stone-washed jeans. Her right eye was pressed shut because of the pressure of her body leaning her face into the wall, and her left eye was open so that she seemed to stare up at me, mouth agape, creating an expression of awe or surprise. Her skin was very blue, with a mottling of bruise around the lower portion of her jawline. And her tongue was like a dark lump between her perfectly white teeth.

Without touching her, I shone my flashlight on her face, taking note of the tiny pink blurs on the now yellowish-white of her eye. They were ruptured capillaries, the telltale result of death by asphyxia. She'd been strangled. I frowned, removed one of my gloves, and placed the back of my hand against her cheek. Stone cold . . . or at least as cold as the surrounding air. Pushing the bottom of her pant leg up, I looked at her white ankle, finding the underside virtually black with lividity where her blood had settled in response to the force of gravity. Then I tried to move her arm, finding her reasonably pliant; rigor mortis had obviously come and gone, meaning that she'd been dead at least twenty-four hours, probably more.

Alexander Kane had died shortly before one A.M. on Friday morning. It was now almost ten-thirty Saturday night. Just about two full days had passed. Judging by the condition of her body, I estimated that the girl could have been killed at any time between late Thursday evening and roughly ten o'clock Friday night.

I stood up and realized that I was trembling. My eyes were teary, and for a moment I felt as if I couldn't move.

Standing there shining my light down at her, I sighed and looked at her face, comparing it in my mind with the young, hopeful lady I'd seen smiling at me from the silver-framed photograph upstairs and suddenly understanding how lucky I was that Nat hadn't shared her fate. I was in the presence of a savagery like I had never personally experienced. And its existence appalled me. What must a person be like inside to be capable of such deeds? And what was I going to do when I found him?

That question finally jump-started me into motion, and after lifting a dishrag off the counter near the sink, I erased the traces I had left of my presence by wiping up the rain I'd tracked onto the porch and into the living room. Then I closed the front door, trotted down to my van, and drove into town.

I parked in front of the sheriff's office and knocked on the door. A light came on inside, but instead of Sheriff Paulson, Deputy Churchill King stuck his face out into the cold, asked what I wanted, and grudgingly let me in. He was dressed in his uniform pants, had grey wool socks on, no shoes, and a white, sleeveless T-shirt, which revealed that he was one of those men who have hair on their shoulders. The lower half of his face was dark with beard stubble, and he yawned several times as he lowered himself into the chair behind his desk, lighted a cigarette, and virtually snarled as he asked again what had brought me to Logan's Town at, "Shit, goin' on eleven o'clock at night! You been drinkin' or what?"

"I've been *thinking*, Deputy," I said, looking down at him from where I stood before his desk. "Ever since my wife was attacked after our lunch with your sheriff, I've been doing one hell of a lot of serious thinking."

The deputy looked at me through a curling lick of cigarette smoke and said, "What do ya mean, attacked?"

I explained to him about Nat. Naturally I left out the part about Larry Fizner and Uri in the bar. I also left out the fact that I'd found the body of a murdered Russian girl in a house not two miles from his office. At the end I reminded him of his statement about not having much "truck" with private investigators, adding that, "I've decided that I don't have much truck with small-town law enforcement officials who don't do their jobs."

"Meaning what?" the deputy asked as I paced up to the window and watched his reflection in the dark glass as a way of reading his reaction while keeping him from reading mine.

"Meaning that all the thinking I've been doing leads me to believe that Alex Kane wasn't the only person who died here Friday morning," I said. "I think you had at least two deaths down here, maybe even as many as four. And you don't know a goddamn thing about any of them."

"Hogwash!" the deputy snorted.

And I turned to him, furious.

"When was the last time you saw the Russians, Deputy King?" I demanded, feeling my spine stiffen and my hands tremble. "Or John Gilbert? Did you know that John Gilbert got rid of the immigrants the very day after his boss was killed? Did you know that the Russian girl painted pictures for Kane to sell in his shops . . . and that he supposedly brought her all the way over from Russia, along with her father and brother, just for the sake of those pictures? And did you know that on the night Kane died, John Gilbert showed up at the hospital at two in the morning just to *make sure that he was dead*? Did you know about any of this, Deputy King?"

"Yeah," he said. "So what?"

"So, have you seen the immigrants since Alex Kane died? Do you know where they went? Do you know who they were? Do you know anything about them at all, other than that they were three foreigners that your town's richest resident was keeping locked up in a house away from everybody else? Didn't it ever strike you as strange that nobody ever saw them step off that property? Didn't you ever wonder what they were doing up there? Didn't you fucking people ever ask any questions?"

Deputy King pulled his legs down from where he had casually propped his feet up on the desk and leaned forward in his squeaky chair to rest his elbow on his knee, look at the floor, and shake his head. "Mr. Hawley," he began in a tone of exaggerated patience, "like the sheriff told you before, we got everything under control. We're even fixin' to make an arrest right after Mr. Kane's funeral. The sheriff figures it's the least we can do, savin' the widow the embarrassment till after her husband's in the ground."

"Arrest?" I asked, temporarily derailed. "Who's he going to arrest?"

The deputy looked up at me with a shit-eating grin and said, "That's official police business. I ain't at liberty to say."

That did it.

"Okay, Deputy, I'm going to give it to you for free!" I shouted, throwing my arm out and pointing at the wall to one side of me. "Alex Kane was doing something with those Russians up in that house! And after he died, his partner, John Gilbert, packed those people up like they were his own personal property and got rid of them. You hear me? *He got rid of them!* They're gone! Vanished! Three nameless people, in a strange country, who don't even speak the language. No friends. No one who gives a shit about them for any reason other than the one thing they know how to do . . . which is paint, Deputy King. Paint, in a very special, foreign way.

"You hear what I'm saying? If I'm not two hundred miles off the mark, and I'm not, then Alexander Kane was using that Russian girl to forge religious icons, gilded with gold, that he then pawned off as the genuine articles, smuggled out of the Soviet Union and therefore worth a ton because they were so rare!"

"You're out of your goddamn mind," Deputy King said, the smile dropping from his face as he stood up and looked me in the eye.

"Oh yeah?" I challenged. "Well, I'll tell you what, I'll make you a little bet. I say that not only was Alex Kane using that Russian girl to make him reproductions of religious icons, but that when Kane died, his partner, John Gilbert, panicked and got rid of the evidence."

"What evidence?"

"The only evidence that could really trip him up—the girl herself . . . and maybe even the other two immigrants as well. But the girl for sure. He killed her, Deputy King. He had to. There was just no other way for him to go."

"How you gonna prove it?" the deputy asked, his expression betraying his interest.

"First, we bet," I said.

"Bet what?"

I placed my hands on my hips, saying, "I'll bet you that if we go up to the immigrants' house, right this minute, me and you, we find at least one body up there, maybe even more. But one at the very least. If we do find a body—and I'll make it even tougher, Deputy—if we do find the *girl's* body, then you give me everything your department's got on the case. And I mean everything: the autopsy protocol, crime scene photographs, dispatch transcripts, the works."

"And what if there ain't no body?"

"Then I'll never set foot in Logan's Town again."

"Ain't good enough."

"What?"

"Ain't good enough. If there ain't no body up in that house, then you keep your ass outta Logan's Town from here on out, after you give me a hundred dollars."

"You want money?" I asked incredulously.

"I gotta go out in the cold in the middle of the night," he replied, pulling the suspenders dangling at his sides up over his arms. "I think that's worth a little overtime. Don't you?"

And I said, "Fine, we can take my car. But don't start spending your money quite yet."

FIVE

■■■■■■■■■

NAT WOKE UP at nine-thirty Sunday morning, and I was there to see it happen. True, I was a little bleary-eyed from being up all night, but I was there, and goddamn glad I was.

I went straight to the hospital from Logan's Town, arriving at two A.M. and clutching two file folders full of paper that I'd xeroxed in the sheriff's office while Deputy King nervously watched for the sheriff from around the curtain by his desk. You should have seen his face when we opened that pantry door. The only thing that surprised him more than the body was my offer to disappear.

"Look," I told him, "I don't want to be involved in this. I've got my own problems. Why don't you just tell the sheriff that, after sitting up all night pondering the case, you went up to the house to check things out and found her yourself? It would look good on your record."

"Really?" was the deputy's reply. "No shit? You won't say nothin'?"

And I said, "Cross my heart."

So after running me back to the office to wait, Deputy King returned to the immigrants' house and stayed with the body until the sheriff arrived to take over the scene. He returned to the office at about one in the morning because the sheriff had told him to, "go back and man the phones," and it was then that he made good on our bet, letting me use the office photocopier on anything I wanted—and what I wanted was everything they had, which, as it turned out after I got a chance to sit down and really look it over, was one hell of a lot. No wonder that fucking sheriff spent so much time grinning, I thought, hunched over the file I'd taken with me and sipping my second cup of vending machine coffee. He thinks he's got it all figured out.

At six in the morning I called first Jerry, and then my dad, just to let them know that I was in Southwest General Hospital's downstairs lounge, waiting for permission to visit my wife. At seven I called Larry Fizner, because I felt that I owed it to him. And at eight I called Jerry again, because I was lonely. At nine a nurse came and got me, saying, "It won't be long now, Mr. Hawley." And she was right.

Nat was in a semiprivate room, which means that she was sharing it with somebody else, which, as far as I could tell made it a semi-not-private room. When I walked in, it was the first time I'd seen her since the second time they'd carted her off to X ray from the E.R., and I was pleasantly surprised to see that she didn't look nearly as bad as I had imagined she would. In my mind, she was lying in a bed that was surrounded by beeping machines with little blips of light quivering in response to her fluttering heart, hooked up to tubes that hung from silver rods, dripping drugs into her veins. But instead I found her resting on her back in bed, looking like Nat, with a cast on her arm. She had a black eye, but it wasn't that bad, and her face was only a little swollen on one side. There were no intravenous tubes anywhere to be seen, and not so much as a single heart monitor beeping by the bed. Just Nat, lying on her back with a white sheet pulled up to her breast, her eyes closed, looking like an angel.

I didn't cry until the nurse closed the curtain to give us some semi-privacy. Then I folded my hands and sat next to the bed, near her head, looking down at her as the tears rolled down my cheeks.

"I love you, Nat," I whispered, tasting a tear as it slid from my upper lip into my mouth. "More than anything else in the whole world, I love you."

They were the same words I had used the night I asked her to marry me, New Year's Eve, over nine years ago. It had been raining in cold, icy sheets that chittered on the apartment's window, there was candlelight flickering like yellow water on the walls, and we had shared a bottle of cheap champagne because it was all we could afford. It was the third time I'd asked, and I'll never forget what it felt like when she said yes.

"I'm sorry, sweetheart," I added, my fingers bunched in the sheet near her uninjured arm. "For everything I've done since then, I'm so, so sorry."

I was talking about my guilt, talking about it aloud because it was driving me crazy keeping it inside. The guilt of being ranked a genius when they took my I.Q. in grade school so that my father could beam with pride and say I was going to be a rich man someday, and never quite making it. The guilt of being the first member of an immigrant family to go to college without having to work two or three jobs to pay for it—because my dad worked three jobs and paid for it for me—only to blow the whole thing by nearly flunking out. The guilt of spending the entire time between my seventeenth and thirtieth birthdays either drunk, hung over, or getting ready to go out and get drunk again.

And, most of all, the guilt of leaving my wife alone during all that time. All those nights when, after working a full day she came home and made me a supper that I would wolf down before kissing her on the cheek and heading out the door. All those nights when I stumbled in at two or three in the morning to find her asleep, alone. All those nights when I was a shit; you can't change those nights, you can't mend them, or alter them, or erase them. You can't get them back. You can't shout loud enough or cry hard enough when that moment of screaming realization falls in on top of you and you see yourself as others must see you . . . and hate every bit of it.

My moment came when my brother drove his Camaro into a telephone pole in a bar's parking lot at two in the morning, after I had tried to punch him out for coming to get me because he knew I was too loaded to drive. It should have been me who was paralyzed that night, not Jerry.

It should have been me who was thrown down the stairs, not Nat.

It should have been me . . . over and over again.

Every single day I'm reminded of my own limitations through the death I see. I know, better than most perhaps, just how temporary life is. And, as a result, I tend to count the days, the hours, and sometimes even the minutes. Minutes wasted, I regret. It weighs on me. Another minute gone, and what did I do with it? Another day passed, and what do I have to show? A week, a month, a year . . . vanished! And for what?

That's my guilt: that for all those precious, irretrievable years when my marriage was new and my wife, who always tried so valiantly to find something to be happy about, was looking to me for love and support, I was asleep at the wheel. I ignored her. I treated her like she didn't count. And still, she stuck with me. That's my guilt: that my brother, who had only wanted to protect me, had lost his legs for his trouble. And still he stuck with me. That my dad, who hoped for so much, and who got so little, still stuck with me. That they all had stayed, despite what I'd done to them, each in turn . . . that's my guilt.

Nat once said that I try to carry too much of the load. That I can't be responsible for the happiness of everyone I know. But I am. We all are. In the end it's all we have to offer one another, it's all we have to give. You are mine, and I am yours, and not one of us can ever hope to find a moment's peace while denying that simple truth. It was a realization I came to when I was thirty years old. And it's the remorse of having missed it for those preceding thirty years that practically turns me inside out.

"I love you, Nat," I whispered again, because it was the only thing I could say that didn't hurt.

I would have preferred to be alone with her when she came to, but it wasn't to be. Shortly after nine my dad wheeled my brother in, both of them looking as if they, too, expected beeping machines. The whole left side of Jerry's face had turned black-and-blue, and he held a bundle of multicolored carnations on his lap that was so big that it came up to his chin. There had to be sixty of them, wrapped in newspaper at the bottom and sprinkled with baby's breath on top. I knew they were left over from the funeral dad had run out of the old Hawley Funeral Home the day before. But that's one perk of being in the business: you get an awful lot of leftover flowers that people don't want.

At nine-fifteen, Larry Fizner arrived, clutching a "Whitman's Sampler," which he had sampled on the way over, and keeping just as quiet as a mouse . . . which was, I knew, the ultimate compliment because it was a gift it cost him so dearly to give.

And just before Nat opened her eyes at nine-thirty, Father Andrew Mylanko, the pastor of the Ukrainian Orthodox Cathedral located down the street from the old Hawley Funeral Home showed up, dressed in his red and gold finery and looking a little pissed because the nurse had told him not to sing.

So instead of a tender, solitary moment shared between Nat and myself, with her eyes fluttering open to find her loving husband leaning over her, anxious with concern, she came awake to a whole crew of people who loved her, which I suppose was even better.

She was very weak, so we couldn't stay long. I held her good hand and told her how much she meant to me; Father Mylanko prayed; Dad and Jerry arranged flowers in every kind of container they could find, including a stainless steel urine pot from under the bed; and Larry sat in one corner, looking solemn and crossing himself every time the priest did. After about fifteen minutes a nurse arrived to shoo us out, saying that we weren't even all supposed to be in there at the same time. But before I left I got a minute alone with Nat, who looked up at me as I kissed her on the forehead. She squeezed my hand, nodded when I said that I loved her, and looked as if she were about to cry. I held her, pressed my face to the side of her head ever so gently, and asked, "Was it that deputy? Is he the one who did it?"

She shook her head, her eyes growing stern as she whispered, "No."

I kissed her again, and then I left, with the nurse on my tail, but not before I got one last look at Nat, lying in that bed, a bed that a stranger had put her in with a single, vicious stroke.

After a lot of sympathetic noises and questions about what there was for them to do to help, Dad and Jerry finally agreed to go back to the funeral home, leaving Larry and I to meet in the same basement lounge where I had spent my sleepless night. There, I described what I had learned about the immigrants, John Gilbert, and the body in the pantry, before summarizing what was in Alexander Kane's autopsy protocol.

"He was drowned," I said, standing as if addressing a board meeting. "According to the coroner, he suffered two compressed disks—let's see, spinal vertebrae five and six—when he slammed into the steering wheel of his car. He apparently hit the top of his head on the windshield, which accounts for the compression fractures, which were supposedly serious enough to affect the rest of his body."

"Paralysis?" Larry asked.

I nodded.

"Is the coroner sure?"

I shrugged, saying, "As sure as he can be, postmortem. There was apparently some pretty significant nerve damage, which is why he removed those vertebrae during the autopsy."

Larry nodded, frowning as I ran through the scenario Deputy King had finally explained to me about Mr. Kane's final moments, which went like this:

Kane's car was forced from the road by another vehicle. When it hit the drainage ditch, its wheels dropped forward, throwing Kane, who was not wearing a seat belt, into the windshield so that he hit with the top of his head, resulting in a compression fracture of two spinal vertebrae, theoretically sufficient to render the lower portion of his body paralyzed. Then, while Kane sat slumped, helpless, and in all likelihood, unconscious, someone pulled him out of the driver's seat, and threw him facedown into the drainage ditch, leaving him to drown. Naturally, Sheriff Paulson had done all the typical investigative stuff he was paid to do, leading him to the conclusion that he had sufficient evidence to arrest a suspect in the crime.

"So, do you think that sheriff knows what he's doin'?" Larry asked.

"I don't know," I said, suddenly feeling the sleepless night trying to catch up with me. "I guess we'll just have to wait and see. But in the meantime, take a look at these."

Opening a second file folder, I spread a series of xeroxed sheets out on the table. One bore the fuzzy, black-and-white images of photocopied crime scene photographs, showing Alexander Kane lying facedown in the ditch. Another was a copy of the property sheet the sheriff had constructed recording the things Mr. Kane was wearing when he died, as well as the contents of his car. Two of the items listed on that sheet had caught my interest. The first was his Rolex wristwatch, which he had been coincidentally wearing, serving to make my story sound all the more plausible to Nurse Hoke at the Wittmere County Hospital. (That watch was presently locked up in the sheriff's safe until such a time as he deemed it appropriate to release it to the family.) The second item was the one I was sure would catch Larry Fizner's attention. As he rose and lifted the page from the table, he ran his eyes over it, stopped, and glanced up at me, saying, "An icon?"

I nodded as I replied, "They found it in two pieces in the trunk of his car. It's painted on a piece of wood about three feet by three feet square, but the front panel had yet to be secured to the back. It's called the 'Our Lady of Perpetual Help.' A stylized Mary holding the baby Jesus. Very famous, very traditional, and very nice."

"You think it's forged?" he asked.

I shrugged, saying, "It would only be considered forged if he tried to sell it as authentic. Before he left I asked Father Mylanko where Eastern Orthodox churches in the U.S. get their icons, and he said that there are people around who paint them. If Kane took orders and sold them as original works of art, then it's a perfectly legitimate setup."

I handed him another photocopied page so that he could see the reproductions of the Polaroids the sheriff had taken of the icon's front and back.

"Judging by those pictures, the icon Kane was carrying was still in the process of being made," I said. "Apparently, it was constructed of two separate pieces, the front held to the back with four wooden pegs that had yet to be put in place. Kane had the thing tucked in the trunk of his car, wrapped up in a blanket, next to this."

I pulled out another photocopied sheet and pointed, saying, "It's a photo album full of color pictures of other icons, all professionally taken and numbered with what look like identification codes."

"It sounds like a fucking catalogue," Larry growled.

I nodded, saying, "That's about the size of it, which doesn't prove or disprove forgery, which I think would all depend on his presentation anyway."

"I suppose there's no indication in the album of where the pictures were taken?" Larry commented.

"Are you kidding?" I asked.

"Does the widow know about this?"

"I don't know."

"How about the kid?"

"You mean about the icon, or the arrest?"

"Either."

"I'm sure he doesn't know about the arrest," I said, pumping quarters into the coffee machine with my back to where Larry sat at the table. "About the other stuff, who knows? But if he knew about the arrest, you can bet your ass that both he and his mother would be screaming bloody murder. And with my luck, they'd be screaming at me. If he knew about the icons, depending on what his father told him—if he told him anything at all—he might not even think they're important."

"So ya know what ya gotta do next, don't ya?" Larry said, putting the Xerox down.

"I've got a pretty good idea."

"How ya think he's gonna take it?"

"I wouldn't be surprised if he tried to run away," I said, sitting down at the table and rubbing my eyes. Suppressing a yawn, I leaned back, sipped my coffee, and added, "Okay, Mr. Fizner, it's time you told me how you knew that Alex Kane was in the art smuggling business. You promised to fill me in, remember?"

Offering me a cigarette from the pack of Camels he'd taken from me in the bar the previous evening, which I declined, Larry lit up and said that it wasn't really much of a story.

" 'Bout a year ago I was workin' a divorce case that involved this honey whose old man was a big shot in some Fortune 500 company," he said. "Supposedly, this guy was loaded to the gills. But in court he claimed poverty, sayin' that he'd made some bad investments that ate up his personal worth. My client disagreed, saying that instead of bein' broke, he'd secretly sunk his cash into an art collection that he had stashed someplace where she couldn't find it. It had to be worth a ton, she said, 'cause during an argument one time, the asshole had blurted out that some of the stuff he owned had been smuggled out of Russia just for him. She said that he spent a lot of time down in Logan's Town, which is practically owned by Alex Kane's antiques company, so that's where I started. One thing led to another, and I picked up on Uri, had a talk or two with Kane, and then everything just dried up. I figured that Kane either got smart or shut down. Either way I was fucked, so I wrote it off as me openin' my big mouth too soon and stuck it in my dead file as a loss."

"So, what do you think about it now?" I asked.

"Now," he said, lifting the Xerox of the icon that had been found in the trunk of the murdered man's car, "I think we've got some pictures of our own to take."

I didn't get back to the funeral home until five. Dad and Jerry had taken care of arranging the flowers for Mr. Kane's wake, which gave me enough time to take a quick shower, get dressed, and set up the equipment Larry produced from his van before Mrs. Kane and her son walked in at six-thirty. I greeted them solemnly, showed them around a little, and then left them alone in the parlor where they stood in front of Alexander Kane's casket—silent, dry, and wordless. At seven I unlocked the front door, where I spent the next two hours greeting those who came to visit and thinking about what was going to happen at nine.

The place was packed from the stroke of seven until well after nine-thirty. It seemed like everybody in Cleveland walked through, including a number of newspaper reporters, and Agatha O'Toole, who was responsible for the "sleuthing undertaker" moniker I'd been carrying around since she first coined it when she mentioned my interest in murder mystery weekend getaways in her weekly "human interest" column two years back. We had more or less run into one another during one of those weekends, and the angle of the undertaker who always seemed to come up a winner at solving staged murders sounded too good to pass up. The fact that I had since gotten involved in solving real crimes only served to add spice to her "discovery." She was constantly asking me leading questions in the hope that I would provide her with more material for her column. After a respectful time had passed, she came up to me and expressed her sympathies about Nat's "accident."

"Where'd you hear about that?" I asked, frankly astonished that the story had gotten around so fast.

Aggie's sixty-two years old, about five feet tall, has frizzy hair dyed a very peculiar shade of lavender-red, and big green eyes that are bright and perpetually in motion. She laughed and asked if I really needed her to answer that question, to which I replied that I supposed I didn't, accepting her condolences but forbidding her to write anything about it in her column. As soon as I did, those sparkling emerald eyes of hers turned crafty, and she leaned in close and said, "So, it's a case, is it? A personal vendetta?"

It made me uncomfortable to think my life could be so transparent even to this all but perfect stranger, so I said, "Absolutely not. I've turned everything over to the police, and that's where it stands."

She smiled crossly and put her hand on my cheek, saying,

"You're so cute when you lie." Then she pinched the flesh next to my mouth between her fingers and held on, squeezing a little for emphasis and adding, "Promise to tell me all the details when it's over, or I'll start scribbling about it for tomorrow's column as soon as I get home."

"But there's nothing to scribble," I protested.

"Then I'll make something up," she said, smiling and pinching my cheek so hard that I lifted my hand and grimaced.

"Okay! Okay! I promise," I said.

"That's a good boy," she said, releasing me with a happy nod. "Now, where's the ham sandwiches?"

At 9:55 I finally got the doors closed, and as Mrs. Kane and her son were removing their coats from the hall closet, I asked them to step into my office. They looked tired and irritable, so I got right to the point.

"I know it's late and you want to get home," I said, loosening my tie. "But we three need to have a talk, and I'm afraid it can't wait. You'll see why in a minute. But first, Edward, have you told your mother yet about the tape you found on your father's desk?"

Edward, dressed in a black suit, with a black shirt and tie, looked a little like a vampire. His complexion was pale to the point of pallor—which I suspected he had embellished with powder—and his blond hair was pulled straight back from his face and tied into a stubby ponytail with a rubber band. His reaction to my statement was to feign confusion while glaring at me with his eyes. But I ignored his silent pleas for secrecy and said, "Well, did you?"

"What tape? What are you talking about?" his mother asked.

"This one," I said, removing the tape from my shirt pocket and describing the interview Edward and I had conducted after she had concluded making her husband's funeral arrangements. As I spoke I watched her face. As I've said before, she was a striking woman, and it was in that instant, when the first sparks of anger snapped in the depths of her auburn eyes, that I really appreciated just how beautiful she was.

"Edward!" she exclaimed, turning to her son once I'd finished. "What's the meaning of this?"

His mouth worked as if he were chewing air, and he lifted his hands hopelessly, looking to me for help. I gave him a little time to squirm, then dropped the cassette on my desk, saying, "There's a sheriff down in Logan's Town named Cornell Paulson. You probably know him, Edward. And if you don't, I'm sure your mother does. He's going to arrest you tomorrow, right after your dad's funeral. He's got evidence linking you to his murder."

"Murder?" Mrs. Kane exclaimed, and in an instant both she and her son were on their feet.

"Yes, murder," I said, taking a seat behind my desk. "Please sit down, Mrs. Kane. And you, too, Edward."

"I don't like your tone of voice," Mrs. Kane exclaimed. "I've got lawyers, Mr. Hawley. Good lawyers who would just love to get a piece of this."

"You're not telling me anything I don't already know," I cut in. "Undertakers are vulnerable because we're easy targets. And that's nothing new. But I'm doing you a favor here, Mrs. Kane. I could have kept my mouth shut and let your son ride back from the cemetery in the back of a police car. He's going to anyway; there's nothing we can do to prevent that. But I thought it might take some of the edge off if you knew that it was coming."

Her expression had grown cool and unreadable. Folding her arms over her breast, she said, "I'm waiting, Mr. Hawley. You've got two minutes before I call out the dogs."

"All right," I said, glancing at Edward, who had slunk back to his chair where he was chewing his thumbnail as his eyes moved back and forth from his mother's back to my face. "I'll give it to you straight, and to hell with tact.

"The way things stand is like this: according to the Wittmere County Sheriff's Office, your husband's car left the state route after striking another car, parked across the intersection. The driver's side bumper of his car had been damaged, as well as the fender and the grill. Paint samples taken from his BMW match samples obtained from the

rear panel of a red, 1991 Porsche 944 titled in the name
of Edward Kane, which was found parked behind a house
owned by the Kane Antique and Collectible Company at
187 South Dovetail Lane, in Logan's Town. The Porsche
was also damaged in a way consistent with its having been
struck by another vehicle traveling at a fairly great rate of
speed. There's also a witness."

"A witness?" Mrs. Kane said, her voice softer, her eyes
looking slightly pained as the crow's-feet in their corners
began to crinkle. "To what?"

"To the fact that your son was driving his Porsche on the
night his father died."

"Who is this witness?"

"A man named John Gilbert."

"Oh, Jesus!" Edward cried.

His mother turned on him and hissed, "Shut up!" Then
she turned her attention back to me and said, "And how do
you know all this, Mr. Hawley?"

"Mrs. Kane," I said, ignoring the question, "a Russian
girl was murdered in Logan's Town, probably on the same
night as your husband, or shortly thereafter. I've seen her
body, so you can believe me when I say it's true. Your
son came to me on the same day you made your husband's
funeral arrangements with a cassette tape upon which he
said his father had recorded a suicide note. He claimed that
it actually wasn't his father's voice on the tape and asked
me to find some evidence to prove it. After we visited
Logan's Town yesterday morning in line with your son's
request, my wife was assaulted, here at the funeral home,
by a man who said that he did it because he wanted us to
start minding our own business.

"Mrs. Kane, this entire affair, from the word go, has
been one cosmically fucked-up mess. And unless we three
sit down and come to some understanding as to a course
of action, your son is going to jail. Maybe for good.

"There. End of presentation. How'd I do on time?"

Mrs. Kane just stood there, looking at me. It was Edward
who finally broke the silence and set things into motion
when he jumped up and said, "Please, Mother! Please! Talk

to him! Tell him, for God's sake! I can't go to jail, I just can't!"

"Tell me what, Mrs. Kane?" I asked, with my eyes settled on hers.

"Sit down, Edward," she said, without looking at him. Then, sighing and brushing her skirt beneath her as she resumed her seat, she asked, "Does the name, New Philadelphia, mean anything to you, Mr. Hawley? It's a little town located about fifteen minutes south of Logan's Town, and it has an airport that's just perfect for landing private airplanes."

I was silent as I listened to her speak, feeling a tension in my spine that I knew was a combination of nerves and fatigue. There was also a roaring in my ears that came, I suddenly understood, from the undeniable reality of how I had already been used by both this woman and her son.

"It was in Logan's Town where my husband dealt with our special collectors," she explained, her hands folded on her lap, her son mauling his other thumbnail as she spoke. "I say special because these people are the cream of our customers. The really serious people interested in only the finest pieces we have to offer. To them, collecting is an art, and they're willing to go to great lengths to get what they want."

"In private," I commented.

She nodded once, saying, "Exactly. Alex would meet them at New Philadelphia, then drive them back up to Logan's Town to conduct his business. The meetings were always arranged in advance, with the details worked out beforehand as well. There was no haggling over price or questions of authenticity by the time the collector arrived. All those things had already been settled. It was all quite brief, civilized, and tasteful. It was always, above all else, tasteful."

As hesitant as I was to interrupt the flow of her words, there was a question that I simply had to ask, which was, "Mrs. Kane, how much longer were you and your husband going to continue pretending to be married?"

Her lips slapped shut and went thin and hard with pressure as she studied my face.

"You haven't cried," I explained. "Not a single tear."

"If an emotional outburst would put you at ease," she responded tightly, "I'm sure my son can oblige."

As if on cue, Edward produced a handkerchief, also black, flourished it like a prop, and let the tears run down his cheeks.

Ignoring him, I said, "Would a divorce have been that financially inconvenient?"

"You wouldn't understand," she replied.

To which I responded, "Try me."

"Why?"

"Because you need me, Mrs. Kane. By this time tomorrow night your son will have been booked, fingerprinted, and installed in a Wittmere County jail cell. Then there's the question of who killed the Russian girl. There's no telling where the blame for that one will land, but I've got a pretty good idea. For strictly personal reasons, I've decided that I might be willing to take your problems on as my own. But before I do, I need to know the truth."

"The truth about what?" she asked.

"Everything. You've been lying to me by omission since you first stepped into my office."

"I didn't realize that the relationship between a widow and her funeral director was so . . . intimate," she said, and I found her inflection unsettling.

Edward, who had finally stopped crying, said, "Her name was Erena. Erena Batilovna. And I knew she was going to be trouble. I just knew it."

I blinked, glanced at Edward, and then back at his mother, who took a deep breath, frowned, and asked, "Do I have to sign a paper or something?"

"What kind of paper?" I returned.

"To hire you," she said, "as an investigator. Come to think of it, I *want* to sign something, and I want you to sign it, too. I'm not thrilled about telling you family details with only your verbal promise as my guarantee of secrecy. I saw you talking to Aggie O'Toole earlier this evening, and a woman like her would love nothing more than to splash whatever dirt you can dig up about my husband and me all over her rag of a newspaper."

I told her that I didn't have any contracts in the office, but that I'd have one in the morning. Reluctantly she agreed to wait, then asked for a cup of coffee. "With maybe a shot of something in it. No, Edward doesn't need anything. Just let him be." She settled herself, seemed to turn something over in her mind, and then looked at her son and asked him a question that almost knocked me off my chair.

"Did you do it?" she said, looking right at him. "Did you kill him?"

With red-rimmed eyes, he simply shook his head.

Then she looked at me and started her story by saying, "I suppose you need to know that we have discussed it, Mr. Hawley . . . Edward and I, that is. We've actually, mother and son, sat down and mulled over the feasibility of killing my husband, who was a bastard. An unmitigated son of a bitch. When I did raise the possibility of a divorce a number of years ago he said that if I ever brought it up again, he'd do something terrible to Edward, who was then just a little boy. Even though he didn't love me, he wouldn't let me go. He never let anything go. He was as much a collector as the people he sold things to. He was manic about it. Edward and I were simply part of his collection. Like that Russian girl you say is also dead, and everything else of value he could lay his hands on. It was the essence of his personality, Mr. Hawley—he collected. I think he'd die before letting go of something he valued. And maybe that's just what happened out on that road Friday morning.

"I always knew it would end up like this. And now that it has, you know, it's almost a relief. But you've got to understand, my son didn't do it. He couldn't have done it. He may have been in Logan's Town that night, but he's innocent, Mr. Hawley. I swear."

"Edward was in Logan's Town when his father died?" I asked, trying very hard to maintain a poker face. But I couldn't keep the irritation out of my voice when I turned to her son and demanded, "Why the hell didn't you tell me about this when you brought me your father's suicide tape? When you came in that morning you never so much as mentioned that you were anywhere near him when he died. Now it turns out that it was your car that knocked him off the road, and you just happened to be hanging around? That doesn't look good, Eddie. It makes me think you're trying to be clever."

"I didn't know!" Edward insisted, speaking in a jagged choke that sounded as if something were constricting his throat. "I swear. It's true that I was in town that night, but I didn't know anything about the accident until the next day."

"So, are you going to tell me what happened?"

"You mean, my side of the story?"

I nodded.

He looked at his mother, and then at his hands. Then he looked at me and said, "I didn't kill my father, Mr. Hawley. I swear I didn't. I didn't tell you that I was in Logan's Town that night because I never dreamed that my being there had anything to do with his death. But now . . ."

He was crying, and I waited, not helping, watching so that he'd know I was unmoved.

Finally he made a show of composing himself and continued. "I went out Thursday night because I wanted to talk to Erena."

"The Russian girl?" I asked, trying to keep the surprise out of my voice. "You speak Russian?"

He nodded.

Another little secret, I thought. The kid was full of them.

"Did she speak English?" I asked.

"Not much," he returned. "I was trying to teach her, but it was going slow."

"Okay," I said. "Go on."

His story from there was reasonably straightforward. Erena's brother's name was Vaslov, and her father's name was Maxym. Edward had gotten a call at home from John Gilbert earlier in the day that Erena was lonely and asking to see him. She was temperamental. Most artists were. Sometimes she got in a funk and his visits seemed to help. She pined for a social life that her present situation in America denied her. Until the difficulty with her passport was straightened out, it was necessary for the Russians to avoid contact with too many people.

"What difficulty?" I cut in.

Edward winced.

His father, he explained, had told the Russians that they had to lay low because the American authorities would deport them if they got the chance. In Russia, he explained, it wasn't unusual to wait five or ten years for an exit visa to be approved. But Alex Kane had pulled some strings and gotten them out by clandestine means. He was going to pull similar strings in this country to arrange their citizenship, but it would take some time to straighten things out. They would have to be patient, he had said. And so far, they had been patient for nearly two years.

"Because of this need for secrecy," Edward said, "Erena's social contact was limited. And she liked to drink, which made her unpredictable. When Mr. Gilbert noticed her swinging toward a bout of depression, he'd call me."

Gilbert had called Edward early Thursday morning, saying that Erena was restless and argumentative. Edward said that he'd stop by after dinner. Gilbert asked if he could make it earlier because Erena wanted to cook. And Edward grudgingly agreed, steeling himself for a long evening of stories from home, a lot of vodka, and eventually a long cry, concluded by kisses, apologies, and thanks for everything he and his father had done for her and hers.

"But when I got there, she was fine," he said, hunching forward in his seat. "Absolutely fine. No booze on her breath. No bitchy mood. Happy as a clam. We ate, talked, and watched a movie. I had some vodka. I mean, even when they were in the best of moods you couldn't not have a little vodka with the Batilovnas. And at about eleven Erena said she wanted to go for a drive. Which was our signal."

"What kind of signal?" I asked.

He looked at me imploringly, as if he were willing the information into my head as a way of avoiding the need of words.

"Just tell him," his mother cut in. "Don't be a baby. I know all about it, and it won't make me faint."

Edward winced, looked down at his hands, and explained, "It was our signal that she wanted to . . . go to bed."

"So?" I said, deliberately making him spell it out.

"With me," he said.

I nodded.

"So?"

"So, we left," he explained, his fingers working nervously, and his eyes snapping toward his mother every couple of seconds.

"You took the Porsche?" I asked, for clarity's sake.

He shook his head.

"No. It wouldn't start. But since we were only heading over to the house on Dovetail, Mr. Gilbert said I could use his van. He said that I should take my time with it, and that he'd see what he could do about getting the Porsche running in the morning."

I sat stiffly upright, trying to picture it in my mind, trying to work it through.

"We were gone quite a while," Edward continued. "But I mean, so what? She was a big girl, and all there was at the house for her was another night alone. I dropped her off at, like, three in the morning. I'm not positive about the time, but it was around there somewhere. The house was dark, and she let herself in with a key."

"She carried a key?" I asked.

"No. There was one hidden in a plastic rock in the garden by the front porch. Erena never went out anywhere, so she didn't need to have a key of her own. They just kept the one in the rock in case they ever accidentally locked themselves out of the house."

"Did you see anyone other than Erena when you dropped her off?"

"Nobody. The house was dark."

"And then what happened?"

"I went back to Cleveland." Edward shrugged. "I had classes the next afternoon, so I figured I'd just go home and get some sleep. Mr. Gilbert could use my Porsche during the day, and I'd return his van that night. Or whenever. With all the vans the company owns, it wasn't like he needed that particular one to haul furniture or anything. I got back at about four, saw the light blinking on my answering machine, called my mom back, and then the whole planet got knocked off its orbit."

"Has Sheriff Paulson heard any of this?"

"No. He never asked."

"And have you seen John Gilbert since it happened?"

"No. I've been in Cleveland the whole time."

"And now it's your word against Gilbert's that it wasn't you who was driving the Porsche the night your father died," I said, thinking aloud.

"Him and whoever else saw me drive into town," Edward agreed.

"Anybody see you in the van?" I asked.

"Sure." He nodded. "John Gilbert, and Erena. I don't know about anybody else. It was midnight, and in Logan's Town they roll up the sidewalks right after dinner."

"Now Erena's dead, her father and brother are missing, and John Gilbert's the prosecution's star witness," I mused, looking at Mrs. Kane. "But why would John Gilbert want to kill your husband?"

"Money," Mrs. Kane answered. "It's as simple as that. With my husband gone, he won't have to split the profits anymore. And with Alex dead, what Gilbert's got to sell will be worth more than ever."

"And exactly what is it that he's got to sell?" I asked.

But Mrs. Kane was on her feet, saying that she had had enough for one night. She would be more than willing to tell me anything else I needed to know. But she'd do it after the funeral.

"I am a widow, after all," she said, with a defiant thrust of her chin. "And there's only so much pressure I can stand. This can wait until tomorrow. Before then, Mr. Hawley, I expect you to produce a legal-looking contract for us both to sign."

I told her that I'd do my best and watched her exit with her son. She was quite a lady, Mrs. Kane. I could hardly wait to see what tomorrow would bring.

SIX

■■■■■■■■

"SHE SAYS THAT John Gilbert's the guy who made most of the contacts with their 'special' clients," I explained the next morning, leading the funeral procession into the cemetery and speaking to Larry Fizner, who was sitting to my right in the Cadillac's front seat, frowning. "And that it was her husband who took care of all the actual selling."

"So, Gilbert made the contacts," Larry grumbled, looking out the window, which was open a crack to let out his cigarette smoke. "How's that supposed to prove that he did the murder?"

I shrugged, saying, "She thinks he lured her son out to Logan's Town, rigged his car so that it wouldn't start when he tried to go home, and then used the car to force Kane off the freeway. Then he let the kid drive back to Cleveland in his van and parked the dented car behind the house where he knew Edward had taken the girl the night before. Actually, when you spell it out like that, it all sounds pretty simple."

"Yeah," Larry agreed. "But the question is, why would he take the chance? If it went down that way, it's as premeditated as hell. And that's the chair any way you cut it. We must be talkin' about a pile of cash to make it worth his while."

"She wouldn't go into the details about that part last night," I said as the cemetery car led us to the grave. "I'm going to her house later this afternoon to see her husband's office, and that's when she said she'd give me the proof I'll need to clear her son. Until then, she said I'd have to be satisfied knowing that her husband was a crook, and that her son is 'innocent of any wrongdoing' . . . her words."

"A crook how?" Larry asked.

"In the minds of some collectors, rarity defines an object's price," I said, all but quoting Mrs. Kane. "The more exclusive the piece, the more it's worth. Alex Kane's talent, at least according to his wife, was that he was able to find one-of-a-kind goodies like nobody's business. And John Gilbert supposedly had a knack for discreetly locating the people who wanted those particular pieces the most. Kane wasn't particular about where his merchandise came from, and neither were the people Gilbert found for him to sell to since they weren't buying for resale, but for their own private collections. It was a match made in heaven, and it drove Mrs. Kane nuts knowing what was going on because she was always worried that one day her husband was going to get busted and piss away their business."

"So Kane was a high-class fence," Larry observed.

I nodded. "But instead of selling hot TVs out of the back of a van, he was selling hot art objects over hors d'oeuvres in the back of a limo. At least that's what his wife says. Now, you stay here and play with your pictures while I go to work."

The pictures I was referring to were of all the people who had come to pay their respects at Alex Kane's funeral the night before. At Larry's suggestion, we had set up a camera on a tripod behind the curtain in back of Kane's casket, running a shutter button on a line along the baseboard of the wall to a side room off the parlor. Larry had been sitting in that room all during the evening viewing, peeking through a crack in the door and snapping a picture every time someone stepped up to the casket. I'd changed the film twice for him on the pretext of adding or moving floral pieces, feeling like James Bond both times. On his lap he had a stack of black-and-white contact prints of the shots he'd taken, four strips of film per page, and a shot glass-sized magnifying glass for examining each frame. He had been up all night processing film in his own private darkroom, he said, which was part of the reason he was feeling so grouchy.

I left him with his glasses perched on his forehead and the magnifier pressed to a page as he squinted one eye and said, "Yeah, yeah, yeah," as a dismissal. Straightening my overcoat, I stepped from the Cadillac, waving for cars in the procession to form two lines so that people wouldn't have so far to walk to the grave, and noticing the dark shape of a police car parked beneath a willow tree a couple of sections down from where I stood.

The procession was huge, 130 cars, and I had used three escort cars to keep it together. It took fifteen minutes for everybody to form up around the grave, and then the minister did his thing, with Mrs. Kane and her son, both shrouded in black, standing to his right, and me, hands folded, head down, standing to his left. When he finished I thanked everybody for coming, invited them back to the restaurant, and asked them to place the flower they had been given atop the casket before leaving. I shook hands with the minister and watched everybody file past the casket for the last time. Then I waited.

The only people left to actually see the arrest were me, Larry, the hearse driver, two guys from the vault company, and Aggie O'Toole, who, displaying a sixth sense for sticking her nose into other people's business, had stayed in her car as everybody else pulled away. Mrs. Kane, Edward, and I were standing at the roadside next to the grave when the Wittmere County Sheriff's squad car rolled quietly up to us, with another unmarked car following behind. Where the second car came from I didn't know. But I assumed it must have been in the procession. As it turned out, it was a Cleveland police detective unit, sent to observe the arrest, since Sheriff Paulson was operating out of his own county.

Edward, assuming the role of sacrificial lamb, held his hands out, wrists together, palms up, head held back and eyes closed, as if he expected the sheriff to manacle him to a chain and drag him behind his car all the way back to Logan's Town. Instead, the sheriff tipped his hat to Mrs. Kane and said, "I'm sincerely sorry 'bout this, ma'am." Then he led Edward to the cruiser, saying, "Oh, cut it out,

Eddie. Nobody's gonna hurt ya." Before closing the car's door, he recited Edward's Miranda rights, then he went over and said something to the grey man from the unmarked car, who nodded and drove away. Then he came back to where I was standing, waiting until Mrs. Kane had been folded into the limousine before turning his attention to me.

We were standing next to the driver's side door of my Cadillac, and just as the sheriff was about to speak, the car's window slid down so that Larry could listen without getting out. The sheriff wasn't smiling, I noticed, and his lips were white. "You wait right here," he said, before returning to his car and retrieving something long and dark from the front seat. It was then that I noticed that Deputy King hadn't come along for the arrest. Stepping up close, the sheriff pointed his finger at my face and said, "You gotta learn to be more careful." He lifted the object he'd gotten out of his squad car for me to see with his other hand.

It was my umbrella.

"You left this by the front door in the alcove last night when you went breakin' and enterin'," he continued, and there was no mistaking how hard he was trying to keep a lid on his temper. "It's got *Hawley Funeral Home* stamped on the handle."

I swallowed nervously, but said nothing.

"When I showed it to Church," the sheriff went on, "his mouth fell open so wide he looked like a fish. Did you really think I'd believe that Church went out to that house on his own? That boy tellin' me that he'd been up all night 'ponderin' the case' was the same as sayin' that he'd decided to grow feathers and take up layin' eggs.

"I could arrest you, Mr. Hawley. You've got that much of a grasp on the situation, don't ya?"

"On what charge?" I asked, my tongue feeling dry.

"I've got physical evidence that you was on the premises where a murder took place." He smiled coldly. "You work it out from there."

"But she was dead when I found her," I protested.

"That's what you say," he returned, throwing the umbrella at me as if it were a rifle. "Now stay out of it! I warned you once. I won't warn you again. Stay the fuck out of it, or you're gonna end up sorry. You're already on my bad side, which I can sincerely say ain't a place you wanna be."

"Edward didn't do it," I said, the umbrella in my right hand, my feet planted firmly on the ground. The temperature had been dropping steadily since the morning Nat and I drove out to Logan's Town with the Miata's top down, and it was now only about thirty-five degrees. The sun was bright in a cloudless sky, and we could see our breath as we spoke. Over the sheriff's right shoulder, I could see his squad car, and Edward Kane's face was framed in the backseat window, his eyes locked on mine.

"You've arrested the wrong man," I added. "You've made a mistake."

The sheriff looked at me for maybe twenty seconds before he said, "We're charging him with two counts of murder, you know. The coroner found fibers on that immigrant girl's coat that match the rug in the trunk of his car. Looks like he killed her someplace else and took her back to the house later. We still haven't figured out where he got the curtain cord he used to strangle her with, but we will. I got search warrants for his apartment, and for his mother's house, too, both up here and in Logan's Town. It's only gonna be a matter of time 'fore we know everything there is to know 'bout what happened the night his daddy died. And in the meantime, Eddie's gonna cool his jets where I can keep my eye on him."

"He didn't do it, Sheriff," I said. "That boy's getting screwed."

"Wanna bet?" the sheriff said, narrowing his eyes in such a way that I instantly understood that he knew all about the wager Deputy King and I had made.

"A hundred bucks?" I asked.

"Yeah," he said.

"You're on."

The sheriff stomped back to his car, opened the door, seemed to consider something, and paused as he was about to lower himself in, glancing my way and adding, "You undertaker boys are regulated by the state, you know. And

I think it's about time an inspector paid you a visit."

"You just go ahead and call the inspector," I snapped back. "See if I care."

Then he drove away, his tires spinning on the gravel.

"Well, I guess you told him," Larry commented from inside the Cadillac as I opened the driver's door and got in. "He won't be fucking around with you anymore, I'll bet."

"Oh, stick it in your ass," I fumed, starting the car and throwing the umbrella in the backseat. "Who's he think he is, getting in my face like that? Fucking hillbilly jerk!"

"Yeah, well, just to cap off a perfect morning," Larry said, offering me the magnifier and one of his pages of contact prints, "take a look at this."

I took what he handed me without looking at him. Still working on what the sheriff had said and what I should have said in return, I put my eye to the magnifier and aimed it at the frame Larry indicated, becoming instantly focused on what I saw. Holding the page to the window to catch the light better, I looked again, pulled the magnifier away from my face, and said, "He was there? Last night?"

Larry shrugged, saying, "We can't be positive, but that guy in the picture sure looks like the suspect composite your brother made with your policeman friend to me."

I withdrew from my shirt pocket the folded photocopied drawing of the suspect that Jerry and Mike Agnello—Michelangelo, to his friends in the Suspect Composite Department of the Cleveland Police Department—had made. They had used an Identikit to painstakingly piece together different features until they had arrived at a face that Jerry pronounced to be that of the man who had attacked him and Nat. That morning Mike Agnello was running the original through a computer program downtown that would exclude any mug shots on file that didn't meet the general parameters established by the composite. So instead of Jerry's having to page through thousands of pictures, the computer would narrow down his choices to only those similar enough to his original to be worth looking at.

Glancing at the composite for perspective, I looked at the contact sheet again, and said, "It's him. It's got to be.

The fucker came to the wake! Holy Christ, he probably walked right past me. If Jerry had been around, he could have blown the whistle on the spot!"

Larry nodded.

"But what's it mean?"

"It means," Larry said, "that he isn't a hired goon, but somebody with enough of an interest in what's happening here to stick around and personally keep an eye on things. In short, it means that the asshole's a player. And since he's a player, we can nail him."

"You thought he was hired muscle?" I asked.

"Yeah." Larry shrugged.

"Why didn't you tell me that before now?"

" 'Cause if he was, we'd never have found him. He woulda just disappeared back into jerk-off land, and I didn't want you to get discouraged."

"I see. So what else haven't you told me?"

Larry looked at me with half a smile but didn't say another word.

As it turned out, the Kanes lived in a huge old house just around the corner from my new funeral home. Berea's a college town, with Lawrence-Wynn University being the area's biggest employer. The house Mr. and Mrs. Kane owned had been the home of the college's first president, and was built in 1868. I'd walked past it a thousand times when I was a student and had always admired its imposing size, ten-foot tall, wrought iron fence bordering the yard, and a stained-glass, cathedral-style window, two stories high, that was the central feature of its forward facade.

The bell was one of those Victorian jobs that you twist like a windup toy, and it made a BRRRRINNNG! sound that was faint coming from the other side of the big oak door. I expected Mrs. Kane, but I got a butler. I mean it. A butler! No shit. I'd never seen a real, live-ass butler before, and I have to admit it took me a couple of seconds to get it back together after he said, "May I help you?" in perfect, subdued tones. I introduced myself, and he said, "Ah, yes. Madam has been expecting you." I followed the guy into the biggest, darkest, coolest house I had ever seen. I mean, this place was magnificent. From the outside it looked big . . . huge in fact. But from the inside, it looked like a genuine, honest-to-God, movie mansion.

I guess it's what I should have been expecting. After all, the Kanes did own a chain of antique stores, so I should have figured that they would keep the best stuff they ran across for themselves. But even forewarned, I was still unprepared for the richness of the house's furnishings. The place looked like a museum, with deep Oriental rugs atop gleaming hardwood floors, intricate, flower-patterned wallpaper—reproduced from the original William Morris prints, I would later learn—plush velvet curtains hanging over fifteen-foot high windows with tassels as big as army boots, and furniture of such size and grace that I couldn't even imagine anyone actually sitting on it. And that was the sensation I finally identified as the most predominant in the house. The place was so thoroughly decorated, and so painfully tasteful, that it was hard to believe that anyone actually lived there.

On the floor around where I stood in the front foyer was a geometric pattern of colored light refracted through the stained-glass window at my back. The colors were predominantly reds and yellows, with a little blue thrown in for variety. It lent the place a slightly twisted atmosphere, being a little too bright, a little too immediate to fully blend in with the decor. The window, I realized, was meant to be seen from the outside, with the light from the house's interior illuminating it at night for the benefit of those passing by. Inside, during the day, its gay colors were more of an intrusion than a pleasure.

Instead of asking me to wait for "madam," the butler led me up a huge, marble staircase, explaining that he had been instructed to show me directly to the "master's" office. Madam would join me when I had completed what I had come to do, not wishing her presence to distract me in any way. I was to indicate that I was finished by pulling the velvet cord hanging on the wall, which immediately brought to mind the "Case of the Speckled Band," one of my favorite Sherlock Holmes stories, and one of the spookiest. As soon as I thought of the word, I realized that spooked was exactly what I was, and I suddenly couldn't wait to get out of there.

Alexander Kane's office was on the second floor, a large, wide room with two bay windows and a chocolate-brown rug interwoven with amber-colored flowers. There was a desk the size of a bathtub against one wall which was flanked by two wooden filing cabinets. A maroon leather chair with gold studs along its edges sat behind the desk, and a couple of other odd pieces were scattered around, including one of those bentwood and wicker love seats in which the "lovers" would sit side by side, facing different directions, like in the old "Addams Family" TV show. Immediately I noticed that there were keys in every keyhole in the desk drawers and the filing cabinets, meaning that Mrs. Kane had kept her word; I was going to be given access to anything I wanted. So, closing the door behind myself, I stood for a moment, drinking in the atmosphere of the place, and trying to get a feel for exactly who Alexander Kane really was. In the back of my mind, I couldn't help but wonder when Sheriff Paulson would be showing up with his search warrant for these premises, the possibility, as remote as it was, that he would be able to drop Edward Kane off at the Logan's Town jail and return here in time to interrupt my search serving to add an air of urgency to everything I did.

Lowering myself into the leather chair, I examined the desk first. Before me I found the personal computer, typewriter, fax machine, and tape recorder that Edward had described, and a Rolodex, carved-wood pencil box, and adding machine that he hadn't. The tape recorder was an old, portable Sony, about as big as a shoe box, with a slot on top for the tape. I looked at it, imagining Alex Kane sitting here, probably drunk, mumbling out his final statement:

"There are a hundred reasons for me to take the coward's way out, and only two reasons not to . . . and they are my wife and son. I'm afraid the numbers just don't add up. So this life of mine is over. That's it. Good-bye."

Opening a drawer I found a whole line of unopened cassette tapes. Removing and unwrapping one, I inserted it into the machine and hit RECORD, repeating Mr. Kane's farewell message word for word. After rewinding the tape and hitting PLAY, I listened to my own voice crackle through the speaker:

"There are a hundred reasons for me to take the coward's way out, and only two reasons not to . . . and they are my wife and son. I'm afraid the numbers just don't add up. So this life of mine is over. That's it. Good-bye."

CLICK!

I stared at the machine, rewound the tape, and played it again.

"There are a hundred reasons . . . Good-bye."

CLICK!

Rewind.

Play.

"There are a hundred reasons . . . Good-bye."

CLICK!

I did it three more times, and every time the result was the same—at the end of the message there was a distinctly audible CLICK, which was the sound the OFF button had made when I pressed it to stop recording. The condenser microphone was located right next to the OFF button, and it had picked up the sound of the plastic snapping down before the machine's spools stopped turning.

I still had the tape Edward Kane had given me in my pocket, and I quickly put it in the machine and played it through.

Nothing.

No click at the end.

"What the hell?" I said aloud, staring at the tape machine and thinking that this absence of sound meant something.

But what?

Rewinding Edward Kane's tape, I turned the machine's volume all the way up and played it again, grimacing as his father's voice boomed at me, distorted by the little speaker and fuzzy with tape hiss in between words. When he had finished speaking, the tape hiss went on for a second and then disappeared. The rest of the tape was perfectly blank. No hiss. No pops. No nothing.

I ejected the tape and looked at it. Then I compared it with the one I had just removed from the drawer. They were the same brand, and both were sixty minutes long. I looked at the rest of the tapes in the drawer and found that they were all sixty minutes, too. Then I looked in the next drawer, and the next. It was in the bottom drawer on the desk's left-hand side that I found, hidden beneath a stack of telephone books, something that interested me.

Pulling out a large, beautifully bound volume, I laid it on the desk and read the title. *Stolen by War: Art's Greatest Loss.* Inside the book, I found hundreds of pictures, done both in color and in black and white, depicting different works of art, in detail, including measurements and material composition, surrounded by thick columns of text. Soon I understood that each page in the book described a separate, missing masterpiece—a sculpture, painting, or manuscript that had disappeared sometime during the Second World War. Artists' names and biographies were listed, as well as the last location in which each piece was reported to have been seen. In two cases, page numbers were circled. And in one place I found a business card acting as a bookmark.

Leopold J. Chimmings, Esq.
Attorney at Law

It was as I removed and read the business card that I noticed that the message light on the answering machine next to the PC was blinking. Card in hand, I rewound the machine's tape and listened.

"Hello, Mr. Kane," a voice began. "Sorry to miss you, but this is Chet Dewine calling, and I just wanted to touch base with you on . . ."

"Yeah, Chet," the voice of Alex Kane, which I instantly recognized from the suicide tape, cut in, "I'm here."

"Screening calls, huh, Mr. Kane?"

"Yeah." A laugh. "You know how it is. What's up?"

The tape went on for several minutes, stopping only when the conversation was over and the line was disengaged. Nothing important—business related stuff about when a couch was going to be delivered: Wednesday next, no dates. Mr. Kane was apparently one of those people who didn't bother turning the answering machine off when he decided to take a call. It was an old machine, I noticed, and if it was anything like the one I had at home—which I never used—you probably had to reset it if you interrupted the cycle.

When it was done playing, I popped out the tape and examined it. It was the same brand as all the others in the desk, and I was tapping it against my front teeth when a thought tried to take shape in my mind. It was right there. Something. Almost. But then it was gone, and I shrugged, thinking, it'll come. I put the tape back in the machine, thought better of it, and replaced it with the fresh tape I'd just opened after slipping the message tape into my pocket.

I was standing, looking through the top drawer of a filing cabinet that was nearly as tall as I am when the office door opened and Mrs. Kane stepped in, looking very different from the way she had the last time I had seen her. It was almost three o'clock in the afternoon, and she had buried her husband that morning. Now she was drunk.

"I thought I was supposed to ring when I was ready to talk to you," I said, glancing up for a moment and then returning my attention to the files in the drawer before me.

"My," she said, fluidly leaning in the doorway with a martini glass in one hand and a cigarette in the other, "the investigator side of your personality is certainly less convivial than the undertaker half. All business either way, though. Stuffy. Like an accountant. I hate accountants, and, come to think of it, I've never been very fond of funeral directors either."

She was wearing a long black floaty thing over another black floaty thing that was cut low over her cleavage and high on her thighs, all lace and sheer whatever kind of material a lady's night wear is made out of. Her hair was brushed back, and she had on a pair of those house slippers women get out of catalogues, black stiletto heels on the bottom and so little stuff on the top—except for a pom-pom of black feathers over each big toe—that they hardly looked like they should be able to stay on her feet. Her toenails were painted a pale pink, which I noticed matched her fingernails. There was lipstick on her martini glass, and a glazed, distracted look in her eyes that made me think that she had had four drinks at least, maybe more. When she stepped into the office, the long gown flowed as if she were underwater, and as she passed me her scent lingered: alcohol, nicotine, and lilac—not unpleasant, but not exactly roses either.

"I'm here to do a job," I said, my nose aimed at the files, "not to make friends."

"That's a shame," she sighed, sitting down in her husband's leather chair and leaning back so that she could put her long, long legs up on the desk and sip her drink. When she withdrew the glass from her lips, the ice cubes in it clinked together, indicating that it was empty. "You sound like my dear departed," she added, dropping her cigarette fizzling into the glass, "eye on the big picture, no time to waste, history and commerce as one."

I looked up and asked her what the last part of her sentence meant.

"History and commerce? It was something Alex started saying after the Berlin wall fell. I remember watching it come down in pieces on CNN, and him looking at me and saying, 'Do you realize what we're seeing, Vic?' He started calling me Vic back when we were dating . . . back when we were kids. I'm only forty-two now. Did you know that, Mr. Hawley? How old are you?"

"Thirty-three."

"Married?"

"Yes."

"You would be. Children?"

"No."

"Tell me about your wife."

"She's a reference librarian for the college—"

"No, not like that. That's how everybody describes everybody when you ask them. Tell me about who she is to you."

"I don't understand."

"Do you love her?"

"Of course."

" 'Of course.' " She giggled. "Is she pretty?"

"Mrs. Kane, I don't see—"

"Is she pretty?" she demanded, raising her voice and sitting up stiffly in her husband's chair.

"Yes," I said.

She seemed to relax, slumping back again and asking, "How often do you make love together?"

"Mrs. Kane . . ."

She moved her eyes to me, making me sigh as I said, "Probably not often enough."

"Alex and I never did," she said, getting up and moving over to give the velvet cord on the wall a pull. The butler appeared so quickly that I thought he must have been standing on the other side of the door. She ordered another drink, asked me if I wanted one, and ordered it for me anyway after I said no. Then, moving around the office in her floating haze of widow's black, she started talking, as if to herself.

"Which isn't to say that Alex didn't enjoy screwing," she said, picking up from where she'd left off before. "He just didn't enjoy screwing me. When we were first married, things were all right. But about five years ago he changed— it was about the time that the business started taking off, and it was almost as if success replaced sex. I was just an object he had added to his collection. He moved me to the back of the shelf, Mr. Hawley. Literally."

Beneath my fingers in the cabinet drawer was a file entitled "Batilovna," and I lifted it out as Mrs. Kane stopped at one of the bay windows on the other side of the room and leaned back, raising her arms in a stretch and moan. Inside the file I found a number of sheets with some kind of drawings paper-clipped to them, stamped pages scribbled over with ink, and a single piece of yellow, legal pad paper upon which were three handwritten columns of figures: the first consisting of what looked like a series of dates, the second apparently being the initials from a number of different names, and the last looking like a row of serial numbers. In the right margin there was more writing, A.M. and P.M. descriptions, long figures containing both numbers and letters—such as JK-417—and even, in at least three instances, recordings of something that, judging by the placement of the decimal point, might have been dollar amounts.

I had just closed the file, having decided that it and the art book I had left out on the desk would accompany me home, when the butler knocked, stepped into the room, and without even glancing at the woman for whom he worked, whose body was defined by the light from the window through the sheer lingerie she wore, deposited two martinis on a silver tray, lifted her empty glass, and withdrew . . . but not before shooting a look my way that was all suspicions and knives.

Lifting a drink, Mrs. Kane draped herself across a chaise lounge in the room's corner and ran one finger around the glass's rim.

"Since my husband's gone, and your wife is in the hospital, maybe you and I should have a discreet little affair," she said playfully, as if thinking aloud. "Just until your wife comes home, and I can find some young idiot to bang me after school."

"Nice," I said, placing the Batilovna file with the book on the desk. "I can see all those years of charm school weren't wasted."

She giggled and drank as she added, "Isn't that the fantasy, Mr. Hawley? The horny widow? Or would you prefer to think of me as *vulnerable*?"

"What about Edward?" I asked, looking over to see her reaction.

"What about him?"

"Aren't you concerned about his welfare?"

"With the benefit of your warning, my lawyers spoke to the prosecutor's office in Logan's Town before he was even arrested. For now he's been denied bail, presumably because I have enough money to finance a dash for the border. But he's the only prisoner in their jail, and considering who he is, I'm sure he'll be very well treated. He's probably safer there than anywhere else anyway. Who can tell what kind of trouble your poking around will stir up?"

"Why did John Gilbert kill your husband, Mrs. Kane? What's your theory?"

"My name's Victoria."

"Why should I believe that your son is innocent?"

"If you suspect Edward, why did you take on the case?"

"Who I suspect isn't pertinent right now."

She sipped her drink, shrugged, and said, "Edward's a sensitive boy, Mr. Hawley. An artist. Beauty means a great deal to him. And the way his father bought and sold beautiful things played on his mind."

"That doesn't answer my question," I said.

Mrs. Kane sighed again, tossed back the rest of her drink, and asked me, "Do you want this or not?" lifting the second drink off the tray as she walked past the table. "Follow me to the vault of all secret knowledge."

Tucking the book and file under my arm, I followed her into the hall and up another flight of stairs to a room on the third floor. She opened the door and nodded for me to enter before her. It was perfectly dark inside, and I was just about to say something when she hit a light switch behind me and a soft, museumlike glow ran down the walls from the ceiling. I held my breath when I saw what was before me, stepping carefully and feeling a sense of real shock.

"They're beautiful," I whispered, truly impressed.

"Pick one," she said from behind me, as if we were discussing a litter of puppies.

"I beg your pardon?" I said, turning to face her.

"I said, pick one. Any one you want, and it's yours. We'll consider it part of your fee. I hate them. Every one. I think they're loathsome."

"But Mrs. Kane—"I began.

"Do you want one or not?" she demanded.

"Well, yes, but—"

"Then pick one."

I turned back to the room, which was immense—probably a ballroom when the house had been owned by the college president. The area was a good fifty feet square, with a high ceiling and polished wood floor. On all the walls, and set up on easels all around the floor, were beautiful religious paintings, icons of the Eastern Orthodox faith. They were large and small, round and square, colorful and grim, but most of all, they looked authentic, which would make them very, very illegal.

"It's against the law in Russia to export any work of art over seventy-five years old," I commented, stepping deeper into the room and feeling an odd tightening in my chest. I was raised a Ukrainian Catholic, though I don't really practice anymore. And these pictures, with their gold gilding and odd, super-formal, supernatural depictions of saints, Madonnas, and Jesus himself, stirred memories in me of masses witnessed through a fog of incense when I was young; tall, frightening priests just this side of divinity themselves, towering over me in triangular smears of perspective and color; and choir voices booming down from the heavens, all bass and modulated melodies of solemnity and grief.

"If you have enough money, there is no law," Mrs. Kane said. "It's a cliché, but it's true. Icons were Alex's special love. I think maybe he liked them so much because, in the old country, people worshiped them as if they were holy in and of themselves . . . so to him, owning one was a little like owning a piece of God. He's been collecting them for years. He even had this room, the 'vault,' was his name for it, fireproofed and wired with its own separate security system. These are the genuine articles, Mr. Hawley. The ones he sold were reproductions."

Something prickled on my skin, and I asked Mrs. Kane to explain her last statement.

"He brought the Russians over from Europe because the girl had a gift," she said. "She could reproduce anything she saw. Alex took orders from churches around the country. He'd put together a catalogue with photographs of the icons he actually owned, and the girl would paint whichever ones the priests chose . . . right down to the streaks and flakes of age that give them that special, old-world flavor.

"Alex used to say that having the Russians here let him sell the same icon over and over again," she concluded. "Now pick one."

Selling the same icon, over and over, I thought, hearing those words echoing in my mind as I strolled through the forest of virgins and babes around me.

"You said that you'd tell me why you're so sure John Gilbert murdered him," I said, my back turned to where she was still standing at the door. "You said you could prove that it was him and not your son. After the funeral, Sheriff Paulson and I had a little confrontation. I stuck up for Edward once, but you're going to have to convince me to do it again."

"Have you chosen a picture?" Mrs. Kane asked, moving between the easels.

"Yes," I said.

"Which one?"

I pointed.

"Ah, the 'Our Lady of St. Vladimir,' " she said, appearing next to me. "Excellent choice. This is a nice one, too. Three hundred and seventy-five years old. Alex paid twenty-five thousand dollars for it."

"Why?" I asked, as I mentally tried to calculate the sum total of the pieces in the room, deciding that it had to be close on a million. "If the authorities ever found out he had it, they'd confiscate it and send it back to Russia. Why would he spend so much money to buy something that he could never admit to having?"

When Mrs. Kane didn't answer, I moved my attention from the icon to her face and found that she was shaking her head slowly from side to side.

"It's all gone," she whispered, her eyes bright and shiny. "Everything we had . . . gone . . . just that fast."

Then she turned and shouted at me, really shouted, the words coming in an agonized torrent that threatened to tear her apart.

"This is what my husband loved, Mr. Hawley!" she exclaimed. "Possession! The vault! It was everything to him, and it gave him the idea that's ruined my life. Do you understand what that means? We owe everything we have to a deception. A filthy lie that we carried with us every day so that we ended up making our own home a fortress against the world. He destroyed what he loved the most *because it was how he made his MONEY!*"

The last word came as a shriek so loud that the butler appeared at the door, his face twisted with concern and his eyes fixed on me. As soon as Mrs. Kane saw him, she screamed for him to get out and slammed the door in his face. Turning, she pressed her back to it, her eyes wild and her lips quivering.

"Alex had a system," she hissed, firing the words at me as if she hoped they'd hurt. "He came up with it years ago, but it was only recently that he perfected it, because the root of it was that he'd have to let go of something he valued . . . that he'd have to destroy something he loved. But once he started, he couldn't stop. It ate at him until all he could do was destroy! Erase! *Burn!*"

Instantly I thought of the pile of ashes on the dining room table in the house where the Russian girl had died, and I held my breath, waiting for Mrs. Kane to finish it, to finally tell me the truth.

"The only reason these icons escaped is because there was no advantage to destroying them," she said. "There's no such thing as a one-of-a-kind icon. There are so many that they've never even been counted. They're only valuable because the Soviets wouldn't let them out of the country, so it didn't matter if he kept them or not. It's only if you can catalogue a thing and prove that it's unique that the value of it really soars."

"What's this got to do with destruction?" I asked, feeling my heart pounding because I was beginning to understand. "And what's it got to do with Edward?"

I think that Mrs. Kane must have seen the knowledge dawning on my face, because something in what she saw when she looked at me seemed to calm her down. Lifting herself from where she had leaned her back on the door, she said, in a voice more composed and sober than before, "Edward hated what his father was doing even more than I did. But neither of us ever dreamed of stopping him because we didn't *want* to! Do you understand, Mr. Hawley? That's why Edward *couldn't* have killed him."

"Because of the money?" I asked.

And she nodded, saying, "Because of the money. We both loved the money. We hated where it came from, but we couldn't bring ourselves to let it go. It was our failing as much as Alex's . . . and in a way we were just as culpable as he. Edward took that girl, Erena, to bed, because his father *told him to*. I looked the other way, because Alex told me that it was important for me to do it, that it was vital that I not interfere. Erena was the key to it all, he said. She had the magic in her hands . . . those were his exact words. She painted icons because it let her use her talents for something godlike. But Alex had other ideas, and he used her to make us rich!"

She had placed both her hands over her heart and was looking at me like a penitent believer before a confessor priest.

"Every time he went to that airport in New Philadelphia, Edward and I knew what it meant—one more fire, one more loss. But we let it go on because we couldn't bring ourselves to put a stop to it. Not that Alex would have listened even if we had objected. He was too far gone, too enraptured with his own schemes and dazzled by his vision of the future. But the point is that we never even tried. Not once. We simply let him go on burning until this was all that was left because he gave us what we wanted! He gave us *anything* we wanted! And we took it all, and let him go on, and on. . . ."

She placed her hands over her face and shook her head.

I went to her, reached out, touched her, and she exploded, slapping my hands away and screaming, "Don't you touch me! Don't you ever touch me!

"I've told you what you wanted to know, but don't you think for one moment that that gives you any rights with me. Don't you think my secrets give you . . ."

Her sentence faded to nothing.

She blinked.

Started again, calmer now.

"My son couldn't have killed his father because killing him would have been like killing his money. You wanted the truth . . . well now you've got it. And what's more, since we're dwelling on the truth, I wish to hell he wasn't dead, because now John Gilbert will get it all. My husband's secret clients will know that whatever Gilbert's got for sale now, it's the last. It'll be worth all the more because of it. And I won't see a dime. That's why I'm sure John Gilbert killed my husband, Mr. Hawley, because he's the one who will benefit. Not me. And certainly not my son."

"But did he burn it all?" I asked.

She nodded as she said, "Until it was in the fire, it was as worthless as the junk in this room. But once he turned it to ash, it was gold."

"Do you know what the last thing he burned was?" I asked.

And she whispered, "No," opening the door and stepping into the hall to where the butler was waiting. "After the first, I decided it was better if I didn't ask."

I walked the two blocks home, feeling a little numb, with the icon she'd given me tucked under one arm, and the book and file under the other. Jerry rolled into the office after I had placed myself in my swivel chair, the painting resting on the desk before me. It was three foot round, and beautiful. When he asked me about it, I told him that it was real. "Bullshit," he replied, forcing me to explain that it was actually an authentic, historic relic, imported from Europe, and all of three hundred years old, given to me by a widow who was definitely not wound too tight. I told him about the room I'd seen filled with other pieces like it, all stolen from the people who saw them not as mere objects, but as physical pieces of their culture. And then I told him how Alexander Kane really made his money.

"It wasn't from antiques," I said slowly, wanting to get it exactly right. "It wasn't even from artwork, really. It was from a lie he told, over and over again. He'd acquire an object, something precious, something that was known to be unique—a painting, a drawing, something recognizable—and then he'd burn it."

"Burn it?" Jerry said, not understanding at first.

"That's right." I nodded. "He brought the Russians over because the girl had a gift for copying exactly what she saw. He'd have her make him a set of forgeries of whatever painting it was that he intended to sell, and then he would destroy the original, also destroying any chance that his forgeries would ever be discovered because, without an authentic masterpiece against which a forgery could be compared, short of the X ray, and chemical analysis done in museums, categorical proof of his deception was impossible. He could sell the same piece over and over again, forgery after forgery, a dozen times or more with complete confidence and impunity."

"But how could two people own the same, one-of-a-kind piece?" Jerry asked.

"They'd never know, one about the other. The objects were illegal; the people who bought them weren't supposed to have them, by law. If they ever did admit to possession in public, the rightful owners would step forward and force them to give up their secret treasures. So these 'special collectors' would have to keep their acquisitions private forever."

Jerry's eyes widened as he began to understand. "That Russian in the bar!" he exclaimed, his arms moving as if he were about to jump up from his wheelchair. "That's exactly the kind of thing you said he was talking about!"

"That's right," I agreed.

"But," Jerry began, his eyes narrowing and his hands clenching on the arms of his chair, "why kill the girl? Mrs. Kane got herself drunk enough to spill her guts about Gilbert . . . okay, I can follow that . . . she was saving her kid. And her story makes sense: Gilbert kills Kane so that he doesn't have to split the profits with a partner anymore.

Fine. But why kill the girl? That would be like killing the golden goose, wouldn't it, Bill?"

"That bothers me, too." Glancing down at a scratch pad on my desk, I asked, "What's this?"

Jerry grimaced, saying, "That sheriff wasn't kidding. He dropped a dime on us to the state licensing board. That's the Ohio Organization of Funeral Professionals' inspector. Name's Rosewood. He called while you were out and said that he'd be stopping by tomorrow morning sometime to discuss a 'serious breach of professional standards.' "

"Fuck!" I hissed, crumpling the note and flinging it into the wastepaper basket behind me. "That's all we need!"

Jerry frowned, glanced at his hands, and said, "There's one last thing."

"Do I want to know?" I asked.

He shrugged, saying, "Probably not, but we may as well get all the shit out of the way in one swell foop. That picture Larry took of the guy who hurt Nat and me didn't match any of the shots Mike Agnello brought from the mug book this morning."

"So we still don't know who he is."

" 'Fraid not."

"Mrs. Kane didn't recognize him either," I commented. "I showed her Larry's contact sheet before I left. She was so drunk she had a little trouble with the magnifier, but she definitely didn't know who he was."

"And you believed her?"

"Yeah," I sighed, "I guess I did. Her son's ass is on the line. Why would she start lying now?"

"So," Jerry said, after a moment's reflection, "what do we do next?"

Staring at the icon on my desk and then glancing at my watch, I sighed, rubbed one hand over my face, and said, "We bring Nat home."

SEVEN

■■■■■■■■■■

SHE WAS WEAK, moved gingerly, winced from pain a couple of times, and asked only for some hot tea after I'd gotten her positioned in bed—Bigelow's "Constant Comment," which we had jokingly nicknamed, "Quietly Constipated," for some reason I now forget. There was something about having her back in the funeral home's living quarters that seemed to fill the emptiness her absence had left, and I got more pleasure out of making that cup of tea than anything I had done in days.

Quincy, our cream-colored Persian tabby with the raccoon tail and golden eyes, raced around like he'd suddenly come back to life. The entire time Nat was gone he'd done nothing but whine and mope listlessly around the apartment, picking up various cat toys, only to drop them as if finding them deficient in some way I was unable to understand. Quincy is Nat's cat. When she isn't around, I'll do for a quick ear scratch or tummy rub in a pinch. But it's Nat he really wants. And having her back had apparently affected him as much as it affected me, sending him purring to the bed, where he all but claimed her for himself, which was great. Suddenly, the apartment felt like home again, not like a hotel room I would occupy temporarily, until an illness passed. But like a place where important things happened on a regular basis.

But when I stepped into the bedroom, balancing the teacup on its saucer and walking like a gymnast so as not to slop it around, I found Nat standing before her closet, naked, trying to pull her favorite nightgown over her head. She was pretty dopey from pain pills, and the cast on her arm made the task all the more awkward. But the thing that froze me in place at the door was that, with both her arms upraised, I got my first clear view of the tape she had wrapped around her fractured ribs, and the bruises that covered her back.

My hands started trembling and I put the tea down on the night table, ostensibly so that I could rush forward and help her get dressed, but really because in another couple seconds I'd have spilled it.

She pulled the nightgown down, saying through her swollen mouth that she didn't want me looking at her because she was "ugly." I told her that, in my eyes, she could never be ugly, and after I had tucked her into bed and brought her her tea, we sat, snuggled close together with Quincy purring on her lap, not speaking, just being us. She was asleep in no time, the cat curled next to her, so I unplugged the bedroom phone, pulled the shades, and closed the door. She was so beautiful, lying with her long dark hair spread over the pillow that, standing with my hand on the light switch, I felt my heart nearly break. When Larry Fizner had asked me what I wanted to do to the man who had hurt her, I had replied that I wanted to kill him. Now, watching my wife sleep, I realized that, for the first time in my life, I sincerely wanted revenge. I wanted to bury the son of a bitch. And I swore, then and there, that I'd chase him until I died. I wouldn't stop until I'd nailed him, and I'd do whatever it took to reach that end . . . no matter what.

I spent an hour on the stair machine in the basement, sweating hard and throwing myself into the workout in a vain attempt to disperse the dark clouds I felt boiling in my soul, because I knew that the key to finding Nat's assailant lay in a mind clear enough to untangle the mess surrounding Alexander Kane's death.

The dates were important, I knew, the strain of the exercise moving the blood through my brain, all that oxygen sharpening my thoughts. Five years ago came to me twice, first because Larry Fizner had cited that time period as when the man named Uri had come to America from the

Soviet Union, and second because Mrs. Kane had mentioned it as the time when the antique business had "really started taking off," and she and her husband had stopped having sex. Two years ago came to me twice also.

The Russians had come to America two years ago. . . .

Which was exactly the time Alex Kane had decided not to buy any more stolen goods from Uri.

It was Larry's contention that Kane had stopped buying because he had found another supplier. That explanation made the most sense because, with Erena Batilovna, the human photocopier, to crank out reproductions for him to secretly sell as unique, one-of-a-kind collector's items, a steady supply of precious, identifiable works of art was his key to the bank. No hot art, no forged copies, no huge piles of cash accumulating . . .

Where?

I pumped harder, closing my eyes and bearing down, feeling a burning sensation in my leg muscles that climbed all the way up my ass.

Kane would demand payment in cash, of that much I was certain. And he'd launder the money through his antique stores.

"Yeah!" I cried, pumping, working, sweating with my head hanging down between my shoulders and my hands on the stair machine's railings. I could see the setup in my mind:

He and his wife started the antique business ten years ago, which was when Sheriff Paulson had said Kane's parents took an early retirement and moved to Florida. (They hadn't attended their son's funeral, I had noticed, making me wonder why.) For five years they did okay, opened a couple new shops, and sold a lot of expensive stuff on commission.

But then, five years ago, when a man named Uri first set foot on American soil, the Kane Antique and Collectible Company started doing better. A lot better. Mrs. Kane even said so. Suddenly, her successful husband was buying a big house, making quite a lot more money than either of them had ever seen, and losing interest in her. She didn't like it. Her son, the sensitive artist type, didn't like it either, but for different reasons. But they both did like the money . . . so much so, in fact, that they bit their tongues and looked the other way. Mommy got a boyfriend. Knowing Mommy, with those legs, she probably got a few. Eddie got an apartment, and went to college, where he majored in Art History, or something equally haute, drove a Porsche, partied his brains out, and probably dealt a little coke on the side to his bohemian friends, just for fun.

(The cocaine dealing was purely an embellishment on my part, of course. But I was on a roll, and I wasn't about to stop for a details check now.)

Obviously the explanation for Kane's sudden success was that he had started moving the hot merchandise his associate Uri was smuggling into the country. And for three years things went fine. But then, out of the clear blue sky, Kane cut off the underground railroad, refusing to buy any more of Uri's goodies. This happened immediately after he "pulled some strings" to get an artistic Russian girl, her father, and her brother, out of Russia, and into the U.S.

"What the fuck kind of strings could Kane know to pull in Russia?" I said aloud, sweat rolling off my nose.

The answer was obvious.

None.

Uri was the one with the strings to pull in Russia. Not Kane. As far as I knew, Kane had never even been to Russia. So why would Uri want Erena Batilovna to come to America? Maybe they were related. Maybe she paid him. Maybe he had a use for the girl and her talents.

They weren't related, I thought, puffing hard. And she certainly didn't pay him. Hell, he was raking it in, in the land of dreams. Where would three peasants from the Old Country get the scratch to impress him? No, he specifically picked those three people because he needed them for something. He had a plan. I grew up watching guys like Uri in my grandfather's bar, and they always had a plan. They were born with one. But it looked to me like Uri's plan had gone haywire. Instead of selling off copies of the stuff Uri smuggled into the country and making an exponential profit on each "unique" item, Alex Kane had cut him out of the picture. After setting the Russians up in a house, he told Uri to hit the road, and kept Erena busy. . . .

"Doing what?" I asked aloud.

Painting copies of Eastern Orthodox icons for priests who had picked them out of the catalogue he had made of his own private collection, a little voice in my mind responded. And copying the other precious paintings Kane's "new supplier" was offering in Uri's place, while his son, on his father's specific instructions, dazzled her emotions by acting as her exotic, American lover.

So Kane was cutting Uri out of all that green after Uri had taken the personal risks inherent in setting up their brilliant little scam.

"No way." I laughed. "Not Uri. Not a Russian. Not ever."

Somewhere, deep inside my Ukrainian heart, there is an inner eye through which I sometimes see the world as my grandfather probably saw it: no bullshit, straight common sense, stripped of delusions, tempered by the simple, prosaic certainty that most people are rotten to the core, and just as selfish as hell.

Uri didn't go to all that trouble only to roll over and play dead when a little Yankee Doodle hotshot like Alexander Kane yanked it out of his hands. Why should he? Kane's setup was a house of cards. All it would take was one puff, one word to the right person about what he was doing, and poof! No more market. No more piles of cash. No more trips to the New Philadelphia airport in the back of his shiny limousine.

But what about Mr. Kane? Couldn't he fight back? Uri was a crook, a smuggler, an illegal alien. Kane could get him deported, or worse. So maybe Uri kept his mouth shut out of fear that Kane would retaliate. Maybe Uri's story was on the level, and I was the one who was full of shit.

"No way!" I grinned, because a new scenario had entered my mind that made me see the whole goddamn thing in an entirely new light.

Wiping my face with a towel, I got off the stair machine and called Larry Fizner's office. It was nearly ten o'clock at night, but still he answered on the first ring.

"Uri lied," I said, after explaining the chain of logic that had led me to my new perspective. "Kane didn't stop buying stuff from him two years ago. They were partners right to the end. Since Kane was dead, all Uri was doing by telling us that story about being cut off was blowing smoke. There's no percentage in being associated with a dead shyster, no matter how much money you made while he was alive. So he fed us all that shit about the art the Russians stole from the Germans because he knew you'd already gotten wind of some of it from your other case. Since you felt smart for knowing some of it, he told you a little more so you'd feel so important you wouldn't be thinking straight when he dropped his bomb about how Kane had stopped buying stuff from him two years ago. It was all a load of shit. Every bit of it. What he really wanted was for us to waste our time looking for Kane's 'new supplier,' who doesn't even exist."

"Jesus!" Larry breathed into the phone, his voice a little thick from his before-bedtime Scotch. "And I ate it with a spoon."

"Can you find him?" I asked.

I could all but see the look in his eye as he said, "I found him once. You bet your ass I'll find him again. Gimme an hour."

I gave him two hours before giving up and going to bed. But at one in the morning he called. I had plugged the phone back in, just in case and his voice, sounding the worse for booze and wear, rasped over the pounding rock beat of a barroom jukebox, telling me to meet him at six o'clock in the morning, downtown, at the West Side Market. I hung up, wondering what kind of shape he'd be in only five hours from now and thinking, I haven't been to the Market since I was twelve years old. Then I rolled over, put my arm over my wife, and really slept for the first time in three days.

• • •

My eyes popped open at four-thirty. Nat was sleeping next to me, lying on her back, with Quincy perched protectively on the pillow near her head. The silver glow of a street lamp outside our second-floor window dusted the room grey through a part in the curtains over our bed. And in that dim light I could just make out the shape of my wife's face, a face I knew so well that, even in perfect darkness, I could still see its every facet in my mind. I wanted to touch her, and I even started to reach out. But I stayed my hand for fear of waking her and got out of bed instead. I had slept for only a little over three hours, and yet I felt invigorated. It had to be her, I thought. Just having her back had literally changed my body's chemistry. My brain was finally working. It was time to get something done.

In the kitchen I fed the cat, listened to my Mr. Coffee gurgle as I drank a glass of orange juice and marveled at the way I felt. It was as if I'd been asleep during those two days that Nat was in the hospital, stumbling along, going through the motions, and missing most of what I saw. I had been preoccupied without even realizing it. But things were going to be different now. I could feel it. The "sleuthing undertaker" was back; and for the first time in my life, I let myself admit that I was excited by the prospect of going out and getting my hands dirty in a case.

Suddenly, as if in reward for my newfound mental attitude, a thought struck me, and I rinsed my orange juice glass, poured myself a cup of coffee—the mug was a gift from Nat and had a caricature of Sherlock Holmes on it—and went into the den where my stereo equipment was set up in an elaborate wall cabinet I had designed myself. Normally, Quincy would have been right there with me the whole time, watching every move I made and chasing cords. But today he ate his breakfast and went back to the bedroom. I understood how he felt, and even considered returning for a couple of hours myself. But instead I hooked up a set of Koss headphones, put the suicide tape Edward Kane had given me into one side of a dual cassette component, put a blank tape in the other side, and duplicated the tape, hitting PAUSE at the end instead of turning the machine off. Then I played my copy through my headphones, smiling all the while.

No click.

There was no click at the end of my copy, just like there was no click at the end of the tape Edward Kane had given me Friday morning. There *was* a click at the end of the tape I had made on the Sony recording machine I had found on Alexander Kane's desk. And that meant that the tape Edward Kane had given me, which he claimed his father had made before going out to Logan's Town to die, had not been made on the Sony machine I had seen.

I was moving so fast now that I was having trouble pressing the right buttons on my equipment. Rewinding the copy tape I had just made, I pulled out a microphone, plugged it in, and repeated Mr. Kane's suicide message as I remembered it, adding another three sentences at the end that I just made up on the spot. Then I got out a fresh tape, put it in the second slot on the recorder, and duplicated my new tape, hitting PAUSE to stop the recording immediately where Alexander Kane's tape ended, and cutting off the additional material I had added. Rewinding the tape, I listened to it very loud through my headphones, hearing the tape hiss created by the microphone cut off exactly at the spot where I had hit PAUSE. Then I listened to the tape Edward Kane had given me. And it sounded the same; the tape hiss ended exactly after the last word spoken by the now dead man, and there was no click recorded by the Sony's condenser microphone of the machine being turned off. The conclusion was obvious:

The tape Edward Kane had given me was a carefully edited copy of a longer tape, made not on an old Sony portable, but on a dual cassette recording component at least as sophisticated as my home tape machine.

"So who edited it?" I said softly, removing the headphones and staring at the cassette player from where I was sitting, cross-legged on the floor in my underwear. "The father? The son? John Gilbert? Who?"

There was no way I was going to work out the answer from the material I had in front of me. But one thing was certainly clear: I had only heard a fragment of whatever it was that Alexander Kane had recorded before his death. Someone had wiped away the rest. Leaving me with two new questions:

Who?

And why?

I shaved, showered, and dressed in a black wool suit with pleated pants and just the hint of a red line interwoven into a block pattern in the material. Nat still hadn't stirred, so I left her a note, woke Jerry up, and told him to look in on her later, making sure she got something to eat and took her pills. Then I took the van down to the Market. It was 5:30 A.M. when I hit the freeway. The morning was beastly cold, the sky still dark, the streets virtually empty.

The corner of Lorain and West 25th Street is one of the centers of ethnic life in Cleveland. It is where the area's farmers and other produce suppliers come to sell their wares. Beneath a roof made of corrugated metal supported by rickety four-by-fours are dozens of stalls, built of plywood, behind which are parked refrigerated trucks filled with anything you could possibly want to eat, fresh from the farm: animals so recently slaughtered that they're still bloody, vegetables so recently picked that the bugs are still confused, and fruits so fresh that you have to wonder where the hell they came from. Restaurant owners, grocery store buyers, and the public all converge on the Market seven days a week, filling the place with a commotion and din that starts at 6:00 A.M. when it opens and goes right through to 7:00 P.M. when the last of the trucks roll away.

But what has always made it so special to me are the voices. Every language in the world is spoken there. When I was a kid, my grandfather used to take me down when he bought stuff for the tavern, introducing me around in Ukrainian as he picked out pickled pig's feet for the jars on the bar, vegetables and sides of beef for my grandmother to make into the soup they served, and live chickens, which he'd load, clucking and squawking, into the back of our station wagon, and keep in the yard until Grandma called for their necks to be wrung. At that time, what you heard was mostly Eastern European tongues, but over the years there's been more Spanish, and Chinese, and Vietnamese, and Arabic creeping in. Until today when you can quite literally find somebody from anywhere in the world selling or buying something for their table.

I found Larry Fizner leaning on a telephone pole, over-coat collar turned up, cigarette sticking out of the corner of his mouth, looking like a secret agent in an old movie. When he spotted me, he took me by the arm into a bus kiosk, sat me down on the bench, and said, "Okay. So what the fuck is going on?"

In response I asked, "When's Uri meeting us?"

"He's not. After our little interview in the bar, he seems to have suddenly started treasuring his privacy. All I could find out is that he comes down to the Market just about every morning, first thing. I figured we could stake the place out, and then decide on an approach together after we talked this thing through."

Brilliant! I thought. Absolutely perfect. Though he was unshaved, had bloodshot eyes, and a sickly yellow tinge to his face attesting to the severity of his hangover, Larry Fizner had obviously been thinking.

"Now spell it out for me," he added, leaning back on the wall of the bus shelter and closing his eyes. "And go slow because I think I might have given myself a brain tumor last night."

I ran through the whole complicated chain of deductions for him one more time, concluding with the discovery of the altered cassette tape I had made just an hour before. To my amazement, even through the fog of his headache, he grasped every detail the first time through, saying, "So, Kane and Uri were in cahoots all along," without even opening his eyes.

"That's right," I agreed.

"And you think this John Gilbert guy greased Kane and the Russian girl, the painter?"

"*Mrs. Kane* thinks it was Gilbert," I corrected, feeling the need to be clear on this point.

"Whoever." He shrugged. "For now, let's use it. So, since Gilbert made the business contacts, he was chummy with Kane, who got his goods from Uri. If it weren't for the Russians, I'd say that Kane would have found it more secure to keep Uri and Gilbert apart. But since Uri obviously had a hand in getting the Russians into the country, and Gilbert was their baby-sitter, it sounds to me like they were all one big happy family. That the way you figured it?"

"Yeah." I nodded, feeling suddenly enthusiastic because Larry was sketching out my line of thought exactly. "Gilbert framed Edward Kane for his father's murder," I added, picking up the thread, "so that he and Uri could inherit the phony picture business and leave Eddie to take the fall."

"So that Russian girl, Erena," Larry mused, pulling in the rest of it, "must have kicked up such a squawk when they started cleaning out the house that they had to grease her, too."

"Right," I agreed, feeling heartsick because of what Erena's death must have been like. "With her father and brother either looking on, or waiting outside, knowing what was happening in the house, John Gilbert strangled her to death."

"But why leave her body to be found like that?"

"Maybe they didn't want anyone to see them carrying her out."

"It was dark. And they'd carried whatever else was in there out already . . . the forged paintings and whatever else. What was one more bundle?"

"Maybe they thought it would be better for Eddie to get blamed for two murders instead of one."

"Maybe. But it seems to me that dumping her in the woods someplace on the way back from Cleveland would have been a lot more sensible."

"Maybe they couldn't."

"Couldn't what?"

"Dump her in the woods."

"Why?"

"She was the old man's little girl," I said, somewhat shocked that the idea had not occurred to him. "Maybe they just couldn't bear to do it."

"And what about that suicide tape?"

"I've got a theory about that, too."

Before I could finish, Larry got up, leaned out of the bus shelter, looked at the people milling around, and said, "We better walk."

So we did, down the street, toward the lake.

"I think Alex Kane was going to end it," I said, once we'd gone a little ways. "I think that when he said, 'this life of mine is over' on the tape, he was really talking about his way of life, and not suicide. I think there was a lot more on that tape, and that either Gilbert, or Uri, or both, doctored it up to sound like a suicide threat and left it for his wife to find. I don't think he was supposed to die on the road like he did. I think that they were going to make his death look self-inflicted, but that something tripped them up. Maybe Kane got wind of their plan and was rushing out to Logan's Town to mess it up. Or maybe Eddie came home and found the tape before they had everything ready. All I know for sure is that that tape was way too carefully planted not to be significant."

"So you think they ended up framing the kid because he was convenient?"

"Exactly. And they might even have gotten away with it if Edward hadn't given me the tape he found. But since they were both down on Lincoln Street cleaning out the house, and he was up here with his mother, they couldn't get to it after the accident on the road fouled things up, so they didn't even try."

"So how come the mother didn't find it? It was her house. Why'd it end up bein' the kid?"

"I don't know," I had to admit. "But I do know that John Gilbert's staying in Logan's Town like he did means that Uri must be the one who's taking care of the Russians up here."

"And speak of the asshole!" Larry suddenly piped up, grabbing me by the arm and swinging me into a recessed doorway so hard I nearly slammed into the glass.

Uri was walking down the street, looking even larger in the early morning daylight than he had in the shadows of the bar. He was wearing a black leather jacket with a tan fur collar, big black boots, and blue jeans. He appeared perfectly at ease, until I noticed his eyes, which never stopped moving, scanning the area around him as if he insisted upon seeing everything in the street first, before it saw him.

My heart kicked into gear at the sight of him, and I glanced around quickly to get an idea of the lay of the place in my mind. He was walking from the west, down Lorain. Too far to have parked a car if he had driven, and there wasn't a bus in sight. In a flash of comprehension I worked it out, grasped how things stood, and knew what we had to do. Turning to Larry, I told him to give Uri a good lead, and then to follow him into the Market.

"Wait until he's got a couple of bags in his arms and then confront him," I said, watching as Uri turned and headed down the Market's first row of stalls. "Rattle him. Ask him outright where the Russians are. Ask him if Erena's throat is still bothering her. Ask him anything you can think of, but get him pissed enough to leave. And then stay on him until he runs."

"He won't run." Larry frowned. "And if he does, I'll never keep up."

"That's right." I grinned, slapping him on the back and pushing him into motion. "You won't. Now get going!"

And Larry did, glancing over his shoulder at me as he crossed the street, and then breaking into a shambling walk with his head down and his hands in his trench coat pockets. When he pulled himself in on himself like that he seemed to shrink before my eyes, and I understood how he had made his living all those years: he almost disappeared when he wanted to, one of life's invisible people, slight, grey, and distinctly, almost aggressively, unremarkable. I watched him fade into the crowd, and then crossed the street myself, working my way down the stalls behind the row I had seen Uri choose.

The Market's smells and noise washed over me, taking me back to when I was a kid, looking up from below at the huge, grinning faces of the men behind the counters, simultaneously scared and exhilarated by so much activity jammed into so tight a space. I was studying those faces now as I went, until, six booths down on the vegetable side of the row, I spotted one that, though older than I remembered, was familiar. Uri was haggling over a ring of smoked kielbasy in the stall across from where I stood. Fishing a quarter out of my pocket, I used it to rap on the hollow-sounding plywood counter, making the man behind it turn, his arms laden with unshucked corn. He looked me up and down, brows furrowed, his lined face frowning for a moment before his dark eyes lit with recognition and he grinned, saying, "Hawlinski!"

I nodded, extending my hand. He handed me a corn, laughed, asked about my grandfather, and removed his cloth cap when I told him that he was dead. He was a burly man in a thick, turtleneck sweater and a raglike denim jacket. He had a scarf wrapped around his forehead, and despite the cold, his face was red and moist with perspiration. Even from across the counter I could smell the thick odor of garlic his body exuded from its pours. Softly, without turning my head, I asked him about the man paying for kielbasy in the stall over my right shoulder. He narrowed his eyes, looked, and made a face of distaste, saying, "Is Russian. Phooey. Is not for you. Forget it."

"You've seen him before?"

"Sure."

"What kind of car's he got?"

"What car?"

"No car?"

"Him? Phooey!"

When I turned, Larry had just made his move. Behind me, the Ukrainian vendor was offering me a special deal on corn as a tribute to my deceased grandfather, and with a wave I told him that I'd be back in a minute. Then I deliberately stepped into a crowd of women in front of a cheese stand offering free samples, getting jostled by their enthusiasm and drawing their indignant exclamations, which, in the Market, blurred into the general babble like sugar dissolving in hot liquid.

Uri looked startled when Larry put his hand on his shoulder, but he visibly relaxed when he saw who it was. From my vantage point amid the cheese-eating women, the big man seemed to relax too much, putting a great deal of effort into appearing unmoved. Larry leaned his head in close and said something that made Uri laugh out loud, seemingly with great ease. But at the same time, Uri picked up his pace, and Larry had to work to keep up with him. I was weaving my way along the stalls about ten yards back, and once I had to physically grab a stranger and position him in front of me when Uri shot those well-schooled eyes of his around, looking for observers. I excused myself through a torrent of Polish abuse and continued, eyes glued on Uri's black leather jacket.

The two men stopped at another stall, and Uri bought more meat. He was taking care of Erena's father and brother all right, I thought, mentally listing his grocery choices so far: kielbasy, bacon, pork chops, and cheese . . . to someone from his part of the world, the staples of a balanced diet. Larry was working hard, I could see, but Uri just grinned, shook his head, and seemed on the whole to be enjoying their conversation. Finally, at a bakery stall, he spoke briefly to the vendor, nodded at a loaf of fresh paska bread that was as big as a basketball, and fumbled with the bags, apparently trying to set them down so that he could get at his wallet. In what was a smooth and spontaneous-looking motion, he handed the two bags to Larry, who took them automatically, shuffling his legs to redistribute the weight while, relieved of his burden, Uri took off at a run, leaving Larry shouting behind.

It was what I had been waiting for. Suppressing a whoop, I leapt over the closest counter to me, skittering around a pile of empty bushel baskets, along the side of a truck, through a hanging cloud of exhaust produced by another idling diesel, and then up and over another counter slick with the running juice of something red—I didn't notice what. As I turned a corner and stopped, I caught sight of Uri, running hell-bent down Lorain, his big boots clumping on the pavement and his leather jacket open and flopping from side to side. Spotting an alley running parallel to the main street, I tore down it, sprinting for all I was worth and pulling up short at the end of the building, where I peeked around and waited until I saw Uri run by, crossing the side street and continuing down Lorain.

I did it again, sprinting like mad and knowing I was passing the bigger man who was running parallel to me on the other side of the building, pulling up short at the side street and waiting. This time he didn't show for a while, and when he did he was walking fast, looking over his shoulder, and blowing like a bull.

I let him go, and after he had passed, I cut down the side street, crossed it, and emerged on Lorain behind him. Keeping my body behind the building, I watched as he quickly walked another two blocks, crossed over to Lorain's north side, and disappeared into an old, brick apartment house. Smiling, I, too, crossed the street, staying in very tight against the storefronts, and tingling all over.

I had known that I wouldn't have far to follow once Larry got him to bolt, because it was my opinion that Uri would be staying someplace in the neighborhood. This was one of the most thickly ethnic parts of town. There were signs in the store windows written in Russian. The smell of cabbage blew through the vents of a café I passed. And on a street corner lay a bundle of newspapers printed in Cyrillic with the crossed flags of the U.S. and Poland fluttering beneath its name. The man behind the corn stand had known Uri as a regular customer but had never seen him drive a car. So if Uri walked carrying his groceries every day, I knew that he wouldn't be walking far. And since he was a regular customer, he wasn't in the area just hiding the Russians. He lived here, at least part of the time, in the most logical, obvious place in town. It all added up. And the logic had paid off.

I had the building. Now all I needed was an approach. Larry would be waiting for me in his yellow van at the Market, I knew. And for a moment I considered running back and getting him. But I decided against it for two reasons: one, I didn't want Uri to slip away while I was gone, and two, I felt things would go better if I flew this mission solo. These were my people, and this was my show.

Stepping into the apartment house's alcove, I couldn't help but notice how well kept the place was. The building was old, but its thick masonry and stone tile was all scrubbed to a gleaming finish. The intercom was a huge, ancient brass affair with Bakelite buttons and a circular pattern of holes drilled into its center acting as a microphone. I found the building's super and buzzed, getting a rather gruff sounding voice that answered indignantly in Russian that it was too early in the morning to be bothered, and that I should come back later. I spoke carefully, saying that I was there on business. The word "business" brightened the super's mood, as I had expected it would. There was a VACANCY sign propped in the front window, and I'm sure he was expecting an interested, potential resident.

The super turned out to be a short, round, balding man with an immense belly, black suspenders, and a white T-shirt. His English wasn't very good, and his teeth were worse. I pegged him at about sixty; although there's a peculiar thing I've noticed about the people who come to this country from Europe as adults, which is that they seem to age very rapidly up until a point, looking as if they are sixty at forty-five, and then not aging any more at all. It's as if they get their allotment of wrinkles and grey hair all at once, and then remain in an appearance time warp for the rest of their lives.

The man had a ring of keys and was already indicating that I should follow him to the elevator to see the wonderful apartment—he called it a "flat"—that he had available, when I stopped him cold with the announcement that I had rehearsed in my mind while I was waiting for him to open the door. He turned to me, eyes darkening, jaw muscles working so hard his ears actually moved, whispering, "K.G.B.?" His mouth hung open.

I nodded solemnly, glanced around as if I expected to be observed, and pulled him over close to the door where I produced my wallet and removed my blue, apprentice investigator's card, and my funeral director's license, laminated in plastic. As I expected, the man couldn't read English, but his eyes fixed on the two impressive-looking seals, one of the state of Ohio, the other of the Ohio Organization of Funeral Professionals, and I explained that I was a representative of the Immigration and Naturalization Service. When he heard I.N.S., he swallowed and took a nervous step away from me, so I took his arm reassuringly and explained that I wasn't interested in anybody but the man I had been following these past two days. He asked for the man's name, wanting to be helpful, but when I said, "Uri Shmetlovna,"—picking a Russian sounding last name at random on the spot—he frowned and chewed his lip.

There was no one by that name in the building he said. Was I sure I had the right place? I nodded, saying that the name I had was the man's real name, and that he had been living under a string of aliases as a way of trying to fool both the government, and, much more importantly, his fellow residents in the community because, and this was vital, *he was still reporting back to the Soviets.*

The man tensed, and two points of color rose in his ample cheeks.

He was aware, was he not, I asked, that the old Soviet government still had factions that were trying their best to destabilize the democratic movement in Russia? Of course. He nodded. Only a fool would think otherwise. And he was also aware, was he not, I said, that these same destabilizing factions fully expected to regain power in the near future, and return the Soviet Union to its former totalitarian state? Yes, he agreed, nodding furiously so that his jowls virtually trembled. It was so! He had been saying it all along, but people didn't listen. They came here and forgot what it was like. Once their bellies were full in America, it didn't matter what was going on at home. But all it took were eyes to see that the Communists wouldn't just play dead, that they would conspire, like they always conspired, and sooner or later there would be another coup d'état, and this time, if the free world didn't wake up and intervene, it would succeed.

"And then it will all start again," he whispered. "The marching, and the slogans."

"The man I'm looking for has been watching you," I said, leaning in close in the European fashion, getting my face right in there amid the garlic fumes and coffee smells. "For *them*. For when things are like they used to be again. But we want to send him back, clip his wings; show him that this time we mean business."

Yes. The man nodded. He was in apartment 403.

"I've suspected him," he confided, and I could see the wheels in his head turning as they fit events into place. "All those trips home, in and out of the country with no questions. And all that money. Where's he get all that money?"

Exactly, I thought. That's exactly what I knew he would be thinking. I knew Uri would be an item in this neighborhood. He'd be a big man, a connected man, a success. But he'd also be watched. Old habits are hard to break. And in a close-knit community people see things.

"He's up there," the man said. "Flat 403."

I thanked him, replaced my wallet, and entered the elevator, telling him to go back to his apartment and to lock the door. He didn't move, and the last view I had as the elevator doors closed was of him standing in that cavernous, gleaming lobby, a pudgy, red-faced little man, clutching a bunch of keys. The news would be spreading through the building within moments, I knew. It would be five minutes, ten tops, before everybody knew that there was an I.N.S. man on the premises, and that this time, he was doing something that made sense.

In contrast to the lobby, the fourth floor was dingy and threadbare. It was still clean, but up here the building was showing its age. I found apartment 403, stopped, and leaned my head in close to the door, hearing a babble of voices raised in anger and fear on the other side. I couldn't make out all the words, but it sounded as if his two Russian houseguests were bombarding Uri with questions, to which he was responding by repeatedly telling them to shut up and calm down. Gently, I tried the doorknob, and found it locked. Then I straightened my tie, settled myself, and with all my strength, rammed my shoulder into the door.

It didn't give.

But it did hurt.

Instantly the voices inside the apartment stopped, and two other apartment doors opened to reveal the concerned faces of residents leaning into the hall.

I was about to put my other shoulder to the door when it opened, and Uri placed himself squarely in my way, gun in hand. Behind him the apartment was empty. The Russians had made themselves scarce. With my attention focused on the gun he was holding, a Browning "Hi-Power" 9mm automatic, I said loudly, in Russian, "It is useless to resist. Your true identity is known."

In my peripheral vision I saw figures emerging from the open apartment doors just as the elevator door opened, depositing at least five large men into the hall. There was the sound of questions, and Uri's name was pronounced, along with the initials, K.G.B. There was also the sound of stamping feet. Uri looked nervous for an instant, then pocketed the gun and grabbed me by the front of my overcoat, using his superior size to muscle me into the apartment so he could close and lock the door.

His first question was logistical. "What the hell did you tell them about me?" he demanded with a mix of fury and concern in his voice.

I told him, in Russian, that since I knew him only as Uri, and did not know his last name, I had denounced him as a K.G.B. operative as a way of finding out what apartment he was in and also as a way of ensuring my own safety. I spoke slowly and clearly, making sure he understood every word. And when I was finished, he said, looking at me crossly as if it were on this point that I had really betrayed him, "I thought you only spoke English?"

"I lied," I said, just as someone started pounding on the apartment's door.

From a side bedroom the other two Russians appeared, looking terrified, drawn by the ruckus in the hall.

"Jesus!" Uri cursed in Russian, running his big hand over his close-cropped hair so that it bristled straight up on his head. "Of all the shit. K.G.B. Fuck! You're going to have to talk to them or they'll smash down the door and tear me apart."

In response, I reached into my shirt pocket and withdrew a three-by-five-inch, black-and-white print of the picture Larry Fizner had taken of the man who had attacked Nat and Jerry. Quite calmly I handed it to him, saying over the violent pounding and shaking of the door, "I want this man."

Uri gave the photograph a cursory glance and asked, "Why?"

"He tried to kill my wife."

"Your *wife*?"

I nodded, seeing that Uri was confused, but also seeing recognition in his eyes.

"Who is he?" I asked.

"Talk to them," Uri said, sounding resigned as he jerked his head toward the door and walked into the kitchenette. "Then we'll work it out," he added over his shoulder.

It took me ten minutes of arguing to calm everybody down in the hall. It seemed that the men in the building had gathered up a squad to come down and teach the "Russian son of a bitch" a lesson about living in a free society where people were free to "kick a little Russian ass." Someone demanded to see the identification card I'd shown the superintendent, forcing me to admit that I was a private investigator and not with the government after all. And also that Uri wasn't K.G.B., and that I'd only said that he was as a way of finding him.

Then I had to argue for my own safety, and it was just when I thought that I was going to end up being the object of their ire, when their anger reached a critical mass where it would either end in violence or dust. Everyone seemed to hold their breath for a second, and then they moved on to the next insult without anyone raising a hand, and I knew that we were on the downhill side of the crisis. For another few minutes I was called a number of rude names, and then, shaking their heads in disgust, the men drifted away, leaving me to go back into Uri's apartment, where I found the big Russian sitting at the kitchen table, with his elbows on either side of a coffee cup, smoking a cigarette, and looking pissed. He still had the gun, I knew. But he didn't seem in any mood to use it anymore. And when I closed the door, the first thing he asked me was, "Why'd you come looking for me? Why can't you just leave me alone?"

"The man in the picture threw my wife down a flight of stairs," I said, opening a cabinet over the kitchen sink and helping myself to a coffee mug. Pouring the coffee from a pot on the stove, I sat down next to him and continued, "He nearly killed her because I asked a few questions in Logan's Town. If it weren't for that, I probably wouldn't have bothered with you, or any of it. But now it's personal. It's my wife. I want him, and I don't care what I have to do to get him. Do you understand?"

"Yes," Uri sighed. "What an asshole."

"Who is he?"

"A chauffeur." He frowned disgustedly, pitching the photograph onto the table and lifting his coffee cup. "A fucking chauffeur. An idiot. A nothing."

"Whose chauffeur?" I asked.

Uri laughed.

"Whose do you think?" he snapped. "What, I look like I got use for a chauffeur? Does it look like I'm the kind who gets driven around? Look at this place!"

I didn't need to. I'd seen it already. It wasn't much, even by an immigrant's standards.

"So where's your money go?" I asked.

"What money?" Uri demanded.

And I told him all about the forged pictures. His face went chalky, and his eyes seemed to be trying to bore right through my head. Finally he said, "So you're some kinda smart guy, huh? Maybe it should have been you to go down the stairs, not your wife. Huh?"

"For you it would have been a lot better if it had been me," I said, concentrating on my Russian to make sure I got all the words just right because it's easy to sound stupid when you're speaking a language that's not your own. Though I'm fluent in Russian, Ukrainian is what I'm more comfortable speaking. But I stuck to Russian, because I wanted Uri to know that there was a lot more to me than what he had thought at first.

"You've got a whole world of trouble on your hands, Uri," I added soberly. "And it's got my name stamped all over it."

"So maybe I should do something to you and make my trouble go away," he suggested.

I shrugged, saying, "Try it."

There followed a very uncomfortable moment that the two of us filled by staring, one at the other, over the kitchen table. Finally Uri shook his head and said, "Fuck. Just fuck. That's it. Fuck."

Then the other two Russians sat down, and we started into the questions and answers.

EIGHT
■■■■■■■■■■■

LARRY FIZNER AND I both arrived back at the funeral home at eleven o'clock in the morning, driving separately, him in his yellow Chevy van, me in my blue Dodge Grand Caravan. We screeched to a halt side by side and jumped out, me feeling triumphant and exhilarated, and Larry anxious for me to share what I had learned while he had sat, smoking in his van parked across the street from the Market, waiting for me to return.

The long black Cadillac parked in the funeral home's lot didn't even register with me until I was inside.

I burst into the office, Larry Fizner in tow, only to find Jerry sitting solemnly in his wheelchair next to the desk as a man I had never met before rose from his seat, extending his hand to shake as the name Rosewood drifted through the cacophony in my brain. Rosewood? I thought. Where the hell had I heard that name before? Then it hit me: he was the funeral home inspector. Jerry had told me he was coming, and I'd put it completely out of my mind.

I tried to gear down, shaking his hand and smiling. Jerry looked positively grim, eyeing me carefully as if trying to warn me about something. I should have heeded that silent warning, I suppose, but I was too cranked up from my interview with Uri and the Russians for diplomacy, and I automatically introduced Larry, who shook hands with a mumbled, "How ya doin'?" and then tried to fade into the background.

Mr. Rosewood eyed Larry with an undisguised air of superiority that hit me wrong, and I suddenly disliked the dapper undertaker and wanted him gone.

Donald Rosewood was probably Larry's age, but the physical differences between the two men could hardly have been more pronounced. Where Larry was short and slight, Mr. Rosewood was a big, healthy-looking guy, with beefy hands and a ruddy, sportsman's complexion that reflected the hours he'd spent in the sauna and on the racquet ball court. He had a slight tan, and his fingernails had been professionally manicured. He was wearing an expensive, brown, three-piece suit; wing-tipped, cordovan shoes polished to a liquid luster; and a thick gold chain around his left wrist. He was holding a clipboard, I noticed, to which was attached a paper bearing a number of black X's. That didn't bode well, which irritated me all the more.

"So this is *the* Larry Fizner?" he asked, as if he were amused by something. "Private investigator's license number OH-3945?"

Larry eyed the man and appeared about to respond when Jerry cut in, saying, "Mr. Rosewood asked for a tour of the facilities, and found a couple of violations of the Ohio Revised Code."

"Really?" I asked, trying very hard to keep my voice even. "That surprises me, considering that we were just inspected six weeks ago, when we first opened. And Mr. Cartright, the *chief* inspector for the organization, gave us a clean bill of health. I've got the inspection form on file if you'd like to see it. He said we were perfect."

Mr. Rosewood smiled, and set to.

"Let's be frank, Mr. Hawley," he said, laying his clipboard down on my desk as if it were a weapon I was supposed to fear. "We've received some very disturbing reports about you in Columbus. Very disturbing. The kind of thing that impacts everyone in our profession."

"And just what is our profession?" I asked, making Mr. Rosewood's smile flicker.

"The funeral business," he said.

"I didn't realize that you were in the funeral business, Mr. Rosewood," I said, opening the cabinet doors on a wet bar I have next to my desk and mixing a cup of instant coffee, which I handed to Larry before mixing one for myself without offering Rosewood anything, on purpose— because I can be a real ass sometimes.

"People in the funeral business usually have funeral homes," I observed, sitting down behind my desk. "You know, with mortgages, insurance premiums, and bills to pay . . . all those insignificant little worries that make self-employment such a joy."

Rosewood ignored me. I was referring to the fact that as the state organization's inspector he lived out of his car and was paid a salary and given an expense account to ride around from motel to motel, without actually conducting any funerals of his own.

"Our organization," he said with exaggerated patience, "is concerned with maintaining a certain level of professional integrity. Our industry is very sensitive to public opinion. And our licensees must always bear in mind that their conduct, both on and off the job, impacts every one of us. Newspaper articles and nicknames? The 'sleuthing undertaker'? I mean really, Mr. Hawley. Do you think you're doing anyone any good by your association with this person?"

He was indicating Larry Fizner, as if just referring to him was enough, in and of itself, to bring me to my senses. I resented it. Larry might not have been the classiest guy I had ever met, but he was my friend. And a protective side of my nature pushed its way to the surface, making me say, "Let's cut the nice-nice and get to the ultimatum, Mr. Rosewood. I've got a full schedule today, and this verbal fencing is eating up my time."

Jerry rolled his eyes, and Larry suppressed a grin.

Mr. Rosewood's face colored a little, and he said, "As you wish." He produced an envelope and laid it on my desk. In it, he said, was a letter from the president of the Ohio Organization of Funeral Professionals, seriously questioning my professionalism and ethics, and warning me that any continuation of my ancillary activities would have a chilling effect on my place in the organization. I asked something about if that meant that they might decide not to accept my dues money anymore, making Rosewood glare.

"I'd take it to heart, Mr. Hawley," he said. "You've got a lot riding on this place. It would be a shame if anything should interfere with your ability to conduct your business."

"That's a threat," I commented, still without having touched the letter he'd offered.

"No threat," he said. "Simple truth."

I rose, cleared my throat, and said, "I took the same qualification exam you did, Mr. Rosewood, and I've been in this business for twelve years. I own this place, and I'll run it any way I see fit. I know the laws. And there's nothing in the Revised Code that says that I can't hold two professional licenses simultaneously."

No, Mr. Rosewood agreed, but there was a statute that specified that, "no license holder will conduct himself in a manner deemed detrimental to the integrity of the profession."

"And we consider complaints lodged against you by law enforcement officials to fall under unacceptable conduct," he concluded.

"That's another threat," I said, rising. "And I don't have time for this. Your objections are duly noted. Thank you for your time."

Mr. Rosewood fluttered around for another couple of minutes, and then left, but not before placing a copy of the paper from his clipboard in my hand bearing the marks of violations he had found while inspecting the building. They were bullshit charges, and we both knew it. But underlying them was the letter I had yet to open. The bottom line was simple: the funeral directing elders had taken offense to my conduct, and if I didn't stop, they'd yank my license. If that happened I could paint the funeral home pink and shove it up my ass for all the good it would do me.

When Rosewood was gone, Jerry asked gravely, "So what are you going to do?"

I considered the question for a second, then said, "Finish my coffee." I headed for the stairs, adding that Jerry should ride his elevator to the second floor because it was time for a powwow. His expression seemed resigned as he rolled toward the door to his apartment, where the elevator that allowed him access to the top floor and basement was located next to his front closet. I stopped him just as he was about to disappear through the door and said, "This'll be it. Okay, Jer? No shit. We'll finish this one, and then never again. How about it?"

He shrugged but didn't reply, as if to say that I'd have to prove my sincerity by deeds, not words. And when I turned to Larry, he looked stricken, asking, "Do you mean it? You're really gonna give up your apprenticeship?"

"Mr. Fizner," I replied, "look around. I've got three quarters of a million bucks' worth of debt in this place. If they yank my card, I'm fucked . . . and so is my brother, my wife, and my dad. My dad cosigned the financing on this little venture. Not only would I go down in flames, but I'd take him, and his credit rating, with me. What choice do I have?"

"You could fight it," he offered.

And I asked, "Why? What's the point? It's not like I'm going to lose something important. Like I'm turning my back on a significant part of my income. All this private investigating nonsense has ever brought me is trouble." I looked at him hard for a second, and then added something that I had been meaning to say for a long time. "Think about it; I almost lost my wife because of this."

"You mean, because of me," he said.

I didn't argue. Semantics weren't important. What was important was that he understood where I was coming from.

"It was fun for a while," I said. "But I'm a grown-up now, Mr. Fizner. I've got to be realistic."

"But you're good," he protested.

"Thanks," I said, heading for the stairs. "But it's not just my ass anymore. It's everybody I love. And that's got to count for something."

I think he was going to continue arguing, but I didn't give him the chance. Instead I told him that if he wanted to hear what Uri had told me about his activities with Alexander

Kane and John Gilbert, then he had better come on, because I was in a hurry.

I ran up about five steps, stopped, snapped my fingers as I remembered something I had forgotten, and turned around, telling him to go on up without me. In the wall I could hear the vibration of Jerry's elevator. And silently, like a man climbing the gallows, Larry Fizner nodded and headed up the stairs. I was breaking his heart, I knew. His time was nearly up. In the funeral business you get to understand stuff like that. You start to see it when it's there. Larry was retired, and alone. He was depending on me to give him another shot at doing what he loved the most, which was conduct his investigations. If I turned my back on my P.I.'s license, I was turning my back on him. If I did that, he'd be dead in two years, I thought. But if I didn't, it could very well be my funeral home that would die. And then what?

I let him go, and then I went and got the icon Mrs. Kane had given me, because it was central to what I'd learned.

They were waiting for me in the living room, with Nat sitting in a chair, a blanket over her knees, her eyes brighter than I had seen them since the attack, and a smile on her face as she stroked Quincy, who was purring so hard that his flanks vibrated where he sat, curled on her lap. The process of organization I was running through in my mind faltered a little when I stepped into the room and saw her there, but we had an audience, so I didn't act on my first impulse, which was to admonish her for being out of bed and help her back to her sick room while clucking like a hen. Instead I smiled and kissed her. Then I placed the icon on a coffee table and cleared my throat. Jerry had parked his wheelchair next to the couch, near the phone, and Larry had dejectedly taken his place in an easy chair near a bay window, symbolically separated from the group.

"Okay," I began. "Here it is."

As preamble I ran through the whole thing, clicking off events in quick succession and tying them together in a working scenario so that we'd all possess the same reservoir of information. I started all the way back with Alex Kane's death, highlighting the suicide tape, my trip to the morgue, Nat's injury, and Edward Kane's arrest. Then I slowed down, and related my interview with Mrs. Kane in more detail, taking pains to make sure that everyone understood the deductive leaps of logic I had made in linking Uri and Alex Kane, which had exposed the lie Uri had told me in the Lakefront Tavern, and led to the chase at the Market.

There I hit a crawl, describing every last detail, right up to the moment Uri started answering questions while his two Russian houseguests suspiciously took seats near his kitchen table, eyeing him, and me, as if we were a pair of magistrates discussing their sentences.

"Maxym Batilovna," I said, "is seventy years old. He was fifty when his daughter, Erena, was born. His wife was thirty, which isn't so unusual in Europe . . . older guys and younger women. Erena's brother, Vaslov, came from Maxym's first wife, who died when she was young. The second wife, Erena's mother, the younger one, is still in Russia. She and her husband don't get along too good anymore, so Maxym doesn't have any plans to bring her to America. From what he says, she wouldn't come even if he was willing to pay for the trip. She thinks America's dangerous, and that all Americans carry guns."

"Oh, come on," Jerry griped. "That shit went out with 'Miami Vice.' "

I shrugged, and went on, saying, "Once I got everything settled in the apartment's hallway, we went at it. Even then Uri's natural secretiveness got in the way, but I nudged him along, and he finally opened up.

"He didn't know that Erena was dead."

"What?" Larry said, sitting up straight with eyes wide.

"That's right." I nodded, stepping into the center of the room. "None of them did. They've had no contact with John Gilbert since the night Alex Kane died. They've been holed up in that apartment. When Uri first got the word that Mr. Fizner was making noises about him on the street, he met us in the bar specifically to send us off on the wrong path. He was trying to keep his connection to Kane and Gilbert a secret. But he blew it."

"I bought it," Larry grumbled, which, for him, was a pretty startling admission of fallibility. For a second it took me aback, but then I saw it for what it was: an attempt to boost my ego and keep me in the detective business. He was sharp, my master investigator. A born sneak.

"Erena's death is where I wanted to start," I said, ignoring Larry's comment. "But as soon as I mentioned it, all hell broke loose. The old man started crying and praying, and the brother went after Uri, insisting that Uri had known all along that Erena had been murdered, and that he had been deliberately lying to keep him and his father passive. They all three started into it, and I was sifting through the babble when Uri slammed his hand into a kitchen cabinet so hard that it splintered right down the middle. The Batilovnas stopped crying and shouting for a second, and Uri filled the gap by saying, 'Fine. If you think I lied to you, go. Leave now. No one's keeping you here.' Which was a lie, too, I think, since I don't believe he had any intention of turning them loose. But it did shut them up, and that was the point."

"It was definitely a lie," Jerry cut in, lifting a newspaper off the couch and showing me the front page.

I walked over and took the paper from him, saying, "Jesus," as I read through the article beneath the banner: "Murder of Businessman and Immigrant Linked." It was the first mention of Alexander Kane's demise, other than the death notice I'd put in the obituary page announcing his funeral, that I'd seen in the news. And it came on the front page, lower right-hand side, tying everything together in a ball that included Kane's position in the Cleveland business community, and the cryptic admission made by the Wittmere County Sheriff's Office that the immigration standing of the dead Russian girl was being investigated— which was all they'd say at the moment. The article's byline read, Agatha O'Toole, and the only thing Aggie hadn't put in was Nat's trip down the funeral home stairs. Scanning the article without turning to its conclusion further on in the paper's first section, I asked, "Am I in there anywhere?"

Jerry shook his head as he said, "Not yet, knock on wood."

"So Edward Kane's story looks even more plausible," I said, dropping the newspaper back onto the couch. "He told me that he dropped Erena off in front of the house somewhere close to three A.M. The place was dark, and there was no sign of anybody being up, he said. He never saw anybody but Erena, who let herself in using a key they had hidden in a phony rock near the front porch. He said that it was the last time he ever saw her.

"According to Uri," I added, sliding my hands into my trouser pockets, "he and Erena's father and brother were gone by then . . . on their way up to Cleveland with a van full of forged paintings."

"You've lost me," Nat said, and the sound of her voice drew my eyes to her automatically.

I blinked and realized what she meant.

"Uri said it went like this," I said, slowing it down. "Edward Kane came to visit, just like he said he did when I talked to him and his mother yesterday. He arrived at about seven on Thursday night. The Batilovnas, Eddie, and John Gilbert, all had dinner and drank a little vodka, just like Edward said they did. At eleven, Erena started moaning about being cooped up, insisting that she wanted to get out of the house. Edward offered to take her for a ride, and they left."

"What about the Porsche not starting?" Jerry asked.

"That part neither Uri nor the Russians can confirm because as soon as Edward announced that he and Erena were leaving, the girl's father and brother, both of whom had been hitting the joy juice pretty hard that night, decided to call it a day, and headed up to their rooms, leaving Gilbert, Eddie, and Erena downstairs."

"So all we have is Eddie's word that the car was on the fritz," Larry observed.

I nodded, adding, "Eddie says that when they went out, the Porsche wouldn't turn over. Wouldn't make so much as an effort. According to him, John Gilbert then suggested that they take the van, offering to look at the Porsche in the morning. But Gilbert told Sheriff Paulson that Eddie got in the Porsche and roared off, taking Erena with him. And that it was the last time he ever saw the girl, alive or dead."

"There's a bit of a contradiction there," Jerry said.

Nat smiled.

"Anyway," I went on, "what supposedly happened next was that John Gilbert noticed the flashing emergency lights out on the street where Alexander Kane's car had been run off the road."

"What time was that?" Larry asked.

"He's not sure, exactly," I said.

"They never are."

"So he goes out on the porch and sees a car in the ditch, an ambulance, and the sheriff's deputy. It's too far away for him to see any details, so he takes a walk down the road, gets about halfway there, and recognizes the BMW as the one his partner drives. He runs back to the house, wakes up the Russians, and calls Uri, who races down to Logan's Town, arriving sometime after one in the morning. They have a heated strategy meeting, Gilbert gets more and more pissed off about Edward not bringing Erena back, and finally goes to the hospital to see for himself that Alex Kane is really and truly defunct. On the way back he stops at the Dovetail Lane house, where Eddie claims he and Erena are spending some quality time together, only to find the place dark and locked up tight. The only option he's got left by then is to send Maxym and Vaslov Batilovna back to Cleveland with Uri and all the incriminating stuff in the house before the sheriff can show up and find it, while he stays behind in the Lincoln Street house to wait for Eddie and Erena to come home. Which, according to what he told Sheriff Paulson the next day, they never did."

"So it's still Gilbert's word against Eddie's," Nat pointed out.

I nodded. "Okay, now here's where things get interesting. Uri told me, with the Russians sitting right there, all teary-eyed after having just heard about Erena's murder, that not only didn't he know about the girl's having been killed . . ."

"Which was a lie," Larry cut in.

"Assuming he saw the story in the paper," Jerry pointed out.

"He saw it," Larry insisted.

"Whatever," I said. "The point is that Uri insists that he and the Russians have been sitting tight in the apartment ever since the night Kane died, and that John Gilbert hasn't gone near them because he's been busy in Logan's Town answering the sheriff's questions and keeping his eye on the antique stores, just like the good businessman he is."

"Why is that the point?" Jerry asked.

"Because he's acting like he's innocent," Nat said.

"Naturally he's going to act like he's innocent," Jerry pointed out.

I said, "That's not what Nat means. What she's saying is that he's acting like he really is innocent. If he killed Erena like we thought at first, why would he keep the Russians around? They're nonentities as far as most everybody in this country knows. He and Uri could have gotten rid of them in any number of ways, from shipping them home, to snuffing them out. But putting them in an apartment to wait for somebody to find them is the last thing he'd do."

"Unless he meant to let things blow over and keep up with the business," Jerry offered.

And I said, "Exactly. He's acting like he believes that Edward Kane really did kill his old man and the girl, and that he's just putting everything on hold until the kid's convicted and put in jail."

"But why would the kid kill his own father?" Jerry asked, the abashment distinct in his voice. Such a thought was sacrilege to him, I knew. In our family, he and Dad are the closest of the close.

I smiled, and removed a screwdriver from my pocket, saying, "This is the good part . . . the part I've been working on harder than anything else. And I think I've got an answer that'll tie it all together."

Stepping over to the coffee table, I lifted the icon and flipped it over so that the painting side of it faced down and its back faced the ceiling. When I placed it back down on the coffee table, Jerry protested, saying, "Hey!" He rolled over and fluttered the newspaper, instructing me to, "Take it easy. That thing's worth a ton." Sliding the newspaper under the icon so that the painting on its front wouldn't get scratched, he returned to his place.

Screwdriver still in hand, I knelt on the floor and said, "Mrs. Kane told me specifically that her husband had been collecting these icons for a number of years. She didn't say how many years he'd been collecting them. But she was adamant about their authenticity. Her husband had made a big production out of keeping them safe in the house, calling the room in which they were displayed the 'vault,' which he had fireproofed and rigged with an independent alarm system that functioned on its own power supply, separate from the rest of the house. The air-conditioning system in that room was independent, too, she said. And the humidity was always kept just so."

Everyone's eyes were on me as I spoke, and there was a feeling in the room like pressure.

"In the trunk of Alex Kane's car, Sheriff Paulson found a small icon," I continued, still speaking slowly so as not to lose anyone along the way, "three feet by three feet square, with the back not yet attached. It was a beautiful little piece, and because Mrs. Kane told me that one of Erena Batilovna's duties was to paint reproductions of the icons her husband had in his collection to sell to various priests who had picked them from a catalogue he'd put together, I immediately assumed that the icon in the trunk was one of those reproductions. I was right, as it turned out. But I was wrong, too."

"Wrong how?" Larry Fizner asked, walking across the room and lowering himself onto the couch just a couple of feet from where I was kneeling so that he was practically leaning over the icon on the coffee table.

"Alex Kane didn't have that particular icon in his collection," I explained, making Larry narrow his eyes in concentration. "It was included in the catalogue as number 212304, but the original wasn't anywhere in the vault, nor was there an empty spot from which it had been temporarily removed. After having time to mull it over, I've decided that I don't think that that icon in Kane's trunk was a copy of an icon he already owned at all. I think that it was the only one he had like it. And that its being included in his catalogue of 'originals' tells us something significant."

For Jerry and Nat's benefit, I explained it further.

"When I was in the vault," I said, looking from one to the other of them, "Mrs. Kane told me to pick an icon to keep. So I walked around the room, looking each one over, trying to decide which one I liked best. They were all beautiful in their own way, but in a file marked 'Batilovna' that I'd found in Alex Kane's office, there were three icons described on a page covered with initials and dates. This one, the 'Our Lady of Saint Vladimir,' the 'Christ the Teacher,' and the 'Triumph of Saint Paul.' The names were just scribbled in the margin of the page, but they stuck in my mind. So when Mrs. Kane offered me one of the icons to keep, I picked this one, thinking that if it was one of the ones that had special meaning to her husband, then maybe it would turn out to have special meaning to me, too.

"I was so preoccupied with that, that it didn't register with me until later that, while I was looking the collection over, I didn't see the original of the icon Alex Kane was carrying in his trunk on the night he died. And even when it did hit me, the significance of it didn't sink in until this morning, when I asked Uri about the materials he's been smuggling into America from Russia. He admitted to the paintings that Erena had been copying because I already knew all about them, so there was no sense in keeping up the facade, but when I asked him about the icons Alex Kane had in his house, he looked confused."

"Confused?" Nat whispered, and I nodded, my eyes fixed on hers as she worked it out in her mind. I could see her sorting through what I'd said, could see her making the same connections I had made, could see from the way the muscles around her eyes tensed and relaxed that, in that moment, she and I were sharing something very intimate. We were sharing a discovery, making it independently, but in the identical manner, a mirror image of one mind seeing itself reflected in the workings of another. It was beautiful, and exciting, and I know she felt it, too, because her pupils dilated, and then her eyes went wide, and she looked at me and smiled as an expression of wonder spread over her face.

"If Uri didn't smuggle those icons into the country," she said, "then the ones in Mr. Kane's vault couldn't possibly be authentic!"

"Bingo!" I said, rapping the back of the icon before me with the handle of the screwdriver and making Jerry start protectively in his wheelchair.

I was going to finish it, but Nat was talking and I let her go.

"If Uri didn't smuggle the icons into the country like Alex Kane told his wife he did," she said, rising from her seat as Quincy jumped first to the floor and then up on the couch where he leaned forward, sniffing at the icon on the coffee table, "then the ones in the vault that he was keeping so safe must have been *made* for him, not stolen. And the only person who could have made them was the girl!"

"Erena Batilovna," I said, standing and reaching my hands out for Nat to take.

"And if the one in the trunk of Kane's car wasn't a copy," she added, "but was one that Erena had painted for him to add to his collection . . . and Uri hadn't smuggled the rest . . . then the whole collection must be . . ."

She took my hands, looked into my eyes, and asked, "The back hadn't been screwed on yet? It really hadn't been put together?"

I nodded, saying, "Two pieces."

"And he told them that he burned the original masterpieces before they sold the forgeries?"

I nodded.

"Oh, Bill," she whispered, "do it. For God's sake, do it now!"

I smiled, let her go, flipped the screwdriver over, and bent toward the icon, ignoring Jerry's gasp as I rammed the tool's end into the soft wood, explaining, "They're held together with wooden pegs . . . just like the real thing."

Working carefully so as not to damage the piece any more than necessary I undid the next two pegs, and then the last until the flat piece of wood that was the back of the icon separated from the front. Then, holding my breath, I wrapped my fingers around the sides of it so that the front and back wouldn't come apart quite yet, and said, "Since these icons aren't what Kane said they are, aren't three and four and five hundred years old, since these are actually brand-new, done for him by Erena Batilovna and treated with chemicals to give them the illusion of age, there was no reason for Kane to take such elaborate precautions to protect them. Or at least that's what I thought. Why would he bother? If something happened to one, he could just have the girl make him another one. So why the vault? That's what I wanted to know. Why the fucking vault?"

Everyone was leaning in close now. We were like four kids leaning over a *Playboy* one of us had snitched from his father's underwear drawer. I think that by that moment we all might have already made the final deduction, but Larry Fizner and Jerry both kept quiet, as if they sensed that it was Nat who should say it. It was Nat, who had suffered the most because of this, before we had even known what this was all about, who should have the satisfaction of putting it into words.

"He needed a vault," she said, "because it was something he was keeping *inside* the icons that he was really worried about protecting."

"I love you, sweetie," I said. Then I removed the icon's back.

Between the two sheets of wood, pressed perfectly flat and affixed with the tiniest of tacks, lay a piece of canvas, about a foot across and two feet high, folded in half. Carefully, with sweating palms and trembling fingers, I gently peeled the top sheet of canvas back, unfolded it, and revealed, nestled inside, yet another piece of canvas, this one only about six inches by nine, cut into an oval, with lightly tattered edges, and a center covered with exquisite color.

We were all leaning close, our heads almost touching, except for Jerry, who craned his neck to see.

"You'll have to trust me on this one," I said through very dry lips, "since I haven't had time to explain how I happen to know the details about what we're looking at, but this portrait was painted in the year 1411 by the Italian artist, Devachio. It was removed from the Castle Renó in the south of France when the Germans invaded in 1940, was put on display in the home of Field Marshal Hermann Goering in Berlin, and disappeared when the war ended. It hasn't been seen in the West since that time. Its estimated value is thirteen million dollars . . . but that's only a rough estimate, since no one ever really expected to get the chance to bid on it again. The man in the picture is the apostle Paul."

"Thirteen million?" Jerry said reverently, as if afraid that the vibrations of his voice might cause the little picture hidden in the icon to crumble into dust.

"That's right." I nodded, unable to take my eyes off the face of the apostle, so beautifully rendered, so elegant, so small. "And though he didn't get top dollar since his customers knew that they probably couldn't resell their purchase, Alex Kane still sold it, or copies of it, five times last year. It was one of four pictures he had Erena Batilovna forge for him before he died. And he kept all the originals hidden inside the icons he displayed in his vault at home."

"But I thought you said that he burned the originals?" Jerry said.

"That's exactly what he told his partners he did. And there's only five people in the whole world who know the truth: the four of us, and whoever killed him. It was either his partner and closest friend, John Gilbert, or it was his son, Edward. Each swears that it was the other, and all we really have as evidence is their word. But now we have this . . . and if we're careful, we can use it to find out which one of the two is lying. Because one of them is. Of that much, I'm positive."

At that moment the telephone rang. Since Jerry was sitting closest to it, he picked it up, saying, "Hawley Funeral Home." Then he furrowed his brow, looked serious, and handed me the phone, saying, "It's Mrs. Kane. The Wittmere County Coroner's Office just released Erena Batilovna's body. She wants you to take care of the funeral."

I took the phone, placed my hand over the mouthpiece and said to the group leaning in around me, "This is perfect. Now listen."

I settled myself, smoothed out my voice, and said hello to Mrs. Kane. She sounded very different from the way she had when she was drunk. Now she sounded reserved and tense as she told me about the call she had just received from Logan's Town regarding Erena Batilovna, explaining that since her husband was listed as the girl's sponsor in this country, she had inherited his responsibility regarding the disposition of her remains. She had known it was coming, of course, but still it was an additional complication she really didn't need. When I asked her exactly what she wanted me to do, she said, "Oh, I don't know," sounding terse and impatient. "Whatever you think is best, I suppose. Just do it and send me the bill. Nothing elaborate, you understand. But something decent. She was a human being, after all. And I'm sure it's what Alex would have wanted."

I agreed, promising to keep the cost down and asking if she'd signed a release. She said no, so I said that before I made the removal I'd have to stop by her house with the proper form. She said, "Fine. Whatever you have to do. Just get on with it."

Before I hung up, I said, "Mrs. Kane?" I held my index finger up to indicate that this was the part I wanted everyone to pay particular attention to. "I know that this probably isn't the best time to bring this up, but there's a matter of business I thought we might discuss."

"What kind of business?" she asked, her voice growing immediately professional, and just a tinge suspicious.

"The antique business," I said. "Well, specifically, the collecting business. This morning I showed that icon you gave me to a certain acquaintance of mine. And it turns out that this man, who is an extremely successful entrepreneur in his own right, is interested in exactly the type of thing your husband collected. As a matter of fact, he said that, if I could find more pieces like the one I showed him, he would be willing to offer a very generous price for as many as I could dig up."

"Does this acquaintance understand the nature of these pieces?" Mrs. Kane inquired.

"You mean, does he know how they came to be in this country?" I asked back.

"Exactly."

"Yes, he does. And their unique nature is part of what he finds so appealing."

"And he can really come up with a serious offer?"

"I guarantee it."

Mrs. Kane was silent for a moment during which I knew she was considering her good fortune in finding an opportunity to dump her dead husband's collection of illegal artwork for a substantial, tax-free profit. Up until this instant she had undoubtedly been wondering how she was going to go about disposing of the icons, knowing their value, but remaining unwilling to engage in the clandestine shenanigans she knew would be necessary to secure anything even approaching a fair market price. In one neat arrangement I had solved both her problems, and finally she said, "Set up an appointment, Mr. Hawley. I'll trust in your judgment regarding this man's character."

I thanked her and hung up, conspicuously skipping over any mention of a commission for finding her a customer and acting as if it were she who was doing me the favor. As soon as the receiver was on its cradle, Larry Fizner said, "So who's this rich collector interested in the grieving widow's goodies?"

I smiled as I said, "You are, Mr. Fizner."

Larry frowned while he worked it out in his mind. Then, when he realized what I was getting at, his grizzled face brightened, and he grinned, nodded, pulled his cigarette away from his mouth, and said, "I like it."

NINE

■■■■■■■■■

I TUCKED NAT back into bed, told Jerry to watch the phone, and sent Larry Fizner off to do some shopping, telling him, "Try to buy something that somebody with money wouldn't be ashamed to wear."

He looked down at himself and then back up at me with genuine astonishment in his eyes, saying, "So what's wrong with what I got on?" His ensemble at the moment consisted of a pair of maroon polyester pants, a white and green plaid dress shirt, and a black bow tie. I had just realized that I was sending him on a doomed expedition, when Jerry laughed from the periphery of the conversation, giving me an idea.

"Jer," I said. "Why don't we put the call forwarding on Dad so you can go with Mr. Fizner and see that he gets done up like a normal human being?"

Jerry was thrilled, Larry Fizner moaned, and I loaded the cot into the van.

After stopping off so that Mrs. Kane could sign a release form, authorizing me to take possession of Erena Batilovna's body, I headed south to Logan's Town, taking the long way, which pointed me north, toward downtown Cleveland. My whole body was humming with adrenaline, and I knew that I was finally on the exact, right, no-shit, don't-try-to-hide-because-I've-got-ya-covered track. I wasn't at the station yet. But my train was rolling. I still had two specific things to do before I picked up Erena Batilovna: one involved John Gilbert, who I had never actually laid eyes on face-to-face, and the other dealt with the man whose business card I had found acting as a bookmark in the bottom drawer of

Alexander Kane's desk in his office at home.

It was going on one o'clock in the afternoon, which was, I knew, lunchtime for the business crowd. But once I'd stepped into the Sohio Building downtown and rode the elevator up to the twenty-second floor, I was told—miracle of miracles—that Mr. Leopold Chimmings had skipped lunch that day, and that, seeing that I represented Mrs. Kane in a legal capacity—I told the secretary that I was a private investigator hired by the widow—he could see me immediately.

Leopold Chimmings, the corporate lawyer engaged by the Kane Antique and Collectible Company, was a dark-eyed man of roughly sixty years of age, with wiry, closely curled grey hair, and very thick glasses that gave him an owlish look. He came out to the secretary's area to greet me after she buzzed his desk, shaking my hand and leading me by the arm into a plush, book-filled room with one wall-sized window overlooking Lake Erie. The air outside was so cold that there wasn't the trace of a cloud anywhere to mar the view. Hovering at the very limit of the dark water's edge was a thin line of horizon I knew to be Canada, a place I had never been, nor had any desire to go to since every time Cleveland got a blast of winter air the weatherman always said that it had come down from there. Canada, in my imagination, has always been a dark, bone-numbingly cold place, where people huddle around tiny, life-giving fires, saving up their money in hopes of one day moving someplace warm.

Mr. Chimmings, squinting through his binocular spectacles, offered me coffee, which I declined, and grew instantly serious when I removed the file folder I had under my arm and laid it on his desk. He asked me what specifically my visit was about. I opened the Batilovna file, standing, ignoring the seat he had offered, and finally said, "November 11, 1991. Do you recognize that date, Mr. Chimmings? Do you recall what you were doing that day?"

He blinked and said that he didn't. Before he could ask the question I knew had already jumped into his mind, I said, "How about the twenty-third of June, 1992? That one ring any bells? It was a Tuesday, I believe."

Again, he pleaded ignorance, and I hit him with one more date before looking around the office and adding, "For someone so intimately involved with expensive works of art, your office is conspicuously devoid of any really nice pieces. One stuffed rainbow trout and a blowup photo of the city skyline seems pretty paltry for a man of your aesthetic sophistication."

"What are you talking about, Mr.—?"

"Hawley," I reminded him. "Bill Hawley. And what I'm talking about is an original Renoir, a Devachio, and a Michelangelo sketch. According to Mr. Kane's records, he sold you one of each."

"He what?" Chimmings asked, snapping off his glasses in surprise, leaving his face looking suddenly naked and vulnerable.

"It's all in the file, Mr. Chimmings," I said, tapping my finger on the papers stacked before me on his desk. "If we weren't so high-class, the two of us, we could more or less say that you acted as Alex Kane's bagman, delivering money and removing stolen property for him to pick up later."

"I don't have to take this . . ." he began, lifting the telephone's receiver and poising his finger as if to ring for security.

"Do we really need to go through the whole song and dance?" I asked, making the lawyer's eyes, which were fixed on me with the intensity of a predator, narrow. "I know the whole deal, and you know I do. I wouldn't be here if I didn't."

"So what is it that you want?" he asked cautiously.

I motioned for him to put the receiver down, which he did.

I began my presentation by expressing my appreciation for what I called "a cute gag," by which I meant the setup that he and Alex Kane had devised for cheating Uri and John Gilbert out of millions of dollars worth of precious paintings, while setting them up to take a very nasty, very inevitable fall.

"I particularly liked the part about burning the originals," I said, finally taking a seat and motioning for Mr. Chimmings to sit down, too, as if suddenly he were the guest and the office was mine. "Whose idea was that, by the way? His or yours?"

"I don't know what you're talking about," he grunted. "But whatever it is, I'm sure that I had nothing to do with it. Now, just where did you get that file, and what exactly is in it?"

"We'll get to that," I said, waving off the question as if the file were suddenly unimportant. "The question here is the money . . ."

"I knew it." Chimmings scowled, leaning back in his leather chair and lacing his fingers behind his head like a man who had suddenly found himself in his own, native element.

It took me about ten seconds to figure out what he meant, and when I did I could feel my face burn as I said, "You've got it wrong, bub. I'm straight."

"Then why'd you come to me?" He nodded, the hint of a smile playing along the corners of his mouth. "If you're such a virgin, why aren't you flapping that file under a cop's nose, instead of mine? And that's saying that there's even anything in there worth flapping."

"Take a look," I offered.

He shrugged without leaning forward.

I didn't like the gesture because it suddenly made me feel as if he were in control, so I decided to let the air out of him. Reaching into my pocket I withdrew a three- by five-inch, black-and-white photograph and tossed it onto his desk. The picture was of him, taken as he stood in front of Alex Kane's casket. He glanced at it briefly, and then at me as I explained the gig.

"I matched it to the picture you've got of yourself in the yellow pages," I said. "I've been looking into your affairs for quite a while, and I know things about you that you wouldn't believe."

From there I described how, on the night he died, Alex Kane had been on his way to the house on Lincoln Street, where, next weekend, according to his own schedule, he planned to burn yet another precious painting, a Goya watercolor of a little girl in a yellow hat. But, as usual, it wouldn't be the original he'd be burning, it would be one of the five forged copies the girl named Erena Batilovna had made for him. The girl, by the way, had been killed on the same night as Mr. Kane . . . as Mr. Chimmings already knew.

"Oh, you *didn't* know that she died on that same night?" I asked when Chimmings raised an eyebrow to indicate his surprise. "Well, now you do. Keep it in mind, because it's important."

"I knew about the girl," he groused, as if my implying that he'd missed something irritated him.

"Good." I nodded. "Did you know her?"

"No."

"I didn't think so."

So, I continued, Kane was going to burn one of the forgeries in place of the original painting, and because the forgeries were so good, no one would notice the difference when he did it, not even the artist herself. Then, as the plan went, Mr. Chimmings would arrive. When?

"This coming Sunday," I announced, answering my own question and referring to the file for verification. "You were scheduled to fly in on a private plane chartered from Wintergreen Chartered Flights, leaving Cleveland Hopkins Airport at six-fifteen P.M. and arriving at the New Philadelphia airport about twenty minutes later. See?" I pointed at the file again. "It's all here. Flight number JK-417, departure time, the works."

"I can't believe he wrote all this down," Chimmings clucked, shaking his head.

"He didn't expect to be caught," I said. "And he certainly didn't expect to die. But what he wrote down isn't what you think. It's all initials . . . see? It's very nearly in code." I turned the file around and pointed. "I only knew what he was talking about because I had put it all together from what I already knew. I figured that the abbreviation CHIM must have referred to the Chimmings whose card I'd found in his desk and also in his Rolodex listing an office number and a number at home. When Mrs. Kane told me that you've been handling the business's legal affairs since it started, I knew you were a man that Alex Kane could trust implicitly."

While I spoke, Chimmings fidgeted, which was good. Nervous people always fidget, and since I was making him nervous, what I was saying had to be close to the mark.

"One of the things that's been bothering me ever since Mrs. Kane told me about her husband burning these priceless, one-of-a-kind paintings," I continued confidently, "is that, if he really was the compulsive, never-let-anything-go type personality she made him out to be, then I just couldn't see how he would ever be able to bring himself to burn up all this valuable shit. Even if he could make a lot of money by doing it. It just didn't seem right. It didn't fit.

"But then I noticed your initials, Mr. Chimmings, listed next to these serial numbers in the file he kept at home. Do you know what these numbers are? They're page numbers. And do you know how I know that they're page numbers? Because Mr. Kane circled them in a book I found while searching his desk. The book's called, *Stolen By War: Art's Greatest Loss*, and it was hidden under a stack of telephone books in a drawer. It lists all the masterpieces that are known to have disappeared during World War Two, and it intrigued me since it was the second time in as many days that I had run across that same premise. While I was browsing through it, I found your business card used as a bookmark on a page describing a missing Goya painting of a girl in a yellow hat, and I also noticed that every so often a page number was circled. It didn't take a genius to see that the numbers in this file and the page numbers circled in that book were the same. And once I made that connection, the rest was easy. When a number appeared next to a set of initials in the file, it was Alex Kane's way of saying that on a certain date, he had sold the owner of those initials a copy of whatever painting appeared on that particular page.

"There were five different sets of initials for each page number listed on the calendar, Mr. Chimmings. Four that I didn't recognize, and yours. Yours, by the way, were the only initials that appeared every time. The others varied, but yours were consistent.

"And that's what made me realize that after he burned a forgery of a famous painting in front of Uri and John Gilbert, Alex Kane would then sell the original, as if it were a forgery as well, to you, posing as just a another customer. You wouldn't give the painting back until later, for which I'm sure you were paid a handsome fee. It was a classic scam, and I don't think I would have ever figured it out, if I hadn't already been looking for it."

"Looking for it?" Chimmings asked. "Why?"

"Because," I explained, proud of myself at the moment and glad for the opportunity to show off, "once his wife told me that Mr. Kane was selling multiple copies of his forged pictures, I knew that the one absolutely essential thing that he would need to keep somewhere was a record of his transactions."

"Why?" Chimmings asked.

"Simple: so that he wouldn't accidentally try to sell the same painting to the same customer twice."

Chimmings frowned.

And I got to the point.

"Mr. Chimmings," I said, "I came here this afternoon because I required the answers to two specific questions. The first regarded whether I was right or not about your involvement in Mr. Kane's scheme. That, you've already answered, although not in so many words. The second question is one to which I would like you to respond with either a simple yes or no. After that, I'll leave you alone. Just one yes or no, and then I'm gone."

"What's your question, Mr. Hawley?" Chimmings asked, bracing himself in his chair as if I was about to ask him to perform some weird sex act.

"Did you and Alex Kane ever use the telephone to discuss the fact that he was planning to divorce his wife?" I asked.

Chimmings blinked as he said, "That's it?"

I nodded.

"That's it, Mr. Chimmings. And it's more important than you can imagine. Did you and Alex Kane ever use the telephone to discuss the fact that he was planning to divorce his wife? Take your time, think it over, and tell me yes or no."

"Yes," he answered without hesitation. "We discussed it any number of times. Alex and Victoria didn't get along as well as they once had." He shrugged. "Maybe it was simply a matter of two people growing apart as they grew older. Or maybe it was him realizing that he suddenly had an awful lot of money to play with, and that he could have any woman he wanted. Most likely it was the latter. I've seen it happen before. It's not a unique occurrence. But for whatever reason, he was planning to divorce her. She didn't know anything about his plan, he said. And until he had his affairs in order and was ready to make an offer as to a settlement, he forbade me from discussing it with her, which wasn't difficult since we hardly ever saw one another. I hardly ever saw him, for that matter. We conducted a good eighty percent of our business over the telephone. He and I only met for lunch a couple of times a year . . . more as a matter of form than anything else."

"Except for when you flew down to pick up the pictures," I offered.

He nodded. "Except for then, of course."

"And the money?" I asked.

"Ah, we're back to that," he returned.

"Yes, we are," I said, rising from my seat and closing the file folder. "Since these transactions must, out of necessity, have been conducted with cash, what I was wondering was whether Mr. Kane slipped you the money you'd need after you had already arrived in New Philadelphia, or if you picked it up before you left. That money was, by the way, the same money that he had been telling his wife he was using to purchase a collection of precious religious icons, which were actually, as it turns out, neither precious, nor religious—at least not the way he ended up using them.

"Anyway, what makes the question of when you got the money important is that if you were, say, keeping it in a safe, say, here in the office, so that it would be handy for when you needed to make a pickup, it might be a nice thing if you admitted that you had it."

He was looking up at me from where he sat, his eyes appearing positively fishy behind his glasses, and a thin, almost imperceptible dotting of moisture adorning his upper lip.

"I mean," I continued from where I had stopped, one hand on the doorknob, "you would need to pay for the pictures you were supposedly buying, wouldn't you, Mr. Chimmings? Alex Kane wasn't in this alone, was he? He had a partner. Two, in fact. And they would want their cuts. Seeing that the transactions would be conducted in cash, his partners would probably want to actually see the sales made, so that they could be sure that Kane wouldn't try to shortchange them. So you'd need to be carrying quite a lot of cash when you stepped off that plane at New Philadelphia. Probably upwards of half a million dollars at a time. That much money's hard to come by. It takes time. And there's a paper trail, records kept by the Securities and Exchange Commission whenever that much currency changes hands.

"So if, for example, you should have a half million dollars tucked away in a safe hidden, say, behind that trout on your wall, it might be a good idea to give some thought to turning it over to the proper authorities when the time seems right. Because I'm going to see to it that the time will seem right very soon, Mr. Chimmings. It's all going to come out, sooner or later. It has to. There's no avoiding it. And considering that you're a lawyer, it would probably be a good idea if you got your own legal affairs in order, too. Although, if your relationship with Mr. Kane is any measure of your average business day, you may just want to take your trout and get out of town just as fast as you fucking can. Because, once the story's out about how you helped screw those rich collectors out of all that money, the cops are going to be the least of your worries. Alex Kane is dead, and you have the disadvantage of an ad with your permanent address listed in the local yellow pages that's got your stupid picture right in it."

"Now wait just a minute!" Chimmings exclaimed, standing up behind his desk.

"See you around, Mr. Chimmings," I said, closing the door behind me as I left. Feeling very satisfied as the little lawyer shouted my name in his office, I smiled sweetly at his secretary and headed for the elevator.

From there I hit the freeway and headed straight south, riding an adrenaline high and grinding my teeth for want of a cigarette, which was pretty typical, addictive behavior, I knew—intense emotions, good or bad, often bring on the "Gimme Monsters." But understanding my cravings on an intellectual level didn't go very far toward changing the fact that *I wanted a cigarette*, and I wanted one *bad*. I had smoked a couple the other night in the bar with Larry Fizner, and that brief encounter was enough to remind whatever alligator part of my brain it is that likes smoke, that nicotine was still out there to be had. Cigarettes, I also knew, are directly linked in my psyche to booze. So by craving a smoke, I was actually craving a drink. Now the craving was awake again, curled in my gut and sending its tentacles through the rest of my body, looking for weak spots it could exploit. Weak spots that sent messages to my brain like, "Hey, what would one beer hurt? You've been straight for three years. You've made your point. We all know that you can do it. So why don't we celebrate?"

Or:

"A beer would help you to relax, and you know that you think better when you're relaxed. You're going to need to do some serious thinking pretty soon. So it wouldn't hurt to be relaxed. Right?"

I think of my cravings, my addictions, as something that rips me in half, so that I become two Bill Hawleys who occupy the same space simultaneously. We, he and I, the dry Bill and the drinking Bill, occasionally have these conversations regarding our behavior. We discuss it. I've been winning lately, but it concerns me that, even after three years without a mistake, the frequency and tone of my inner dialogues really hasn't changed all that much.

Maybe I was naive, but I expected things to get easier as the distance between my last hangover and the present moment increased. I thought it would be like taking a trip, with the way I was when I drank being a physical location, and the way I am when I'm sober being like a bus carrying me someplace else. Every sober day would be like another hundred miles traveled by the bus so that, eventually, I'd leave that place I started from so far behind that I wouldn't even remember what it looked like.

But it doesn't seem to work that way, at least not for me. Like I said, every drunk is different. Maybe for some of those guys who go to A.A., twelve steps cover enough ground to do the job. But my bus, traveling full tilt every single day, just seems to circle my hometown. I feel like I'm going someplace, all the sensations of movement and accomplishment are right, but all I have to do is look out the window, and the place I left behind is there, as big as life, and I think that's the way it'll always be.

Gripping the steering wheel so tightly that I all but sprained the muscles in my forearms, I pulled up the one mental image I've learned to depend on during my really rough moments: I thought of Nat, and the promises I'd made to her. And it kept me going, straight down to Logan's Town, with no stops along the way.

Erena Batilovna was waiting for me at the Wittmere County Hospital, I knew. I also knew that since she was an obvious homicide, Dr. Webster, the county coroner, had already had his way with her. I had a pretty good idea what kind of condition she'd be in when I got there, so I wasn't exactly in any great hurry to get to that part of my day. I had one more stop to make before the hospital, and though it promised to be on the tricky side, I was looking forward to it a hell of a lot more than I was the inevitable prospect of gazing down at the horror of what I knew would be left of the pretty young Russian girl who had had the "magic in her hands."

The Country Notions shop, where Ochre Kane, Alex's father, had raised his son, was located on Birch Street, off the Logan's Town central circle and next to a smaller shop that was also owned by the Kanes. I parked my van up the street and out of sight, so that anyone looking out the shop's front window wouldn't see it. Then, turning up the collar on my coat, I started walking, passing the shop once, then again, and then finally working my way up the driveway to a parking lot tucked in behind the building. I was looking for a couple of specific things, and I found the first as soon as I turned the corner.

Behind the shop was a paved area reserved for customer parking, with room for about fifteen cars, and a pair of metal garage doors against the back of the building, one of which was opened. I strolled across the lot, looking through the open garage door and seeing a white Ford van with the words, *Kane Collectibles*, painted in blue script across the side. From what I could make out, there was another van just like it parked farther on in the garage, behind the closed garage door. And a third was parked outside, with its back doors open as a tall, lightly framed young man in jeans and a dark blue parka stood, nodding to another shorter and considerably more stout man who pointed at a clipboard and then at the van, as if giving him instructions. Behind the two men the garage was packed full of furniture, some covered with sheets, some uncovered, some with price tags, some without, and some bearing big yellow stickers that said, SOLD, in bright red letters.

The younger man was Richard Hickle, the "chauffeur" that Uri had identified from the picture I'd shown him, and the older man was, I assumed, John Gilbert, the original object of my visit. I hadn't expected to see Hickle. And seeing him now, the man who had attacked my wife, the man whose identity had motivated everything I'd done these past few days, I had to mentally fall back and regroup, get a hold of myself, and say aloud, quietly but with conviction, "Not now. Soon. But not yet."

The magnitude of my reaction, the physicality of it, the positive substance of my anger, amazed me because I've never in my life engaged in a really violent act. That's just not part of my personality. Truth be told, I've never really even understood violence; I've never seen where it ever solved anything. It's always been the recourse of stupid people, in my opinion, the action of someone without the sense to think through the consequences of their behavior. But in that instant, looking at Richard Hickle and knowing what he had done to the woman I love, a revelation struck me with such thunderous force that I was left, quite literally, amazed.

Sometimes, the consequences of violence are worth the deed!

That thought scared me, because I knew that at its root it wasn't the product of calculation, but of emotion. I was thinking for that instant with my glands, letting a chemical—adrenaline—interfere with my view of reality.

And then I had another revelation.

Thinking with your gut is just like drinking, because in both cases you're letting a chemical, in the one instance alcohol, in the other adrenaline, influence your behavior. Neither the drunk, nor the man enraged, really knows what he's doing. Violence done in the heat of passion is violence done by a mind impaired. If I was to be truly devoted to my vow of living a sober life, which was ultimately a devotion to seeing the truth about the things around me without the distortion of chemicals to smooth over the edges, then getting a rein on my emotions had to be a part of the process. What good was swearing off booze if I was going to let myself get stoned on rage?

It was all or nothing.

So when the rage came bubbling up from my gut, I squelched it.

Or at least I tried.

I was standing there, a man in a black cashmere coat hanging to his knees, black trousers, and shoes shined to a mirror finish, hands in pockets, talking to himself, when John Gilbert lifted his eyes from his clipboard and looked toward the center of the parking lot, at me. He said something to Hickle that I couldn't make out, causing the younger man to turn his head, which made me look away since, though Gilbert had been conspicuously absent from Alex Kane's funeral, I had photographic proof that Hickle had been at the viewing, and I didn't know if he would recognize me or not. Then Hickle slammed the delivery van's back doors, got behind the wheel, and drove away, leaving Gilbert to tuck the clipboard up under his arm and step my way, saying, "Can I help you?"

As he approached I got the measure of the man: about five feet eight inches tall, probably about 180 pounds, fifty-five to sixty years old, thick, reddish-brown hair, brown eyes, a smooth, handsome face with few wrinkles, and a thin nose and mouth, neither too large, nor too small, but nicely symmetrical, giving his face a well-meaning, almost harmless appearance. His clothes advertised his success in life without being overt. Overall he looked like an amiable, trustworthy salesman.

When he was close enough I bid him good day, in Russian. He blinked, smiled, and said, "Pardon?" And I could tell from the look on his face, not the look he was wearing when he spoke, but the one that had crossed over his features in the fraction of a second before he recovered from his initial surprise, that he hadn't understood a word of what I'd said. Assuming a thick accent, I said, "Excuse me," with a polite, European nod, explaining that I had been sent to find a gentleman named Gilbert. "Mr. John Gilbert," I said. "On a matter of business."

"What kind of business?" he asked.

And I nodded toward the garage, saying, "How you make your living."

I followed him inside, through the garage door, and as we made our way toward the front of the building where he had his office, I took the opportunity to meander around a little, looking things over, and noticing that, at the far end of the shop, just past the second white delivery van, there were three empty parking spaces. One for the van presently making its deliveries, I assumed, one for the van that Edward Kane had driven back to Cleveland on the night his father was killed, which was presently in the hands of the police, and one more.

Gilbert had just reached the door leading from the rear storage area to the front of the shop when I stopped him by saying that if it was all the same to him, I'd prefer to conduct our business right where we were since it was an obviously private place. He turned, looking blankly at me and pulling his hand back from the doorknob as he said, "Go on."

Ah, I thought. A man accustomed to business conducted in "private." Mr. Gilbert and I were going to get along just fine.

The gist of it was simple, I explained. I was the representative of a certain party who, having heard of the unfortunate death of Mr. Alexander Kane, had instructed me to approach Mr. Gilbert, as Mr. Kane's business partner, with the offer of a transaction.

"What kind of transaction?" Gilbert asked.

Moving through the sea of couches, divans, dining room tables, and hutches scattered on the concrete floor, I said, "One concerning a little girl in a yellow hat," affecting my Russian accent and keeping my voice soft, in a refined, experienced way. At one point I stopped, placed my hand on a particularly nice breakfront, looked it over appreciatively, and said, "Very nice indeed." Then I turned to give Mr. Gilbert the full force of my attention as I added, "This little girl is a Goya, by birth. We understand that you and she are acquainted."

I had to give him credit. Even though I had obviously blindsided him, Mr. Gilbert recovered beautifully and keyed in on the single most important aspect of my offer that would affect him as an individual.

"Who is this interested party?" he asked.

I shrugged, saying that I wasn't at liberty yet to say. Once certain guarantees had been given, I added, we could get down to a more detailed accounting of ourselves. But for now, he would just have to be satisfied speaking in general terms.

Gilbert didn't like it, I could see. But he was interested. I knew he'd be interested since, with Erena Batilovna dead, his supply of forged paintings had, at least temporarily, dried up. The Goya of the little girl in the yellow hat that I had seen listed in Mr. Kane's folder as the next painting to be burned and sold might well be the last that Gilbert would ever have at his disposal, unless Uri could find another forger with Erena's talents. But now, more than ever, despite his desire to make as much profit as he could from his final offering, Mr. Gilbert had to keep in mind that he was a witness for the prosecution in a murder case, and as such, he would need to keep his nose absolutely clean.

At that moment a terrible clatter of something that sounded like a school bell rang, interrupting our conversation and making Mr. Gilbert practically throw his clipboard straight up in the air. He smiled apologetically as he explained that it was the telephone, rigged on a bell so that it could be heard in the garage. A moment later a buzzer sounded, and Gilbert excused himself, saying that the phone call had obviously been for him. Disappearing through the door leading to the front of the shop, he apologized again and promised to return in a moment.

As soon as he was gone, I started moving.

First I scanned the upper recesses of the ceiling, looking for security cameras. There were none. Then I moved quickly through the tangle of furniture in the garage, looking things over as fast as I could as I searched for one specific item, which I found, and grabbed, just as the door opened and Mr. Gilbert reappeared.

It's awful when you get caught. You never know how much the person doing the catching actually saw, so you're left with that terrible moment during which you have to stand there, looking as innocent as you can, waiting to find out how much you got away with and how much you're going to have to explain. Essentially, Mr. Gilbert had caught me red-handed. The thing I'd come hoping to find was wrapped around my right fist, which was hanging at my side as I said, "You have some very nice pieces here," in a way that I hoped transmitted an impression of perfect ease.

He looked at me in what I was sure was a cross way, and then glanced over to the spot where I had been standing when he left. The particularly nice breakfront upon which I had commented earlier stood to one side of me, and a dry sink with a copper basin rested between Gilbert and myself so that my hands were hidden from his view. As soon as he moved his eyes from me, I stuffed my hand into my overcoat pocket, and then made sure that my facial expression was neutral so that when he returned his attention to me I'd be ready.

As I had expected, his present concerns for security were overshadowing his taste for currency, and even though he was very curious as to how I knew about the little girl in the yellow hat with whom he was acquainted, he said, with regret heavy in his tone, "I'm sorry, but at the moment I'm afraid you've caught me at an incommodious time. I sincerely wish I could accommodate your interest, but I'm afraid it would be unwise for me to even consider your offer. With time, I'm sure we can speak again. But for now, I'm going to have to pass."

Very well, I said. I would relay the message. Thanks a lot, good-bye, don't get up, I know my way out.

I had just stepped through the open garage door to the freedom of the parking lot when Gilbert's voice stopped me, making my heart pound. Both my hands were in my coat pockets as I turned, seeing him approaching me through the maze of furniture separating us, and I must admit that in that moment, with my right coat pocket stuffed full of the thing I had just stolen, the thought of simply making a break for it crossed my mind. But I didn't. I stayed put. When he stopped just a couple of feet from me and extended his hand, I was convinced that I'd blown it. I was sure that he wanted back his stolen property, and I was about to pull it out of my pocket and give it to him when his face softened and he said, "No hard feelings? You understand my position?"

I shook his offered hand, trying hard to hide my relief as I said, "Of course. Your discretion is to your credit. I'm sure you'll be seeing me again."

He looked relieved as he pumped my hand, his grip firm and friendly. Then he glanced over the parking lot and asked about my car. When I told him that I had left it on the street, I thought that he'd follow me, but he was more delicate than that. He watched me from the front window of the shop instead. I could just make out his dark form, very much in the way I had seen Deputy King observing Nat and me as the sheriff gave us our original tour of town that preceding Saturday afternoon. With his eyes on my back the way they were, I was glad I had chosen to leave my van up the street, out of his view.

Once I was in the driver's seat, I gave myself a couple of minutes' worth of deep breathing, letting the tension in my neck work its way out a little as I concentrated on the darkness behind my eyelids and thought, Okay, that's number two for the day.

But I suddenly realized that I now had one more stop to make before I went to get Erena. The really hard part of this whole thing would come tonight, I knew, which was when Maxym Batilovna would see his daughter for the first time since her death. Though legally Mrs. Kane was the person in charge of the arrangements—since officially no one even knew that Maxym and Vaslov existed—I felt I had an obligation to the girl's family to offer them the chance to arrange her memorial service, which was going to be a bitch. But, at the same time, it would also bring Uri to the funeral home, and Mr. Gilbert's obvious lack of understanding when I had greeted him in Russian had brought up a new wrinkle that I wanted very much to discuss with that big, sneaky, lying, Russian son of a bitch who had had things his own way for too fucking long, and who was in for one hell of an unpleasant surprise as soon as I got home.

Old Nicholas, the junkyard dog, barked his brains out when I stepped up to the rear of the sheriff's office and walked past his fence. The Country Notions antique shop was visible from the front of the office, and I didn't want to take the chance that John Gilbert would see me going in to see the sheriff after our little talk, so I knocked on the office's back door, and entered the building through the interrogation room. Deputy King showed me in, and his expression declared his animosity for the trouble I had gotten him into with his boss more eloquently than any words he could have chosen. I just followed him in and let the tension be. There was nothing I could do to fix it anyway, so I didn't see any point in wasting time fucking with it.

Sheriff Paulson didn't stand when he saw me, but just stared from where he sat behind his desk as I stepped up and dropped the thing I had stolen from the Country Notions shop's back storage area onto the magazine he had been reading when I came in. The sheriff looked down at the length of decorative gold rope curled atop his issue of *Field and Stream*, his neatly trimmed moustache twitching and his hands steady on his desk.

"I thought it would turn out to be curtain rope," I explained. "But I was wrong. It came off a chair."

"Where'd you get this?" the sheriff asked.

Before I answered, I wondered if Edward Kane's cell was within earshot of the office. Deciding that it probably wasn't, I responded, "It matches, doesn't it?"

"I asked you where you got it?" the sheriff returned.

"And I asked you if it matches or not."

"I can't tell just by lookin' at it."

"Well, I can," I said. "I haven't run any forensics or anything, but I can all but promise you that this piece of rope is the mate to the one that was wrapped around Erena Batilovna's wrists and neck. It's about three feet long, Sheriff, which is the same length as the one used to kill the girl. It's the same color, and I took it off the right side of a French provincial living room chair. Though that chair had a peg and a hook on its other side where a matching piece of rope would hang, it didn't have another piece on it. I think that the piece that was supposed to be there is in a plastic bag marked 'Exhibit A' in a drawer someplace in this office. What do you think? Could that maybe be the case?"

I let the sheriff go for a couple of seconds during which his lips grew pale and his eyes studied the rope so intently that I thought he'd hurt himself. Just as I was sure that he was about to let his anger out, I said, "I got it from across the street." I pointed at the window to my right that faced the Logan's Town city circle. "You can see the place from here, as a matter of fact. You're the one who first showed it to me, Sheriff. Mr. Kane's father owned it, you said. Remember? The Country Notions shop has a rear storage area in a garage around back. There's a bunch of furniture stuffed in it. There's also room for a whole fleet of delivery vans."

"Are you sayin' that the Batilovna girl was killed in that garage?" the sheriff asked.

I shook my head.

"No. She was killed in one of the vans."

"One of the vans?" the sheriff protested. "That's bullshit! The boys from the Cleveland crime lab have been going over the van that Eddie drove home since we arrested him, and they haven't come up with so much as a hair to prove that she was ever anywhere near the thing."

"Think about it, Sheriff," I said. "Your own coroner said that he found carpet fibers on Erena's coat that matched samples taken from the trunk of Edward Kane's Porsche 944. It's been my experience that a girl on a date very rarely chooses to ride in the trunk of her boyfriend's car. But the funny part is that the coroner didn't find anything in the trunk of that Porsche that belonged to the girl . . . no hair, no dirt from her shoes, no nothing.

"And then we have the rope that was used as the murder weapon coming from the garage across the street from your own office.

"Between the carpet fibers from the Porsche, and the rope from the garage, I think it's a pretty safe bet to say that things were set up to look as if Erena Batilovna's body was transported some distance before it was placed in the pantry of the house on Lincoln Street.

"Which presents us with a logistics problem. The Country Notions shop is at least three miles from the Kane's house on Lincoln Street. And the house on Dovetail Lane, where you say you found Edward Kane's Porsche parked the day after Alex Kane died, is at least five miles from either place. Edward Kane went home to Cleveland in a delivery van. And you've got the van to prove it. According to your own interviews, no one saw him walking any of those miles between the shop and the two houses anytime that night, or the next day. And, more importantly, no one saw the Porsche . . . a bright red, conspicuous sports car, on the street anytime after the accident.

"You also said that John Gilbert's already sworn to you that he stayed in the Lincoln Street house until eight-thirty in the morning, waiting for Kane to bring the Batilovna girl home. If that's true, then Edward Kane must have planted the girl's body in the house sometime after John Gilbert left. Leaving the question of how he could have gotten the body into the pantry, returned his Porsche to the house on Dovetail Lane, and then picked up a delivery van all the way back in town, without being seen, in broad daylight, by himself."

"And how'd he wipe that van so clean that a forensics squad can't find a trace of the victim ever bein' in it?" the sheriff asked rhetorically. And then, moving his eyes to me, he added, "I'll bet you think you know. Don't ya, Mr. Hawley?"

"Yeah." I nodded. "I think I do."

Leaning back in his chair and lacing his fingers atop his stomach, Sheriff Paulson told Deputy King to pull up a seat for me. I accepted the chair, sat, and waited while the sheriff gathered his thoughts. Finally, leaning forward again and lifting the rope as if it were a dead snake, he said, "So, how'd you do it?"

"I just walked in and grabbed it," I replied.

He smiled as he shook his head and said, "That ain't what I'm askin' and you know it. Who drove the second car, Mr. Hawley? Somebody must have. Just tell me that much."

I shook my head, leaning forward in my seat and getting very serious.

"Sheriff," I said, "I want to put it *all* on the table. Everything. Me and you, face-to-face, no more crap. I've gone as far as I can without you, and you've gone as far as you can without me. Together, we can finish this whole thing off and be done with it once and for all. Separately, there's no telling how long this shit could drag on. And I don't see how either of us has any interest in wasting any more time."

The sheriff agreed, telling me to, "Get to the part with the proposition."

"How did you know there'd be a proposition?" I asked.

And he barked out one harsh laugh before he said, "There's always a proposition, Mr. Hawley. With a guy like you, that's how it works. You're a smart ass. Now, now." He lifted his hands to cut off any protest. "I don't mean that in a shitty way, necessarily. It's just that, if you thought that you could go it alone, that's just how you'd do it. But you comin' here to hand all this over like you did, well, that can only mean that you either need something from me, or you need me to do something for you. Since you seem perfectly capable of acquiring anythin' you want, that leaves me doin' you a favor as the only other logical motivation for this neighborly little visit. And since you ain't so dumb as to think that I'd do you any favors for free, I'm figurin' that you came in here this afternoon lookin' to make a deal. Now, how'd I do in the deducin' department?"

"Just perfect, Sheriff," I said, suddenly liking the man a good deal more than I had previously.

"What about our bet?" he asked.

"I'm willing to wave it." I smiled.

"No way," he said, lacing his fingers over his stomach. "We'll talk about your deal, but the bet stays on."

I shrugged and said, "Whatever."

"Now gimme the hard part first," he said. "What do I gotta do?"

"Let Edward Kane out of jail," I said, deciding that the easiest way to go about this was also the quickest.

Deputy King's jaw dropped open when I said it, and I thought that he'd fall over. But Sheriff Paulson didn't react with even a hint of surprise. Quite the contrary. He responded as if he'd just been waiting for me to say exactly what I'd said, nodding in a contemplative way and looking down at the rope as he asked, "And what do I get?"

"All of it," I said, scooting forward in my seat and leaning on his desk. "Kane's killer, Erena Batilovna's killer, and a whole bunch of other stuff that'll make you look like a mighty big fish when it hits the press."

"When?" he asked.

"How about now?"

"That sounds 'bout right."

"So is it a deal, Sheriff?"

The deputy was looking back and forth from the one to the other of us, but we both ignored him.

The sheriff glanced up at the ceiling, and then at the window, saying, "Right across the street from my office, huh?"

"That's right," I agreed.

"Okay, Mr. Hawley," he said. "Looks like you've got yourself a deal. But if it don't work, it's gonna mean your ass, and probably mine, too. The only one who won't get hurt's Church here." He cocked a thumb over his shoulder to indicate the deputy, adding, "And that's only 'cause the boy ain't got a clue. Ain't that right, Church? You ain't quite up to speed just yet, are ya?"

Deputy Churchill King shook his head from side to side, saying, "Sheriff, right this second I ain't even sure 'bout the question."

"Innocent as a babe." The sheriff grinned. Then to me he said, "See why I knew he couldn't have gone out to Lincoln Street on his own? I'll have to go through Eddie's lawyers though, make it all look good and legal. That okay with you?"

"Fine," I said. "The sooner the better."

"So when do you want him to walk?"

"No sooner than nine o'clock tomorrow morning, but no later than noon."

"Whew, you got yourself a real set of balls, workin' things out that close before you even knew whether I'd go along with it or not."

"It's not necessarily that, Sheriff. It's just that I personally can't take it anymore. If you're willing to give me a hand, we may as well line them up and knock them down before we end up with another body to deal with. Or worse."

"Worse?" he asked.

I nodded.

"You're really on a roll, ain't you, Mr. Hawley?" the sheriff commented.

"Sheriff Paulson, when I was younger I worked for a private ambulance company. What I mostly did was carry bodies for funeral homes, but every once in a while we'd get an emergency call. Then we'd go racing off with the lights flashing and the sirens blaring, thinking we were really doing something. But in the back of my mind I always knew that the really significant event had already happened. Whatever the accident or trouble that was at the root of it all was, the really important part was already over. We were just going in to clean up the mess.

"And I suppose that's exactly what me and you are doing here, Sheriff. A lot of complicated and expensive shit's been going down around here, and it's finally slopped over and made a mess on the floor. We can clean it up before it gets any worse. But only if we work together."

"Okay," the sheriff said, rising from his seat. "Start talkin'."

And I did.

TEN

■■■■■■■■■

I CALLED UNCLE Joe the minute I got Erena Batilovna on the prep table. You never call an embalmer until the body's at the funeral home. That's one of the first rules you learn in the business. The temptation is to call as soon as you learn that you've got a job so that the embalmer can come right out and get started. But sometimes a body will be delayed in transit, and the embalmer will end up standing around and waiting. That only has to happen once for you to learn that it's a lot better for you to have to wait for the embalmer than for the embalmer to have to wait for you. It's professional courtesy, especially when the embalmer has to get out of bed at some ungodly hour of the morning to come down to an empty funeral home and glower at you— the glorious asshole who just woke him up two hours early for nothing.

I got the first of the two calls I was expecting within an hour of getting home. It came from Mrs. Kane, and she was positively exuberant about the news that her son was to be released from jail.

"Ten-thirty tomorrow morning," she exclaimed. "Oh, Mr. Hawley, I'm so pleased . . . and I'm sorry about any trouble I might have been to you. Sheriff Paulson said that it was you who convinced him to agree to the release, and I think it's wonderful."

It wasn't that they were dropping the charges, she added. It was just that the Wittmere County prosecutor, at the sheriff's suggestion, had decided to let Edward make his bail. With the case having been covered in the local newspapers, she said, quoting exactly the pretext Sheriff Paulson and I had worked out in his office not two hours before, it was felt that he could be trusted to show up on his arraignment date. I thanked her for the kind words, and finished up by asking if three o'clock tomorrow afternoon would be okay for the meeting she had agreed to regarding the sale of her husband's icon collection. She fumbled for a second, sounding as if she were about to give me the brush-off, but then she seemed to reconsider, saying, "Certainly, Mr. Hawley. Anything you say. I'll be expecting you at three. And regarding your fee . . ."

There I cut her off, saying that the case wasn't over yet since her son still had to face an arraignment in the Wittmere County Court next Monday, and adding that, as far as I was concerned, the gift of a precious, authentic Russian religious icon was more than fair compensation for my trouble.

I had no sooner hung up the phone with her, than it rang again, and I answered it, saying, "Hawley Funeral Home, Bill Hawley speaking."

It was Uri. He had gotten the message I had left for him at the number he'd told me to call if I needed to speak to him again. He didn't have a phone in his apartment because he said they were too easy to tap. Behind his voice I could hear traffic noises, and I thought that he was probably calling from the phone booth across the street from his apartment.

I told him that he should bring the Russians to my funeral home in three hours because I had Erena's body and it would be ready to be viewed by then. When he asked, "Why should I do this?" I said that I thought that it was only right that Erena's father and brother should make her funeral arrangements. Uri grudgingly agreed, asking for directions and saying that they'd be there at nine.

"Good," I concluded.

Then I hung up and went upstairs, finding that there was a strange man waiting for me in my living room.

It took me about thirty seconds to realize that the stranger was actually Larry Fizner, who was standing there, looking at me through a pair of gold-framed, wire-rimmed glasses, wearing a charcoal-grey suit, black Italian shoes, a cream-colored shirt, and a subdued, floral print tie tucked into his vest. His hair had been cut, and now he was brazenly, unashamedly bald on top, with his grey hair trimmed neatly around the crown of his head, and those awful tendrils he normally had oiled across his scalp a part of history. I walked around him, staring, and he returned my look, moving his head and keeping his eyes on me. Nat was sitting in a chair off to one side of the room, and Jerry had his wheelchair parked next to her. Larry's clean-shaven face looked remarkably distinguished without the black plastic frames of his old glasses. And shorn of his lemon-yellow sport coat and bow tie, he suddenly didn't look like a dried-out derelict anymore, but had become instead a very passable imitation of a respectable, retired professional.

"What do you think?" Jerry finally asked.

I simply shook my head as I completed my circuit around Larry and stopped, moving my hands out at my sides and then letting them fall with a slap on my thighs as I said, "Amazing."

"What do ya mean, amazing?" Larry grouched. "I look like a sissy."

"You look fantastic," I said. "I'm not kidding. The women are going to go crazy."

"That's what I told him," Nat chimed in.

And Larry grumbled, "That's just what I need, a bunch of old biddies trying to drag me to bingo games. This is shit. And I ain't payin' for it."

I glanced at Jerry, who rolled his eyes and said, "For all his griping, he picked out most of it himself. Turns out that Mr. Fizner really hasn't got bad taste after all. What he's got is arthritis."

"Arthritis?" I asked.

"The hinge on his wallet freezes up and causes him terrible pain when he tries to open it."

"Well, I'll be," I said. "A cheapskate."

"That ain't true," Larry cut in. "I just don't see no reason to spend good money on clothes that I'm just gonna mess up anyway. In my line o' work, I'm hard on my clothes. Why should I piss money away? Goddamn it! Quit lookin' at me like that, you asshole!"

"You can put a tuxedo on a monkey," I said, shaking my head. "But underneath, he'll still be a monkey. You're going to have to watch your language if we're going to pull this thing off."

"You just worry about your own goddamn language, and let me worry about mine," he said.

I shrugged, adding, "That's better. Anyway, you and me got some talking to do downstairs. Come on."

I reached out my hand to take his arm when Nat cut in that she wanted to know what was happening.

"What do you two need to talk about that Jerry and I can't hear?"

I told her not to worry. But she looked at me with that searching expression of hers, and I knew right at that instant that I was skunked.

"Okay," I said, giving up any pretext of a lie. "There's an outside chance that things might end up getting a little rough tonight."

When Nat looked at me, there was a deep sadness in her eyes. The doorbell rang. I buzzed the intercom to let Uncle Joe in. And Larry Fizner said, "Well, if there's gonna be any rough stuff, the first thing we oughta do is order a pizza."

We all looked at him, and he added, "Hey, carbohydrates. Ya need 'em for energy."

So Jerry said, "Why the hell not?" And Nat didn't say another word.

Uri pulled in with the Russians at exactly nine on the button. He was driving a white, *Kane Collectibles*, Ford van and wearing the same black leather jacket he had been wearing the day before. Maxym and Vaslov Batilovna emerged from the back of the van and entered the funeral home with bowed heads and expressions that reminded me of beaten animals. They were terrified, and nervous, and refused to meet my eyes with their own, preferring to look around as if they expected to turn a corner at any moment and find a body stretched out on the floor.

In Europe, funerals are run differently than they are in this country, and in many places the tradition is still to have the actual viewing in the house of the deceased. The priest will arrive on the morning of the funeral, say some words, and then everybody heads out to the cemetery before coming back and eating for the rest of the day. One of the things recent immigrants are always fascinated by are American funeral homes. There seems to be a richness to the big buildings that they find both appealing and intimidating.

I showed them into my office, asked them to sit down, and opened a fresh file on my desk. That movement really put the old man on edge, so I closed the file, and explained to him, in terms as simple as I could manage, that his daughter had been released to me, and that I was offering him the chance to give her a decent funeral.

"He hasn't got any money," Uri cut in harshly.

I turned my eyes to where the big man was sitting and said, "Who said he needed any? This is between me and him. Now butt out."

Uri's face reddened, and Maxym Batilovna sat, shooting glances out like sounding lines, looking for a reference point.

Returning to the old man, I explained that there would be no cost for the funeral. That I didn't expect anything from him in return. And that, if he wished, everything could be done strictly in private.

He looked at me with big, wet eyes, and asked if he could see his daughter's body, which was what I had been expecting since he first walked in. I knew that there wouldn't be any thought given to actually setting up the funeral until he'd seen her, so I nodded, stood up, and said, in Russian, "She's in the back. I've covered her with a sheet, but you'll need to choose a dress for her later. Is your son coming?"

Vaslov stood and squared his shoulders as if I'd challenged him in some way. His fists were clenched, and looking at him at that moment, I realized that I had never seen him when he wasn't holding his hands at his sides, balled into fists, as if he were perpetually ready to fight.

He put his arm through his father's as if to support him, nodded, and followed me out of the room. Uri came behind, and together the three of us moved down the hall to the prep room.

Maxym Batilovna gasped when he saw his daughter. She was lying on the prep table, covered with a clean white sheet from her feet to her chin, her long, brown hair cascading over the end of the table and hanging in a fan. Her eyes were closed, their long lashes still sticky with glue, and her mouth was set in a noncommitted smile, the lips full and pink with fresh makeup. I had found her in pretty much the condition I had expected when I undid the plastic bag the Wittmere County Hospital had placed her in after her autopsy. And when Uncle Joe had asked me over the telephone what kind of shape she was in compared to Alex Kane, who was the last person he had embalmed from that part of town, I had replied, "About the same. But at least they left her eyes in." Everything else was gone. She had literally been cut into pieces.

Now she was beautiful. Uncle Joe had even managed to mask most of the rope burn across her throat. It was still there, of course. You can't make something like that completely go away. But with a high-necked dress, she'd be fine.

Mr. Batilovna's knees gave out and he sagged. Luckily his son already had a grip on him, and by the time I realized what was happening and reached out, he had already started pulling his father back up. We held him for a moment before he pulled away from us and approached the table under his own, stubborn steam, head held high, back straight, like a soldier, marching. There he stood for a long time, his hand laid upon his daughter's cold shoulder, his face shining with tears. His son stood behind him. Uri remained at the door, out of the way, as did I. Uri wheezed a little when he breathed, I noticed in the silence. Too many Marlboros.

When the Batilovnas were finished, we returned to the office and made Erena's funeral arrangements. They were simple. There would be a one-hour "viewing" the following morning and a mass at the Ukrainian Orthodox Cathedral. I had already explained the situation to Father Mylanko, and he had agreed to say the mass even though, at the time, we didn't know if the girl was Orthodox or not. Mr. Batilovna was flabbergasted that an Orthodox priest would be willing to do something like that, and, on the spot, he vowed to make compensation to the church by donating an icon that he would paint especially for them—an offer that I noted in my mind as explaining how Erena could forge all those paintings and still have time to paint the icons I'd seen in Alexander Kane's "vault." The answer was simple: she hadn't. It was her father who was responsible for the religious objects so dear to Mr. Kane's heart. I told him not to worry about making compensation, but he insisted, so I let it be. Then I asked Uri to step out into the hall with me for a second to discuss another matter, excusing myself politely and leaving the Batilovnas to mix themselves coffee at the wet bar by the desk.

"This way," I said, leading Uri toward the garage.

"For what?" he asked.

"You'll see," I said, indicating over my shoulder that he should follow. "I found something at the Lincoln Street house yesterday night, and I wanted to see if you could tell me what it is."

I opened the garage door and let Uri step inside. He was no sooner past me than the sound of flesh slapping flesh banged through the echoing air of the big, empty room, and Uri stumbled to one side, holding his jaw and looking at Larry Fizner, who had hit him with a roundhouse right, as if he were amazed. I stepped forward, ready to speak. But Uri let go of his jaw and raised one hand. In that instant Larry moved, producing, as if out of thin air, a length of two-by-four that he must have fished out of the pile of broken and cut boards we had in one corner of the garage, left over from when the funeral home was built and intended as starter wood for the fireplace we had in the downstairs lounge.

With a whistling sound Larry swung the board forward, catching Uri's arm as he moved it up to block his face. I shouted, "No!" This wasn't how we had agreed it would go at all. This was too much. I hadn't intended for Uri to suffer a beating. But it all happened so fast that I couldn't do a thing to stop it.

Larry hit Uri hard on the arm, slapping it down with the board and producing a terrible cracking sound that confused me for an instant, then sickened my stomach. Uri screamed and grabbed at his arm, staggering back as Larry advanced on him, swinging the board around and positioning it for another shot. Before Uri could even move to defend himself, Larry brought the board whistling around again, catching the big man on the left elbow and all but spinning him around with the force of the blow.

Larry was out of his new duds. He'd put on his old clothes because, "I'm tellin' ya, there's no sense in fucking up the expensive stuff on a jerk like this." So, in that instant, under the harsh fluorescent lights of the garage, he looked like a crazed bum, beating a bouncer.

Uri's shoulders shrugged as if he intended to lift his hands to defend his face as Larry stepped in on him yet again, board upraised, but his arms didn't move. They hung in a strangely limp way before him, as if they were no longer responding to his commands. With a shout Uri tried to move his head to one side as Larry brought down the board, but the motion was pathetically feeble compared to the efficient savagery of Larry's aim. The blow caught Uri on the side of the shoulder, smashing his collarbone and buckling his knees as the board snapped and broke in half. In another instant the big man was down, lying moaning on the concrete, his arms cocked at crazy angles over his chest and stomach, his head rolling from side to side as his wide eyes searched while his lips formed the Russian word for "Why?" over and over again.

Uri was mouthing it, but I was saying it, in English, loud.

"Why?" I shouted, stepping up to Larry, who had pitched away what was left of the two-by-four and was staring at where Uri lay. "You said that you were just going to clock him one on the jaw. You said that you just wanted to shake him up . . . to get his attention! Why the board? Why the fuck the board?"

"You saw him," Larry said, stepping past me. "I nailed him with my best shot, and he didn't even flinch. In another minute he'd have killed us both. Now he can't. Capish?"

I didn't like it. As a matter of fact, I hated it. But Larry was right. When it came to this stuff, he was always right. Looking over my shoulder to the closed garage door as if I expected the other Russians to appear at any instant, I stepped up to the phone, saying, "I'm calling 911."

"In a minute," Larry said.

"I'm doing it now!" I shot back.

"I said, in a minute!" Larry hissed, stopping my hand two inches from the receiver with the sheer power of his voice.

Uri was out cold, and Larry was bent over him going through his pockets. I stepped up tentatively, watching Uri breath, and feeling a tight fist of fear clench in my chest as Larry removed the Browning "Hi-Power" automatic I had seen the big Russian brandish in his apartment earlier that very morning.

"He's a trusting soul, bringin' a rod to make funeral arrangements," Larry said, pocketing the gun and moving over to the water spigot. There was a five-gallon plastic bucket we use for washing cars sitting next to a brush on the end of a stick, and Larry turned on the hose and filled the bucket almost half full. As the water ran, he added, "When he comes to, you ask him your questions fast and loud. I don't care what else he says, or what else he does. I don't care if he cries, or pukes, or pisses. You stay on your questions. You hear?"

I was trembling as I watched Larry step over the big man, the wash bucket held with two hands over Uri's unconscious face.

"Couldn't you drown him like that?" I protested just as Larry was about to pour.

Larry stopped and looked at me hard, saying, "What's with you, Bill? You goin' weak in the knees or what? This son of a bitch lied to us. That girl in there's dead, and Nat came damn close to endin' up the same way! Now, be a man!"

I nodded, unable to speak. My whole body was stiff, and I felt as if I were watching a dream. Uri was lying on my garage floor with broken bones. *Broken bones!* I'm not talking about bruises. I'm not talking about movie violence with slapping sounds and stuntmen falling into balsa wood saloon chairs. I had just seen Larry Fizner take a three foot length of two-by-four and beat the living shit out of a man, leaving him crumpled at my feet. And now that same Larry Fizner was going to bring that man around so that I could interrogate him. . . .

Oh God!

I felt like a fucking Nazi!

The water hit Uri and made him sputter. He shook his head from side to side, spraying water from his nose and mouth as he reflexively tried to sit up. When he did he grimaced, growled through clenched teeth, and dropped back down, his head striking the concrete with a moist thump that made his shoulders buck and his legs twitch. His arms had hardly moved, remaining where they were, folded across his stomach. And his eyes were vaguely staring around as if he were slipping back into unconsciousness as Larry slammed a hand between my shoulder blades and said, "Go on! Do it!"

I stepped forward, tried to speak, but squeaked instead. Uri moved his eyes to me as if trying to focus. I cleared my throat and said, in as distinct a voice as I could manage, "You lied, Uri. You've been lying all along."

Uri shook his head in the negative, and then started coughing pathetically.

I shot an imploring glance at Larry, who pulled a fierce face and mouthed the words, "Ask him!" between his teeth.

I swallowed and squatted down next to Uri so that he could see me. From there I looked him in the face and said, "John Gilbert doesn't speak Russian." I was concentrating on my own voice as a way of getting through this. If I can just spit it out, I was thinking, then it'll all be over that much faster. The quicker I do it, the quicker it'll end.

"You lied, Uri," I said. "John Gilbert wasn't the Russians' baby-sitter. You were. How could it be John Gilbert when he doesn't speak Russian? It doesn't make any sense."

Uri was looking at me now, his lips motionless, his eyes fixed on my face.

"You were already out there that night, Uri. You weren't up in Cleveland like Gilbert said you were. You were already in Logan's Town. It wasn't Gilbert who called you when Alex Kane's car ran off the road, it was you who called him. That's why Gilbert went to the emergency room at two in the morning—he was checking to make sure that you were right about Kane's being dead. With something that important, he had to see it with his own two eyes. If he'd been in the house he'd have seen it on the road and he wouldn't have needed to make a trip to the hospital.

"You called him, Uri. He didn't call you. You were the one who was already in the house, not him. You lied. And so did he. You've both been lying all along."

"Just ask him!" Larry growled. "Fuck the explanations!"

I waved him off impatiently, keeping my eyes on Uri, who was keeping his eyes on me.

"You were there with Erena, her father, her brother, and Edward Kane," I said. "You were out there with them all evening, and eventually Eddie and Erena left. Then there was the accident, and you went outside and saw that it was Alex Kane's car in the ditch. Then you called John Gilbert so that he could come in and run the damage control.

"Eddie says he brought Erena back at three in the morning. John Gilbert says that he never brought her back. The only thing that both their stories have in common is that neither one of them mentions you. In both cases, you were long gone, and so were the Russians. With all the rest of it, they're both protecting you, Uri.

"Why?

"Why would both Eddie and John Gilbert go to so much trouble to protect you?"

Uri didn't answer. Instead, a determined look came over his face, and his cheeks reddened with exertion. To my utter amazement, he groaned, set himself, and sat up, just moving from the waist. He supported himself on his left arm, which Larry Fizner had smacked on the elbow. The right arm he held across his lap. His head leaned to one side at a funny angle, and I noticed that he was breathing carefully.

Uri licked his lips and then puffed a drop of water off his tongue, saying weakly in Russian, "The asshole broke my collarbone."

"Tell him to speak English!" Larry Fizner said.

"I said, your mother's a whore," Uri growled.

Larry grunted behind me.

"Can you stand?" I asked him.

"I think so," Uri said, reaching his hand out for me to take as he added, "if you help."

I was about to take his hand when something made me hesitate. Uri was sitting on the ground, soaking wet, head hanging to one side, looking up at me with his hand extended for my aid, when I said, "I asked you a question. You haven't answered it yet."

"A hard ass, huh?" he asked, lowering his hand.

"What were you doing before Kane died?"

"And if I refuse to answer? Are you going to hit me again?"

I didn't respond, and neither did Larry.

Uri's eyes moved from me to Larry and back. Finally, with a tone of angry resignation, he threw his hand out again and said, "Okay already! Enough! Help me up, give me a drink, and let me alone. I'll tell you anything you want to know. It's all fucked up now anyhow. What's the point in lying?"

I took Uri's hand and pulled him to his feet. He was extremely heavy and very solid. Larry had been right, fully functioning and mad he would have torn us both apart. Or used the gun. Or both. He staggered a little when he first came upright, and using his good arm, he leaned on my shoulder, making me sag under his weight. He was turning himself as if to head for the door when I stopped him with my hands, making him look at me to see what was wrong. Our faces were only inches apart, and I could smell the sweat and car soap on his skin as I said, "No lies, Uri. I mean it. No more lies."

"He was going to fuck us," Uri said, looking me hard in the face as if challenging me to dispute him. "He was going to take off and leave us holding the bag. How's that? Now do you understand? He was going to fuck us, and we were talking about doing it to him first. Okay?"

"Whose idea was it?" I asked.

Uri said, "The kid's. Eddie's. It was Eddie's idea. He wanted to screw his dad."

"What made you believe him when he said it? What kind of proof could he have that his father was planning to do you wrong?"

"A tape. He had a tape of his dad's voice."

I nodded, satisfied that Uri was coming clean. If he was willing to mention the tape, he was willing to tell the truth. And then, as if the effort of revealing secrets so long held was more than his system could stand, he sagged against me, his eyes rolling up in his head and his mouth dropping open. He wasn't unconscious, but the pain of his broken wrist and clavicle was soaking his enormous constitution. His face went ashen, and I said quickly to Larry Fizner, "Help me! He's going into shock!"

Together we got him into the office and Larry pulled a bottle of Seagram's out of the cabinet under the wet bar as I moistened a towel with cold water and applied it to Uri's face. Uri must have drunk a full cup of whiskey, straight from the bottle Larry handed him, before he leaned his head back against the wall, sighed, and said, "Better."

"When you're ready, I know a doctor who won't ask questions," Larry said.

Uri nodded as he replied, "Then let's go."

"In a minute," I said. "I've got a couple more questions."

"Oh, Jesus," Uri cursed before taking another slam off the whiskey bottle.

"They're easy questions," I added. "Who killed Alexander Kane? And where was John Gilbert when you called to tell him that Kane was dead?"

Uri sighed and rested the bottle on his knee.

"Nobody killed Kane," he growled, grimacing as he moved his head to look at me. "It was an accident. Or at least that's what Erena said . . ."

"Erena!" I cut in.

And he nodded, which was a mistake.

"Goddamn!" he exclaimed through clenched teeth over the pain of his broken collarbone. After another shot he handed the bottle back to Larry, saying, "That's enough." Then he continued, "Eddie and Erena were just leaving. We'd all worked ourselves up pretty good over the tape the kid had found of his father telling his lawyer how he was going to divorce his mother and run away . . ."

"The tape Eddie had found in his father's answering machine at home?" I asked.

"Yeah," Uri agreed. "He'd left the machine on while he was talking, or something . . . I guess he did it all the time. Eddie found it, and it had his father telling that lawyer of his how he was gonna fuck us all. In another couple of days he was gonna be ready to go. And then we could all eat shit and die."

He made a ticking sound with his tongue to express his displeasure.

"So Erena and Eddie left. Then what?" I asked.

"According to what Erena said, they got in Eddie's car and made it to the intersection when they noticed another car coming. Eddie saw that it was his dad, and being all worked up like he was, he decided to confront him about what was on the tape. He waited a couple seconds, and then pulled the Porsche out to block the intersection. But instead of just pulling over, his father slammed on the brakes, hit the Porsche, and ended up in the ditch. Eddie and Erena got out just as Alex Kane opened his door and fell facedown into the water.

"It was not murder . . . really. Unless not pulling him out is murder. They let him drown . . . or at least Eddie did. He sent Erena back to the house to tell me what happened. I came out, found Kane just like Erena said, and went back inside."

"To call John Gilbert?" I offered.

Uri frowned, saying, "No."

"No?" I said.

"No."

Maxym and Vaslov Batilovna had jumped from their seats when Larry and I first helped Uri into the room. Their eyes had gone wide and their mouths had dropped open, and there had been the briefest instant there when I thought that maybe we would have trouble with them, because it seemed to me that the younger man, with his clenched fists and intense expression, was preparing to come to Uri's aid. But I had offered to bury Erena for nothing, and they had seen Uri and me talk like civilized men over the kitchen table in the big Russian's apartment. So instead of interfering, they had more or less fallen back, retreating to the periphery, from which they were straining their ears to listen, trying to pick up a word or two of English that they could understand.

Larry had positioned himself between Uri and the Russians, as if he had made a strategic decision. And, just as Uri had said that it was not John Gilbert who he had called after seeing Alex Kane's dead body lying in the drainage ditch, the door between the office and Jerry's apartment swung open and Jerry rolled in, really blowing Maxym and Vaslov's minds. Jerry didn't say anything about being brought up to speed, and he didn't comment on Uri's condition. He just moved close to the desk and watched, his face hard, his eyes cold and attentive.

"If you didn't call John Gilbert after seeing Alex Kane's body," I said, kind of as a way to help Jerry pick up on where we were, "then who did you call?"

"That deputy they call the Church," Uri said.

Although I was trying to keep myself on an even keel, I was unable not to sound surprised when I said, "Deputy King? Why the hell would you call him?"

"Because I wanted him out there first and not the sheriff," Uri said, looking at me as if I had suddenly gone completely stupid. "What, you think you can do what we were doing in a town so small like Logan's Town without somebody to watch out for you? Are you that dumb, or what?"

"And you didn't think you could buy the sheriff," I said. "So instead you bought the deputy!"

"Right."

"Oh, fuck!" I said, turning to Larry Fizner. "To get Sheriff Paulson to let Edward Kane out of jail, I went to his office this afternoon and told him everything! And that goddamn deputy was standing right there when I did! Why the hell didn't I think of it? Damn it!"

I slapped myself hard on the forehead, and then turned, staring at the office wall as if I had been suddenly endowed with X-ray vision, imagining, just a block away, the house in which Mrs. Kane lived, with her husband's "precious" icon collection. Deputy King knew what I was planning to do with that collection tomorrow afternoon because he'd been standing there while I explained it to the sheriff. If he, or John Gilbert, or both, were going to do anything about it, they'd have to do it tonight because by tomorrow afternoon, the whole scam would be blown sky-high. It was ten o'clock and very dark. Through the window over my desk I could see flecks of snow drifting past the glowing haze of a street lamp at the parking lot's edge. In that instant I made up my mind.

Turning back to Uri, I asked quickly, "Last question. What did you guys burn on the dining room table?"

Uri looked at me blankly as he replied, "Nothing."

I nodded, saying, "That's what I thought you'd say. Mr. Fizner, I've got to talk to you for a second."

Larry and I left the room, leaving Uri slumped painfully in his seat, and the Batilovnas huddled close together against the wall while Jerry watched over them all from his wheelchair. Closing the door, I grabbed Larry's arm and pulled him into the funeral home's front foyer, which was large and dark, lit only by the silver-grey bands of light coming in through the two tall, narrow, rectangular windows which flanked the massive front door. Those windows cast long strips of light over the floor and up the wall, creating ribbons of flower-patterned detail. When we were well away from the office door I grabbed Larry's shirtfront in my fist and said, "First, I don't want you ever, ever doing what you did tonight on these premises again! Do you hear me? Never again! No assaults, no violence, no rough stuff, nothing! Do you hear me?"

Larry broke my grip with a quick flourish of his arms. He was several years older than me, five inches shorter, and at least seventy pounds lighter. During all the time I had known him, I had never actually touched him, I realized at that moment . . . not so much as to shake hands, I don't think. And it was remarkable to me just how hard and strong he was. His chest beneath his shirt felt like an oak plank. And his thin arms, when they hit my wrists to break my hold, felt like broom handles. He straightened his shirt and rolled his shoulders to readjust himself, his face side-lit by the street lamp outside, his old, horn-rimmed glasses looking as if they weighed about ten pounds so pronounced were they on his nose. "Like I'm gonna start takin' orders from you," he said indignantly.

I pointed my finger in his face and snapped, "Fuckin' A you are! This is my place! They're not closing me down because of some bullshit you pull in my garage. You got it, or what?"

He looked pissed, but he was listening. He didn't reply, and I didn't have time to argue.

"That's all I've got to say," I concluded. "That's it. From here on out, I'm going it alone. You're out of it. Everybody's out of it. This is mine, and then it's over, for good."

"Right," he grumbled.

"Just take Uri to that doctor and get out of my life."

Larry looked at me in the dark and asked, "Is that really what you want?"

"Yes."

He nodded, clucked his tongue, and said, "Fine. You got it. You're an asshole anyway." He turned and threw the office door open so hard that the knob slammed into the wall. "Come on," he said to Uri, grabbing his arm and pulling him out of his chair so hard that the big man protested. Larry didn't respond. He just dragged Uri out of the room, with the other two Russians first looking my way, and then at Uri's back indecisively for an instant before they fell in behind. Through the window I could see the four of them get into the van and drive off.

Then I said to Jerry, "Call Sheriff Paulson and get him up here. Don't talk to anybody but Paulson, understand? Nobody but Paulson! If that deputy answers, ask for the sheriff. Understand? Just tell Paulson to haul ass . . . *and I mean now!*"

"Where are you going?" Jerry asked as I pulled a jacket out of the cabinet next to the wet bar and thrust my arm through one sleeve.

"Just do it!" I snapped, unfairly. "And don't give me no trouble!"

Then I was gone, running through the swirling snow in the parking lot for all I was worth.

I cut across the lot and leapt over the wire we hang between a pair of posts across the side street entrance when we're not busy. My head was alive with racing thoughts as the connections between the people and events surrounding Alex Kane's death finally fell into place. Uri had answered it all for me when he admitted that it was the deputy, and not John Gilbert, who he had called first on the night Kane died. That admission had done it, and it had also scared the shit out of me.

The air was bitterly cold, and I was puffing like a locomotive by the time I stopped running and started approaching the Kane house at a crouched, careful walk. The jutting, skeletal pattern of the wrought iron fence bordering the sidewalk was as black as a spider's web in the moonlight, and the points along the fence's top looked like arrowheads arranged in a row. There was a low line of shrubs along that fence, and beyond, illuminating the yard, the front of the big old house was ablaze with red, yellow, and blue light filtering through the stained-glass window I had admired since college. The front door was open a crack, and as I made a quick circuit around the grounds, I found a car in the driveway out back. It wasn't Mrs. Kane's Lexus. It was a white Ford van.

I had been assuming all along that the story of Alex

Kane's death was absolutely accurate up until the time that his body was taken to the hospital. The reason I had assumed such a thing was that since the sheriff and his deputy were on the scene with the paramedics in the ambulance, I didn't think anyone would be able to tamper with or change any of the physical evidence of the accident. But with Uri's admission that Deputy King was more or less on the payroll of Kane's merry band, I realized that none of my previous assumptions were valid. The manipulation of the facts had begun the instant Edward Kane got in his Porsche and hit the ignition.

The easiest point of entry to the house was the open front door, so I climbed the porch steps, trying to see into the large foyer through the lace curtains. There was something in there, on the floor. Something.

Should I ring the bell?

Should I just barge in?

What if I was wrong?

I glanced over my shoulder at the street, opened the storm door a little, and stuck my head through, trying to hear what was going on inside while I aimed my eye at the band of light coming through where the inside door hung ajar. I couldn't hear a thing. But the object I had seen as a blur on the floor through the curtains resolved itself into a shoe. . . .

A shoe, attached to the end of a leg.

Setting myself, I pushed the door open, finding Mrs. Kane's butler lying on his back on the floor. His arms were flung out at his sides as if he had been crucified, and his head was turned away from me. I stepped up to him quickly, crouched, and found that he was still breathing.

So that was the tack they had taken. I had figured they could go one of two ways: share the wealth, or not. The butler's condition made it obvious that they had chosen not.

Suddenly, I realized that I was unarmed. So, rising from the butler's body, I looked quickly around the huge front room for anything that might serve as a weapon. My mind did a quick inventory of the things one might expect to find in a typical suburban household, running down the list for objects with the potential to inflict serious physical injury. Immediately I thought of the kitchen, and the knives it would contain. But I abandoned the idea almost as quickly as it had come. It takes a special kind of person to stab another human being. The wounds are horrible, and the deed done up close, eyeball-to-eyeball. As furious, scared, indignant, and motivated as I might have been at that moment, I still couldn't delude myself into thinking that I could do such a thing. I'd pull back, hesitate should it come to that, and in the face of someone who had been able to cold-bloodedly pitch my wife down a flight of stairs, I'd end up on the losing end because of it.

That's who I was expecting, by the way.

Richard Hickle.

Maybe John Gilbert, too.

But Hickle for sure.

There was still no sound to indicate that the house was at all occupied, and a sudden fear for Mrs. Kane's safety had just struck me when my eyes settled on the great fireplace on the front room's far wall. There was an ornate set of black iron hearth utensils hanging on a freestanding tree, and I ran over to it and lifted the poker, which was probably three feet long, had a very heavy, shiny brass handle with a knob at the end the size of a golf ball, and was tipped with a wicked looking arrow-shaped head with a clawlike hook on one side. It was surprisingly heavy, probably because it was so large—in direct proportion to the fireplace itself, I assumed—and there was something about its weight in my hand that gave me a feeling of formidability.

Turning, I approached the main staircase of the house. As I've described before, it was, like everything else in the place, massive and overdone. At its bottom, the stairs were a good twenty feet across, narrowing as they ascended to the second-floor landing to probably ten feet wide. They were made of bright white marble, shot through with cream-colored swirls, and worn smooth by the years. And there was a magnificent, carved mahogany bannister on either side, culminating at the top in two posts, four feet high each, surmounted with the carved images of squatting gargoyles, with folded griffin wings and grotesque, jutting tongues. I raced up these stairs—all thirty some odd of them—poker in hand, heart pounding in my chest, and my mind focused on the third floor, where the deceased Alex Kane had seen fit to construct his "vault." It was there that Richard Hickle would be. Maybe John Gilbert, too. But it was Hickle I was looking for.

I stopped at the second-floor landing to listen.

Still nothing.

Stretching on either side of me was the main hallway of the second floor. Alex Kane's office was to the left. At the end of each side of the hall was another shorter staircase, curving around, leading to the third floor. Quickly, but with as much stealth as I could manage on the hardwood floor, I ran past Kane's office, shooting a perfunctory glance inside, and then pulling up short at the bottom of the curved staircase to listen.

Finally, the sounds of movement. Nothing spectacular. Nothing particularly dramatic. But someone was doing something upstairs.

Sliding my left hand along the bannister, feeling the poker's handle slick in my sweaty right palm, I crept up the stairs, straining to make sense of the sounds of snapping coming from above. Still there were no voices. Just the snapping sounds, which, as I reached the top, resolved themselves into something sensible.

Deputy King stepped from inside the vault just as I was about to move to the door. He stood there, mouth hanging open for an instant, his gun conspicuously jutting from his holster, his sandy-brown uniform pants and chocolate-brown leather jacket serving to make him look righteous and in charge. I felt instantly absurd with my lightweight jacket, necktie, and fireplace poker. But in that instant I caught a glimpse of Richard Hickle in the room behind the deputy, and I said very softly, "It's over, Deputy King. The sheriff's on his way."

"Innocent as a babe," had been Sheriff Paulson's description of Deputy King. "The boy ain't got a clue." Well, the sheriff had been wrong on that score.

Dead wrong.

The deputy went for his gun without gracing me with a response.

He went for his gun!

I don't know if you've ever really paid any attention to guns in your life, other than the bullshit, Hollywood BANG-BANG that it seems every American is inundated with from the moment of conception, but real guns, in real life, are real scary. They're enough to make you piss your pants. I'm speaking from experience here. There's no romance, no glory, no sensation of anything but sheer, unadulterated panic when you see that terrible, blue-black steel barrel sliding from its leather sleeve and realize that it's death, pure and simple, that's pulling its nose up to sniff the air in search of the scent of your blood.

I was an instant away from deep shit.

So I threw the poker.

I don't think that's what the deputy expected me to do. I think that, given his experience, he probably figured that as soon as he had his hand on the grip of his gun, I'd fold up and go passive. Or maybe I'd run. That really would have been a mistake, because I'm sure it would have been like trying to run from a dog. A guy like Deputy King would shoot. He'd have taken a couple of casual steps forward, set himself as I fumbled down the stairs with that goofy, bowlegged run you instantly fall into when you're trying to move down stairs at top speed without falling on your face, and put a round right between my shoulder blades. Then he'd have made up some story about hitting a fleeing felon, and because of his khaki-colored shirt and shiny badge, the people who really count—the ones with badges similar to his own—would believe him.

So I threw the poker, overhand, with all my strength, just as his gun cleared its holster. I didn't even think about it. I just did it. And I could tell by the look that came into his eyes that it was the last thing Deputy Churchill King expected me to do.

The iron rod made a very satisfying whistling sound as it passed my ear. I was only about five feet away from him, so it was impossible for me to miss. And the poker was heavy, as I've already mentioned. But still and all, I didn't expect it to stick. I swear, that's not what I expected it to do.

It was a shot that looked as if I knew what I was doing. The poker left my hand and flew like a missile, hitting the deputy on the right side of his chest, just near the ball of his shoulder joint. And it stuck there. The sharp-tipped end bit through his leather jacket, and the whole rod remained jutting from him as he stumbled back with an "Oof!" dropped his gun, hit the door frame, and grabbed at himself.

"Jesus Christ!" he screamed as the poker came out, bloody-tipped in his trembling hands.

Behind him both John Gilbert and Richard Hickle had appeared, looking at me over the deputy's shoulders with eyes that were at first surprised, and then enraged. Hickle moved first, pushing the deputy, who was more or less fixated on me, poker still in his hand, wavering on his feet, out of his way. He came directly at me as I righted myself from where I had bent to retrieve the deputy's gun. And before I could pull the gun up and aim it at anything significant, he hit me, pushing me back with both his hands so that I ended up landing hard on my ass as he raced past me and down the stairs.

John Gilbert was shouting Hickle's name as the boy ran, and he, too, emerged from the room, stepping more gingerly around Deputy King, who was still looking at me as if I'd betrayed him in some way. But from where I was sitting on the floor I lifted the deputy's pistol and said, "Don't."

Gilbert looked at me, confused for an instant since the last time he had seen me was when I was speaking with a Russian accent in Logan's Town, offering to buy his secret art treasures. He almost said something. I could see the questions forming in his mind. But finally his confused glare gave way to an expression of contemptuous comprehension, and he said, "Oh, kiss my ass," before making to follow his accomplice. But at that instant a screaming demon hit him from behind, flying out of the vault like a stroke of lightning, and before I could even get to my feet,

Mrs. Kane was on top of him, beating at him with her fists and shrieking like a mad woman.

For a second I considered pulling her off, but instead I followed Richard Hickle.

That son of a bitch . . .

Richard Hickle.

I had a gun.

And he was running.

I couldn't shoot him. I knew in my heart that I couldn't do that. But at the same time, I knew equally well that I couldn't just let him get away.

Mrs. Kane was screaming, and John Gilbert was shouting, and Deputy King was silent behind me as I thundered down the hall stairs and onto the main landing of the second floor. There was a figure at the top of the grand staircase, and I headed for it, wondering why the man was just standing there instead of trying to escape . . . just standing there . . . not moving at all.

Suddenly I stopped cold in my tracks, halfway to the stairs, my arm dropping the gun to hang at my side, my entire body deflating as I recognized Larry Fizner, who was looking at something in his hands. He didn't seem to notice me as I approached, but remained fixed on what he was holding, which I realized when I got closer were his black plastic, horn-rimmed glasses, broken into two pieces. When I was about ten feet from him, he glanced up and said, "I'm glad I bought that wire-rimmed pair this afternoon. These are shot." He put the glasses back on, balancing them on his nose. One of the arms had been broken off, and they stayed in place only if he cocked his head to one side.

"Where is he?" I asked, though I already knew.

Larry was standing at the very top of the stairs.

In response to my question, he indicated the stairs with a slight movement of his head that made his glasses slip so that he had to catch them.

I handed him the pistol when I stepped up next to him, and then I looked down the stairs. From where I was standing they spread out before me in a huge, white crescent, looking like a ski jump slope in those camera shots they show on the Olympics to impress upon the audience the courage possessed by the participants. At the bottom of the stairs, looking very small and crumpled, lay the body of Richard Hickle. Motionless. Twisted.

"He tripped," Larry commented.

I didn't say a word. Instead I just stood there, gazing down at the man who had hurt my wife, realizing that Larry had just done something I could never have done. As badly as I might have wanted to, I never would have been able to do it.

"Is he alive?" I asked, finally taking my eyes off Richard Hickle's body and looking at Larry.

"Who cares?" Larry replied.

Just then Deputy King staggered down the curved stairs from the third floor and shouted, "Will somebody do something about this crazy bitch before she kills somebody?"

And that's when I knew that it was really over.

ELEVEN

■■■■■■■■■■■■■

ERENA BATILOVNA'S FUNERAL was held the next morning starting at eleven o'clock at my funeral home, with an eleven-thirty mass at Father Mylanko's Ukrainian Orthodox Cathedral. Stepping into the front foyer, dressed in my best black suit and feeling a little better for having been able to sleep in late that morning, I looked over the crowd of people who had decided to attend the funeral, feeling a certain pride for the dignity of the Ukrainian people and the sense of community they obviously held in such high regard.

Father Mylanko had announced the circumstances of Erena's death during the previous evening's liturgy, and fifty parishioners had decided that she shouldn't go into the ground alone. They didn't know her at all, but they had come anyway, because it was the right thing to do. Maxym Batilovna was at first surprised and then moved nearly to tears when as he stepped into the foyer he was greeted by the president of the church council, who expressed the condolences of the parish and invited him and his son to have lunch in the church hall after the funeral, a courtesy arranged by the good church ladies, who donated the food and labor.

Mrs. Kane and Edward both attended, looking so amazingly different that they hardly seemed to be related at all. Mrs. Kane was virtually beaming with happiness because of her son's release. She had been up late the previous evening making statements to the police. This morning she didn't say a word about our adventure, other than to say that she had never imagined things would go so far. Edward just couldn't seem to keep himself from scowling at me, as if instead of being the instrument of his deliverance, I had done something to confuse him. I spoke little to either of them. But when Mrs. Kane asked what exactly I had said to Sheriff Paulson that would so radically change his mind about her son's innocence, I told her that later, after the funeral, when I came over with the man who was interested in her husband's icon collection, I would be glad to explain everything. She didn't make any verbal response to my promise, but simply looked at me, nodded, and stepped into the parlor to join her son.

Larry Fizner also attended, wearing his new suit and glasses. He wore the suit, he said, not for me, but for Nat. And when he shook my hand, I said, "Thanks again, I mean, for coming back last night. I know I acted like a prick. But . . ."

"Forget it," he replied, as if he were embarrassed. "Just file it, okay?"

"It's filed," I said earnestly. "And believe me, I won't forget. I'll make it up to you someday, Mr. Fizner. I owe you one."

The last player to arrive was Uri, whose right arm was in a sling. He held his head very erect, and I could see the impressions of strapping tape beneath his shirt and jacket where his collarbone had been wrapped after being set. He didn't so much as look at me, and I returned the courtesy, choosing to ignore him, too . . . until later.

In total, we ended up with over seventy people at the funeral, and the church donated the grave. Erena looked peaceful in the pink dress Nat had chosen for her, nothing like the horror I had picked up at the Wittmere County Hospital. My last memory of her was of an expression of serene repose. I had never even met her, and yet I felt her loss. I'd seen the pictures she had painted, and they were truly magnificent. It was a sin the way she had died. If there is a hell, it's exactly the place the souls of those people who can end such a life should receive as their reward. Death is enough of a terror, with its finality and unswerving emptiness, without the intervention of men to rush its arrival. Life is precious, and to end it, I feel in my heart, is for any man the unpardonable sin.

Nat, Jerry, and I all attended the entire funeral. We even went back and had lunch at the parish hall. Other than a few inquisitive glances, no one commented on the presence of the dozen or so police officers who joined us, laying back and observing the crowd. The police presence was most heavily felt at the luncheon, where the officers positioned themselves at the exits and silently kept an eye on those who came and went, while quietly eating the stuffed cabbages and pirogies they were offered on paper plates.

When we got back to the funeral home, Sheriff Paulson was waiting.

"Are we ready?" he asked, shaking my hand in the parking lot before introducing me to the chief of police from Berea, who was a big, amiable man with an inquisitive, open face. Behind him, in the sheriff's car, sat Deputy King, fresh from the hospital, and John Gilbert, neither of whom so much as lifted their heads.

With a nod I said, "Yeah. Let's do it."

Together we all trooped over to Victoria Kane's house. When she opened the door to let us in, she looked surprised to see the sheriff . . . but not nearly so surprised as she did when she saw John Gilbert and Deputy King enter with a uniformed cop walking on either side. The look she directed at me said clearly, "What's going on?"

And I offered simply, "I'm sorry about this, Mrs. Kane. But it's something that's got to be done."

It was like a classic scene from an old mystery novel, the group that gathered in the third floor vault that afternoon, with the memory of Erena Batilovna's funeral still so fresh as to color the atmosphere with an invisible hush. There was a yellow police ribbon strung across the door to Alexander Kane's special room, which I undid as I passed. Two cops carried Jerry's wheelchair up the stairs so that he could be a witness to the conclusion of this affair, and Nat stood silently next to where he had parked himself near a wall, watching every move I made with sparkling, intense eyes.

Those present around me were Maxym and Vaslov Batilovna, Victoria and Edward Kane, Sheriff Paulson, Deputy King, Nat, Jerry, and at least a dozen cops, including the city's chief of police. Larry Fizner stood blocking the door. And Uri, who entered last, also accompanied by a policeman, completed our contingent of players. Around us, the room lay in exactly the condition it had been when the police arrived in response to my 911 call the night before. Broken pieces of wood were scattered over the floor, and at least a dozen icons lay smashed in splintered, gold-dusted heaps. The only significant member of the cast not present was Richard Hickle. He was in the hospital with a broken back, charged with assault, and badly battered. Mrs. Kane's butler had chosen not to attend. He had been about the only person who had been given the option. The rest had been compelled to come by the presence of the police.

"First off," I said, sliding my hands into my trouser pockets and clearing my throat. "Just so everyone here understands what's happening, let me say that last night Mrs. Kane was forced by Richard Hickle, John Gilbert, and Deputy Churchill King to disconnect the alarm system which protects these premises, so that these men could do what they did to the icons you see broken on the floor. Why they did what they did reflects the truth about what the deaths of both Alexander Kane and Erena Batilovna really meant. And because of the cooperation of Sheriff Paulson and Chief Doyle, I've been given permission to do what I'm about to do."

Heads turned in the group as people looked around to see the reactions of those around them. Mrs. Kane was holding onto her son's hand. And Edward, who was wearing the same black clothes that he had at his father's funeral, assumed a wide-eyed expression that I could only interpret as fear. He looked just as guilty as hell, and from the way his mother hovered over him, I think she had picked up on that look and was unconsciously preparing to protect him.

"Ladies and gentlemen," I said, more loudly and with as much authority in my voice as I could muster, "I'm going to start from the beginning, because I think each of you might understand a particular part of why we've all ended up here today, but I doubt if there's anyone who understands it all."

"Just get to the part about who I should arrest," Sheriff Paulson, who had actually removed a pair of handcuffs from where they had been dangling from the back of his leather-weave belt, growled from where he stood next to Edward Kane, who flinched at the volume and menace of the lawman's remark.

Mrs. Kane tightened her grip on her son's arm protectively. And Larry Fizner moved his attention over those standing before him with all the menace of a prison guard.

Ignoring the sheriff's demand, I said, "This whole thing started when Edward Kane came to me with a cassette tape that he claimed was his father, predicting his own impending suicide. How could a reasonable person believe, he argued, that his father would leave such a tape, go off into the night, and then die in an auto accident? Wasn't it too much of a coincidence to be credible, especially since his father was such a wealthy and powerful man?"

Edward Kane was nodding his head, as if confirming the absurdity of such a position. As was his mother, loyal to the end.

I ran my eyes over the group and said, "Well, I didn't credit it. So I went to the county morgue and used a voice spectrograph analyzing machine to check the voice on the tape against a sample I was sure was Alex Kane's, finding that they matched."

Sheriff Paulson interrupted, demanding to know how I just happened to have an authentic sample of the dead man's voice in my possession. When I told him how I'd gotten my test tape, his eyes narrowed as he obviously tried to picture me squeezing a dead body's chest in my embalming room. They all looked at me like that, and I let them. Then, when I thought they had stared long enough, I continued. "Though that spectrograph ribbon wouldn't be considered acceptable as evidence in a court, it was enough to convince me that Edward Kane was telling the truth. It was his father on that tape. So he was right; it was an awfully interesting coincidence that his father should die accidentally on the very night he apparently was planning to take his own life anyway.

"Now, Alex Kane's car was forced off the road in Logan's Town, coming to rest in a drainage ditch," I continued. "And his body was found facedown in that ditch. The county coroner's determination as to a cause of death was that he had drowned. He had suffered two compressed spinal vertebrae in the accident when he flew forward in his seat and struck the top of his head on the windshield. According to the coroner, those injuries were theoretically sufficient to render him paralyzed and incapable of leaving the car once it had come to rest. The implication, therefore, was that he had been dragged from the car, thrown into the water at the bottom of the ditch, and left there to drown.

"In the trunk of his car was found an icon similar to the ones hanging on the wall behind me. And because the car he had struck before winding up in the ditch belonged to his son, Edward, who coincidentally happened to be out in Logan's Town that night—which he conveniently neglected to mention to me the first time he described what he knew of his father's death—Sheriff Paulson naturally suspected that son first and foremost. That suspicion led to Edward Kane's arrest, and that arrest led Mrs. Victoria Kane to hire me to prove her son's innocence.

"It was her contention that John Gilbert actually killed her husband. . . ."

"I did no such thing!" Gilbert insisted. "That's a dirty lie!"

Mrs. Kane turned and was on him in an instant, accusing him afresh. He defended himself loudly, and to calm them both I said, "That was Mrs. Kane's *contention*. I didn't say it was a fact."

Both Mrs. Kane and John Gilbert looked my way, and glancing at her, I continued. "When I first started my investigation, Edward Kane told me that he had been summoned out to the Lincoln Street house by John Gilbert, who was acting as the baby-sitter for the Batilovna family. . . ."

At the mention of their name, Maxym and Vaslov perked up.

"The Batilovnas," I continued, "were three Russian immigrants, in this country illegally, as well as secretly, in the employ of Alex Kane. . . ."

"Only one of 'em is here illegally," Sheriff Paulson cut in. "I got a fax this morning from the Immigration and Naturalization Service sayin' that there were never any visas issued in the name of Batilovna by their department. But an Alexander Kane was listed as the sponsor for *two* immigrants from Russia named Maxym and Vaslov *Liski*. There was no girl included in that listing. Just the men. So I assume Erena was here on phony papers. I don't even know for sure that Batilovna was her real last name. But it's for sure Kane didn't sponsor her."

This last piece of news broke my heart, and I had to consciously steady my voice as I said, "Erena was a gifted artist, whose greatest talent was painting exactly what she saw, down to the most minute detail.

"Keep that word, 'gifted,' in mind, ladies and gentlemen, because anyone can simply copy a picture. Any above-average art student can produce a fairly impressive version of an old master's trademark work.

"But Erena's talent went well beyond any understanding we might have of what precision really means. She was special . . . truly. Her eye was flawless, and her technique invisible. She was able to paint in such a way as to mimic the geniuses of the past without a single seam to expose her work as anything but authentic. She was so good that even trained professionals, studying what she made with the concentration of a scientist, pronounced it genuine, again and again. It was her job to forge the pictures provided to her by yet another Russian immigrant—a man named Uri, who, though he tried to keep it a secret, has the last name Chevinski. We can thank Mr. Larry Fizner for that piece of information. We can thank Mr. Fizner for quite a bit more than that. But I'll get to that in a minute.

"Now, Uri Chevinski had been in the phony art business in Europe long enough to know all the tricks of treating canvas and wood with the right chemicals to make Erena's paintings look physically old, and it was his equipment that took the most time to remove from the Lincoln Street house on the night Alex Kane died. But no matter how carefully treated a canvas might be, what's painted on it is the key. And Erena, according to Alexander Kane himself, 'had the magic in her hands.'

"Not that Uri didn't have his own, unique talents, too," I added. "What he could do was acquire priceless masterpieces that were originally stolen by the Nazis during the Second World War and which have been hidden in Russia ever since."

Now Uri was looking at me, and his eyes were so hard and filled with anger that I could practically feel them boring into my skin.

"Apparently what Mr. Kane was doing," I went on, ignoring him, "was having the girl, Erena Batilovna—since that's the only name I know for her I'm going to assume that it's authentic—forge a number of copies of the precious pictures Uri Chevinski smuggled into the country for him. Then he was burning the original, as a way of ensuring that it would never resurface to serve as a point of comparison that could expose his forgeries, and then he was selling those forgeries, in secret, to a number of wealthy art collectors who each thought that they were purchasing an authentic, one-of-a-kind masterpiece.

"Since the original owners of these masterpieces would still have a legitimate claim for their return should they ever resurface publicly, these collectors were bound by necessity to keep their acquisitions absolutely to themselves. And Mr. Kane profited magnificently by selling the 'same' picture over and over again.

"That was the plan. And its accuracy is not in dispute here. But we need to understand it before any aspect of Mr. Kane's death can make any sense.

"Now, as I've already said, Edward Kane claimed that he had been summoned out to the Lincoln Street house, where the people known as the Batilovnas lived, because Erena Batilovna, the linchpin of his father's scheme, was feeling lonely and irritable. According to Edward, whenever the girl got that way, John Gilbert would call him and he would go out and soothe her. His devotion to soothing her went so far as to take her to bed, which he had been ordered to do by his father. It was imperative that the girl be kept happy. And though he never came right out and said it, Edward Kane himself was obviously Erena's reward for not making trouble. He was her pretty American beau, and I believe that she was probably in love with him. Perhaps not because he was particularly matched to her in any spiritual way, but because, locked up in that house with her father and brother . . .

"Her father and brother . . ." I repeated, shaking my head thoughtfully. "That's what I thought these people were originally. But that relationship doesn't fit with the facts. Instead, let us imagine that Maxym and Vaslov weren't related to Erena by blood at all. Instead of brother and sister, let us imagine that Erena and Vaslov were lovers, perhaps even husband and wife.

"Since it's obvious that it was Erena who was the vital part of Alexander Kane's plan, and since Maxym and Vaslov Liski are in this country, standing here with us today, we've got to assume that it was Erena who used her influential position to insist that they be brought along. It makes sense, really, when you think about it. Erena is starting a new life in a new country, she's young, and in love. So when she moves she brings with her a lover from Europe and that man's father, who I'm sure she would see as her future *father-in-law*.

"But once she got to America, things changed. She was disappointed by what she found here. Instead of a life of freedom and ease, Erena Batilovna was locked up in a house for nearly two years, kept from seeing anyone but the people she had escaped from Europe with, and always afraid of discovery and deportation. Being confined for that long, under those conditions, would surely go a long way toward making the prospect of marriage to a wealthy American lover seem like salvation. After all, what could Vaslov offer her, compared to Edward Kane? How could a poor boy from Russia compare to a catch like Eddie?"

I paused and looked Edward Kane directly in the eye, saying, "You were your father's carrot. John Gilbert was the stick. And Uri was the priest and confessor who had brought her over from the Old Country with promises of luxury and wealth. Once she was here, the promises were slow in materializing . . . so they were using you to keep her satisfied, playing on her feelings, and extending to her a hope for a future that she would never know. She *could* never know it, because she was too dangerous for them. Because of her drinking and her unpredictable artist's temperament, she was a potential problem. She wasn't trustworthy; there was no telling what she might do or say.

"Which is why they couldn't afford to let her out of their sight for so much as a minute. Looking at it now, I think that she was fated to either end up back in Russia, or, much more likely, dead, from the moment she set foot in that house. And I think you knew it, Eddie. I think that you knew what you were doing all the way through."

Edward Kane was shaking his head insistently, but I paid him no mind.

"I don't care what you say, Eddie," I told him. "I can't prove that you knew, but I know that you did. Since you were aware of what your father was doing with the paintings, since both you and your mother have admitted to being aware of it, I just can't believe that either of you was so naive as to believe that what you were doing was anything but a charade. Your mother knew you were making love to that girl at your father's command. And Vaslov, her former lover, who lived in the same house and owed his very presence in this country to a love she had once had for him, a love that had grown cold, knew it, too. How's that look to you, Eddie, once you step back and really examine it? What conclusion do you think a reasonable person is going to draw from that situation other than that Erena was in the company of wolves?"

He seemed about to speak, but I wasn't interested in anything he might have to say, so I turned and looked at the icons behind me as I continued with my story.

"So in line with my scenario," I said, "we have, on the night that his father died, Edward Kane visiting the Lincoln Street house and watching movies with the Russians and John Gilbert. Erena was feeling romantic, and after she passed a supposedly secret sign to Eddie, the pair excused themselves on the pretext of taking a ride to drive over to another home owned by the Kanes on Dovetail Lane, where they would go to bed together.

"But according to Eddie's version of events, when they tried to start his Porsche, they found that it wouldn't turn over. So instead of the bright red sports car, they took one of the company's white Ford vans, a vehicle so common around Logan's Town that it was all but invisible.

"They remained at the house until well after midnight, says Eddie. And then, at about three o'clock in the morning, he took Erena home, kissing her good-bye and leaving her, very much alive, in front of the house, as he drove home in the van. He was, according to him, completely unaware that his father had been killed earlier that night. He found out about it only when he arrived back at his apartment in Cleveland and checked the messages on his answering machine. He went straight to his mother's house, but she had already gone to the funeral home to make her husband's funeral arrangements. So he wandered around, crying because of his loss, entered his father's study, found the suicide tape, played it, and decided to bring it to me, having read in the newspaper that I was a detective.

"Is that about it, Eddie?"

The young man nodded.

And I said, "Well, it's too bad that you're sticking to your story now, because it's a lie."

He was about to protest when I cut him off by raising my hand and shouting, "It's a lie, goddamn it! Don't try to shit me anymore because I'm not as stupid as you think!"

He shut up and looked at me, terrified.

"But in Eddie's defense, I must say that not all of his story's untrue," I said, a little more gently. "It's just that the ratio of bullshit to reality is exactly great enough to make it look premeditated . . . and that ain't good.

"And now to you, Mr. Gilbert."

The man's eyes narrowed, and the two policemen near him reflexively leaned in a little closer.

"Your story starts off pretty much the same as Eddie's, but you say that instead of taking a van, Eddie's Porsche started up fine. Then you say that he and Erena drove off, but that Erena never came back. When Alex Kane died on the road, you saw the ambulance lights through the window of the Lincoln Street house and went looking for Eddie on Dovetail Lane to tell him what had happened but found the place dark and empty. You maintain that you have no idea where Erena and Eddie went. Nor do you have any knowledge of how the girl's body ended up in the pantry of the house on Lincoln Street. Is that correct?"

"It is," John Gilbert said.

And I replied, "Too bad. Because you're lying, too."

He looked at me with surprise written all over his face. But before he could speak, I said, "You're lying and you know it. It's just that your lies are more subtle."

Turning to face the group again, I added, "What really happened out on that state route the night Alexander Kane met his death is this:

"There was an accident, no individual was directly to blame for what happened, and no crime took place until Erena Batilovna was murdered.

"That single act was the only crime anyone in Logan's Town committed on the night Alex Kane died."

"But what about all this picture forging?" Sheriff Paulson asked.

I replied, "Ahh, that brings us to the heart of this problem. When I first started looking into Mr. Kane's affairs, his wife brought me into this room as a way of explaining her husband's personality. I think that this vault was meant as a kind of symbol that would illustrate exactly the kind of man he was better than any words she could have chosen. He was a collector, a man who amassed beautiful and precious things and kept them hidden away in a special, secret place all for himself.

"That was an important point, and to emphasize it she showed me these icons, each one of them hundreds of years old, and each one of them worth tens, if not hundreds of thousands of dollars because of the fact that the Soviet Union doesn't allow pieces of their artistic history to be exported out of the country. Supposedly, given that there must be fifty icons displayed on these walls, Alex Kane took precautions in the design of this room to keep them safe. Fireproof walls, separate burglar alarms, careful climate control. All to make sure that these precious icons remained secure.

"The problem is," I said, turning and lifting the icon of the "Christ the Teacher" off its hook on the wall, "when I spoke to Uri Chevinski, the man who supposedly brought these valuable pieces into the country, he insisted that he never smuggled icons for Alex Kane. He swore that he didn't know anything about so much as a single one. Now, Uri had lied to me before. As a matter of fact, looking back, I see that very little of what he told me was ever anywhere near the truth.

"But the significant thing about his lies has always been that they've been calculated to achieve a particular end, which was to distance him from Alex Kane and make it appear as if Uri's role in what was going on in Logan's Town was something very different from what it actually was. Denying that he ever smuggled icons didn't do anything to further that aim, since he had originally told me that Alex Kane had purchased just this kind of thing from him up until two years ago. The stories didn't jibe, meaning that since both of them couldn't be a lie, one of them had to be true.

"So which one was it? Did he, or didn't he, smuggle the icons?

"I decided that he didn't, because there just wasn't enough of a market for them to make it worth the risks. Alex Kane was doing very well selling freshly painted versions of these ancient pictures to churches around the country, so why bother sneaking in the real thing? It would be a waste of his time. Which means that these pretty chunks of wood, so carefully kept in this vault away from the prying eyes of the world, aren't priceless at all. They're beautiful, worthless junk!"

With that I spun, the icon gripped firmly in my hand, and with all my strength I lifted it over my head and smashed it into the wall. The wood splintered with a loud crack beneath the force of my first blow. But when I lifted the icon again and smashed it a second time, the whole thing disintegrated into splinters, leaving in my hand a single length of broken wood, at the end of which hung a tatter of white canvas.

Both John Gilbert and Edward Kane dove forward out of the group in response to my action, shouting and bodily pushing me aside. They were shocked by what I had done, and each of them was crouched, picking through the junk on the floor, unfolding the rumpled canvas and lifting pieces of something torn and tattered from amid the splinters I had made.

"My God!" they were mumbling. "Oh my God!"

They each had a piece of something in their hands when I said, "This is what was really going on the night Alex Kane died."

Both men were looking up at me from where they were kneeling on the floor, but my attention was fixed on Edward Kane.

"John Gilbert knew about the hidden pictures because I told Sheriff Paulson about them yesterday afternoon," I said. "Deputy King was working for your dad, Eddie. He was keeping an eye on things and taking a salary under the table. Since you were in jail, and therefore beyond his reach, as soon as he heard about the hidden pictures, he ran right to the only boss he had left, who was John Gilbert, and he told him all about this great, secret treasure just waiting in this room to be had. Which is why he, and Richard Hickle, and John Gilbert ended up smashing icons out here last night.

"If Mr. Gilbert had known that the pictures were hidden in the icons before, he wouldn't have waited until last night to come for them. He'd have been here long before now, and then he'd have been long gone. And because Deputy King knew that I planned to expose the secret of these icons today, using my friend Larry Fizner as a phony collector interested in buying them, it was imperative for Mr. Gilbert to get out here before I had a chance to blow the whistle.

"But you, Eddie . . .

"What made you so upset when I broke that icon?"

Edward Kane rose to his feet, two torn pieces of canvas hanging limply in his hands. Every eye in the room was on him, but his eyes were on what he was holding as he said, "It was worth millions. And you destroyed it to make a point . . . to trap me, you ruined it completely!"

His face snapped up and his eyes were blazing. His hands trembled and his lips quivered; his entire body was alive with a rage so deep and personal that I thought for sure that he was going to go for me, then and there.

For the benefit of those who were watching, I said, "Alex Kane was a collector. This room proves it. But what he was collecting in this place wasn't precious, ancient religious objects, it was something far more secret and valuable. Inside three of these icons he hid three original masterpieces: a Renoir watercolor, a tiny Devachio portrait, and a Michelangelo sketch. The icon found in the trunk of his car on the night he died was slated to hold a fourth masterpiece, which would have capped off his collection. The pictures he burned in front of his partners weren't the originals, as he said they were. They were forgeries. He was burning a forgery so that his partners would think the originals had been destroyed, and then he was selling the priceless masterpieces to a planted collector for peanuts compared to their actual value, so that he could keep these treasures for himself.

"That's why he built this vault. What he was protecting here wasn't worth hundreds of thousands of dollars—it was worth millions."

"And you just *ruined* one!" Edward Kane screamed, the tatters of canvas still in his trembling hands. "*Look at what you did!*"

"What I did was uncover the truth!" I shouted back at him, my own anger bubbling up like boiling water. "And the truth is worth a lot more than money! But you wouldn't understand that. Not you, or John Gilbert, or your father. None of you would know what the fuck I was talking about when I say that the truth has a value, because to you, the lie was everything. You and your father, and your mother as well, you all lived off lies. They were the commodities you sold. Nothing you did was ever anything but a lie, and now you're holding the last one in your hands. The last lie. The last laugh.

"Don't you get it yet?" I asked, pointing at the pieces of canvas Edward Kane was clutching so protectively. "Are you really that dense? Don't you see?

"Uri!" I said, turning and seeking the big Russian out of the group with my eyes. "Are you going to tell him, or should I?"

Uri's face darkened with his rising blood, and the tension in the room stretched even tighter.

"What are you talking about?" Edward Kane asked behind me. And then to Uri, he said, "What's he talking about? Huh? What's going on?"

Uri and Eddie were locked in a grip of mutual dependence, and I wasn't speaking to them, but to everybody else as I said, "It was because of the precious pictures hidden in these icons that things happened the way they did the night Alex Kane died.

"Alex Kane had been hoarding these pictures for years, and there was one last one yet to have. A Goya watercolor of a little girl in a yellow hat. Uri had smuggled it in from Europe, he said, and Erena Batilovna had spent the last six months making the five copies that the group would need to sell to its special collectors. Alex Kane would burn one last forgery, sell that priceless Goya to his undercover collector, and have in his possession four masterpieces that would have a combined total value in excess of seventy million dollars.

"His plan from there was simple:

"He intended to take his pictures and leave. He and his lawyer had been hiding funds and moving money for months. At the proper time, he was going to announce his desire for a divorce, make a settlement offer, and go, leaving his wife and son the peanuts he had not amassed for himself in secret accounts, and eventually offering his four, hidden masterpieces to the French and Italian governments. Faced with the opportunity to recover such important and heretofore lost classics, those governments would gladly pay a substantial reward."

"What's he talking about, Uri?" Edward Kane asked again, as if I wasn't standing there, saying the things I was saying.

"Alex Kane would have profited from the sale of the forged pictures," I continued, "and then he'd be paid again when he returned the originals to their rightful owners. His partner, John Gilbert, would be left with a lot of explaining to do to the people to whom the forgeries were sold, and Alex Kane would be a hero, living safely, and no doubt comfortably, in some unnamed country—probably a hot one. He would have gotten away with it, too, if it weren't for his bad habit of letting his answering machine run after he'd picked up the phone. Eddie found a tape in that machine of his father discussing his divorce plans with his lawyer, and he took that tape out to Logan's Town and played it for Uri and the Batilovnas last Thursday night.

"That," I shouted, turning on Eddie, "was what you were doing out there the night your father died! You weren't comforting anyone! You were exposing the lie your father was living, and plotting a way to ruin his plans."

Even accused, Eddie was still looking at Uri. And I could see in his face that he was beginning to understand, and despair.

"John Gilbert wasn't even in the house," I went on, more for the people who were watching than for Eddie. "He didn't speak Russian, so how could he have been the Russians' baby-sitter? No. You were the one who spoke Russian, Eddie; it was your major in college. I called the registrar and asked. You've had three years of it. Top of your class. One of their most motivated pupils . . . and no wonder!

"You stayed until about eleven, and then you left, taking Erena with you.

"But in the car she spoke to you, didn't she, Eddie? To her, things looked like they were unravelling. You were mad at your father, you and Uri were plotting things without including John Gilbert. Alex Kane was going to betray you. She was scared. She was alone. She loved you, and she may even have thought that you loved her. Outside, in the driveway, or maybe in the car, she spoke to you, probably with her arms around you, her head on your chest, and she cried. She cried and admitted her fear, said that she didn't want to be sent back home to Russia, expressed her terror of jail.

"She was an artist. Jail would kill her spirit. Further confinement, this time in a real prison, not an isolated house in the country, was more than she could bear to imagine.

"So she told you something, didn't she, Eddie? Because you were someone she could trust, because she had been to bed with you, because she loved you, she told you something that night, there in the German sports car your father had bought for you . . . the eighty-thousand-dollar car that you tooled around in like a prince. . . .

"She told you what your father had been doing, didn't she, Eddie? She told you that she knew that the pictures your father had been burning weren't the originals but were actually forgeries.

"Didn't she, Eddie?

"Didn't she?"

"Yes!" Edward Kane screamed at me, finally pulling his attention back from Uri and looking me in the eye. "She told me! She said it! She wanted us to get married, and she was making her secret a present to me. She was drunk out of her mind and trying to talk me into running away. She wanted to go that night, that minute, anywhere, she didn't care. She said that I had a lot of money. She thought I could take her away and that we could disappear. She was crazy. . . ."

"That's right," I agreed. "She was crazy because she thought that it was her that you wanted . . . when it wasn't. You didn't want her . . . you never wanted her.

"And when she told you that your father had been pulling a fast one, you realized, probably at that moment, what the vault he had built at home meant. Didn't you? You knew that it was the man posing as Erena's father who was painting those icons your father was collecting at home. You probably even wondered, more than once, why he was taking such good care of them when all he had to do was ask and Maxym Batilovna, nee Liski, would make him another one. But when she said that he was burning forged pictures and keeping the originals, you knew that he had to be storing those precious masterpieces somewhere. And you thought of the vault. You saw those pictures in your mind, and you thought of the vault.

"You probably had the vault in your eyes when you saw his car coming. There you were, sitting in the Porsche he had bought you, feeling cheated. Here he came, and he had millions hidden away . . . millions that he wasn't going to share. You deserved that money. He was your father, and you knew what he was doing, and if for no other reason than you shared his secret, you felt that you deserved a share of that wealth.

"So you were going to confront him with what you knew. You saw his car coming, and you pulled out to block the intersection, but instead of stopping, he panicked and ended up in the ditch."

"I didn't kill him!" Eddie said in a low, pleading voice, as if he had finally come back to the topic at hand, which was a murder accusation made before at least a dozen cops. "I swear I didn't."

"I know, Eddie," I said. "He hit your car, you got scared when he didn't move behind the wheel, and you ran back to the house with Erena to tell Uri what had happened. While you were gone, your father tried to get out of his car; he was hurt and dazed and probably didn't even know what he was doing. But he opened his door and fell out, where he drowned while you were up at the house. He probably was paralyzed, at least his legs must have been. But his arms worked well enough to get him out. And by the time you all came back, he was dead. Uri kept you away from the body. He kept everybody away from the body, which is why the sheriff didn't find any footprints in the mud . . .

which is why I knew you didn't kill him.

"And then you left.

"The Porsche was dented, so you and Uri drove over to your father's shop downtown, got a van, and then dropped the Porsche off at the house on Dovetail Lane. Uri told you to take the van home, and that he would handle everything. He'd fix it with Deputy King. Everything would be okay if—and this was really important—you stuck to the story he told you to repeat, no matter what happened. He told you exactly what to say, about the Porsche not starting, the whole routine. He'd fix it somehow with Deputy King, and as long as you stuck to your story, everything would be okay.

"But it wasn't okay . . . because someone killed Erena Batilovna that night. And that created such a mess that it was decided that you would need to be the fall guy for someone else's mistake. You were expendable. Up until that time you were the promised reward they used to keep Erena on an even keel. But with Erena dead, there was suddenly nothing for you to do. So, while you were on your way back to your apartment, preoccupied with your father's death, and probably even more preoccupied with the knowledge that now only you and Erena Batilovna knew about the treasure he had hidden in his vault, Uri and the Russians were setting you up for a fall."

"So who killed her?" Sheriff Paulson asked. "For Christ's sake, who did it?"

I turned to Uri and looked at him.

"Well?" I said.

And he looked at me, genuinely surprised.

Next to him were the Russians, Maxym and Vaslov. Stepping over to them, I looked at Vaslov, Erena's ex-lover, standing there, not quite comprehending what was happening but sensing enough to know that he was in some kind of trouble. His posture was defensive, his fists were clenched. Those fists had been clenched every time I had seen him since Erena's death. Reaching out, I took his right hand and lifted it. He resisted, glanced around, found the police looking at him, and relaxed a little.

Then I said simply, "She was strangled. It takes a lot of effort to strangle somebody to death. You have to pull very hard. You have to be very sure of exactly what you want."

With that I squeezed Vaslov's hand, and his fingers unfolded to reveal an angry red welt across his palm, serrated with the impression of a thick rope's weave.

"The sheriff has the rope," I said. "There were traces of skin and blood on it where the killer held it to pull. It'll be all they need."

Turning, I continued addressing the rest of the people in the vault.

"Originally, I thought Erena had died in the furniture store garage," I said. "Because that's where I found the chair from which the rope that was used to kill her had been taken. But then it dawned on me: the Kanes were in the business of selling furniture. And the vans were used to *move* it.

"That's why Eddie didn't just take the van that was parked at the house instead of riding over to the furniture shop and getting another one—because it had furniture in it.

"And . . .

"The Russians needed to get the evidence out of the house. There were forged paintings inside, and other incriminating material. They needed to move it, so they threw it in the van after Uri drove off with Edward Kane. By this time, Erena was hysterical. Drunk and unreasonable. Probably screaming. Surely scared out of her mind. She didn't want to go anywhere without Eddie. Where had Eddie gone with Uri? Why hadn't they taken her? Didn't they realize that Alex Kane was dead and that the American police were going to be coming? Didn't anyone see?

"Yes, Vaslov saw, and he was frightened. They were all frightened. There was a dead American lying in a ditch. They could be deported . . . or worse. Erena was still screaming. Even out in the country, they couldn't let that go on. There was another house across the field. It was a long way off, but with the way she was carrying on, who knew how far her voice would drift? So Vaslov tried to shut her up. Soon they were all screaming. He hit her. She didn't stop. He forced her into the van and closed the door. She was probably sitting in the chair inside the truck, and that chair had two lengths of decorative gold rope hanging off it. He took one, wrapped it around her throat, and . . . maybe he threatened her with it, or maybe he intended to tie her up. If she'd calmed down, who knows? Maybe, looking up at her former lover with drunken, terrified eyes, if she'd calmed down, she'd still be alive. But she was famous for her temper, which was so fiery that I think Vaslov's threats enraged instead of intimidated her. Whatever the details of what happened next, the results are undeniable.

"Vaslov made a very bad mistake—he let his threat become reality, and he killed her.

"He killed her," I repeated.

"She was right there before him, the key to everything. Alexander Kane was dead, Vaslov was scared . . . and something more. She had rejected him. She'd loved him once, loved him enough to refuse to leave Europe without him and his father. But once they got to America, things changed. She didn't want him anymore. She made him move out of her bedroom and into one of his own. She started sleeping with an American. A rich, spoiled brat of an American to whom Vaslov felt himself superior in every way . . . except one.

"Money.

"And it was that one thing that he couldn't give her that Erena wanted more than anything else.

"He was seeing it all in that moment, feeling it all, with that rope around her neck, ostensibly as a threat, but then for real. And he let himself have his revenge. He probably would have rather had Eddie in his grip, but Erena would do. She was fated to die anyway; no one even knew she was in this country. She was the only one with a phony visa, so obviously she had never been fully trusted by the rest. She had been fated to die, and she did.

"And once she was dead, her body was carried into the house, and every paper with her name on it, every passport or letter, every photograph or piece of writing to come from her hand, was burned. I found the ashes on a cookie sheet in the dining room. She was dead, and her name had been erased. She was alone forever, a nothing as far as anyone living would ever know. Any truth of her life had been erased, and she, like the paintings she made, had become a lie. Maxym Liski, the man who had played her father for the benefit of the curious Americans in Logan's Town, even put on a show of grief, first in my prep room when he first saw her body, and then this morning at her funeral. He cried very convincing tears because to these people their lies were more important than that girl's life."

Vaslov was looking at me, his palm open, pointed up so that the wound he'd burned into himself virtually glowed. In Russian I whispered, "We all know what you did."

And any light of hope in his eyes went out. Dropping his head, he looked down at the floor.

Letting go of his hand, I turned and said, "So . . . that's it. Uri came back to find Erena dead. Though he was angry, he had to deal with the realities of their new situation. So he and Vaslov moved Erena into the pantry and closed the door. . . ."

"How do you know that?" Sheriff Paulson cut in.

"When I found her body Saturday night she was leaning in the corner of the pantry, with the angle of her limbs fitting perfectly into the space around her. Originally, we all had the unspoken conviction in our minds that it must have been Edward Kane who had killed her . . . and if that was the case, then he must have done it someplace else and returned the body later. Since John Gilbert said that he stayed in the house until morning, and Eddie was seen at my funeral home the following day at eleven, I figured that he must have kept the body somewhere, like the trunk of his Porsche—because of the carpet fibers the forensics guys found on her coat that matched the carpet in his car's trunk—and returned it late the next day.

"The problem is that rigor mortis would have set in by then. A dead body's joints and muscles start stiffening within eight to ten hours after death. If Eddie tried to put her in that pantry the afternoon after she died, she'd have been as stiff as a plank. When I found her Saturday night, even though rigor mortis would have probably been gone by then, since it goes away after about twenty-four hours, there would have been evidence that she had been placed in one position but had settled into another. Her clothes would have been disarrayed, there would have been marks on the wall left as she slid, there would have been something to indicate that she hadn't remained still after death.

"But there wasn't any evidence like that at all in that pantry. As soon as I saw her, I knew that she had been placed there immediately after she was killed, while her body was still warm and pliant. That meant that whoever killed her had to have had unimpeded access to the house. And if we believed John Gilbert when he said that he knew nothing of Erena's murder, and we understand that it was impossible for her to have been placed inside after he arrived, then we're left with the inevitable conclusion that she must have been placed in the pantry before he got to the Lincoln Street house."

"Then you've believed that John Gilbert was innocent all along?" the sheriff asked.

I nodded. "Yes."

"Why?"

"Because he had nothing to gain from murder. He wasn't going anywhere. He had already made a substantial amount of money from Alex Kane's forged-painting scam. His business and his life were all here, and in Logan's Town. And he was making himself available as a witness for the prosecution. If he was involved in any way, that position would have been untenable. He was bound to have been exposed. No, his behavior was too upright, too correct. It was just too accurate in its detail to be a deception. Nobody lies that well, especially when there are other options. . . ."

"Like what?" my brother, Jerry, asked.

"Erena could have disappeared. Why leave her body to be found?" I said.

"That's a good question," Jerry said. "Why would they leave her?"

"Because Uri was scared," I said, looking at the big Russian. "When he drove Eddie to the furniture store garage, he was dealing with one situation. When he got back to the Lincoln Street house, he was dealing with another. Vaslov must have told him what Erena had been saying when she was upset, so he must have assumed that she had told Eddie the same thing. Uri thought his secret was out, so he decided that the only thing he could do was set Edward Kane up for a fall, and get John Gilbert to go along with it. Uri had already convinced Eddie to stick to one version of events, and then he convinced John Gilbert to stick to another. That way, Eddie would be out of the way and unable to act on the information he thought Erena had given him. And John Gilbert would use his good name to keep Uri out of the investigation. Uri still had the last five forged paintings in his possession, don't forget. And they were worth a lot of money. It was vital that Eddie be discredited, so that the information Uri thought Erena had revealed would be discredited as well."

"And what is this information?" Uri asked contemptuously.

"What Erena actually told Eddie," I said, keeping my gaze fixed on Uri, "is that she knew that the paintings Alex Kane was burning were not the originals like he said they were, but phonies, like he was selling for big money. That was earth-shattering news to Eddie, enough to make him take extreme action.

"But what she didn't tell Eddie was the one thing Uri feared she would say the most. And that was the fact of *how* she knew Alex Kane was pulling a fast one. If she'd have revealed that secret to Eddie, he wouldn't have gotten upset when I broke the icon just now. Would he, Uri?"

Uri didn't respond. There was sweat on his forehead, and his lips had gone a little pale.

"Have you figured it out yet, Eddie?" I asked, glancing over at the young man and finding that he, too, was looking at Uri Chevinski.

"No?" I added. "Okay. Then here it is:

"Erena Batilovna knew that Alex Kane wasn't burning original masterpieces because she knew that there weren't any original masterpieces to burn. She'd painted them all. Every goddamn one of them. In Europe, before they ever even came to this country, she had painted four pictures, probably copying them out of a book called, *Stolen by War: Art's Greatest Loss*, a copy of which I found in Alex Kane's desk drawer when I was searching it after he died. That's why her copies were so perfect: she could reproduce the masterpieces that Uri was able to 'smuggle' in because she was copying her own work. The originals were hidden in some politburo member's basement somewhere in Russia anyway, and the chances that they would ever be found were practically nil.

"When I first met him, Uri tried to distance himself from Alex Kane by telling me that Kane hadn't bought any smuggled material from him in almost two years. When I asked him how anyone could ever trust a man like him enough to buy anything he had to offer, he said something that has stuck in my mind ever since.

"What he said was that before a person can tell a lie, it's important to first come up with a lie that the person hearing it *wants* to believe.

"Uri could tell Alex Kane anything he wanted, and Alex Kane, with his eyes full of dollar signs, would believe it because he *wanted to*! So would the 'secret' collectors buying the stuff. They'd believe they were getting something wonderful and unique, because that's exactly what they wanted to believe. What kind of experts could these people be, anyway? What kind of collector buys something he knows is stolen and that he knows he can never even admit that he has? How would he ever realize a profit? What if they were ever stolen again? They couldn't even be insured.

"So there were never any masterpieces to start with," I concluded. "This whole thing has been a lie, in a lie, in a lie. And both Alex Kane and Erena Batilovna paid for that lie with their lives."

The shriek that filled the vault then startled me. I had expected some reaction, but not the one I got.

It was Edward Kane who was screaming. The sound that came out of him was like a siren, or the shrill, hideous wail of a bird of prey as it dives in for the kill. It was an agonized, brutal, hopeless kind of sound that welled up from inside him and tore through the room, cutting into my heart like a knife. His face was perfectly white. His eyes were big black holes. His mouth was a round, dark nothing, spilling his frustration out in a single, sinuous note. We all looked at him, shocked for an instant. And then he moved.

It was a lunge of total abandon. He didn't care who saw him do what he did. He didn't care what the consequences of his actions were. He wasn't thinking anymore. He was seeing, I knew, all the things he had expected to gain, all the profit, all the wealth, all the independence and freedom and power he had felt so certain were his, slip and fall, shattering on the hard floor of reality in a single, smashing stroke.

The pictures weren't worth a dime.

His father was dead.

His future was shot.

He went for Uri like an animal. But there were policemen all over the room, and they were a lot bigger than him. He was just a waifish, lightly boned, little rich kid, and they were tough, hard-nosed guys who had never had his advantages. Eddie made it about four steps before he ran into one of those cops. And in about ten seconds more, he was in the grip of three of them. He was screaming, and crying, and struggling, throwing spit and tears and curses in a stream around him that, remarkably, everyone in the place seemed to ignore. There was a feeling in the room like something had ended, and glancing around, I realized that something had. The dream was over. The lie exposed. All that remained was to finish it. And I did, as quickly as I could.

"Sheriff Paulson," I said, "Vaslov Liski and Uri Chevinski moved Erena's body into the house as soon as Uri got back from dropping off Eddie's Porsche and getting him a van to take back home to Cleveland. The reason your forensics people haven't found any trace of the girl in the van Eddie drove is because she was never in it. The van in which she was killed is the one that Uri's been driving since the night of the murder.

"John Gilbert didn't spend the night in the Lincoln Street house," I added, stepping over to my wife and taking her hand. Edward Kane had stopped struggling and was watching me with tears and snot smeared on his face. "He came when Uri called him, too late to see Alex Kane removed from the accident scene. So he went to the Wittmere County Hospital at two in the morning to make sure that his partner was truly dead. And then he went home. The only thing he can be charged with is lying to you about the Porsche not starting. I guess you could call that attempted murder, since it would have been his testimony that would have convicted Eddie, if his case had ever come to trial.

"But that's all you can charge him with. You can't even say that he was selling stolen property, since the paintings he and his partner, Alex Kane, were selling, weren't stolen. They were junk. It's no crime to get a good price for what you sell. The buyer has to beware. Especially in the antiques business. Plus, I wouldn't expect that you'd be able to find anyone willing to come forward and press charges anyway. He's clean.

"And so is Eddie, except for leaving the scene of an accident."

"Then why did he make the tape?" Sheriff Paulson asked. "If he wasn't involved in anything, why'd he come to you with that tape of his father?"

"Ahh," I said, turning and looking at Eddie one last time. "The tape. That tape was worth about seventy million bucks to our boy. When he got back from Logan's Town it was late . . . or early, depending on how you look at it. He had left a little after midnight, and he didn't get to my funeral home until almost eleven in the morning. That's a long time to be alone in an apartment, thinking.

"His father was dead," I pointed out. "He knew that much. He didn't know that Erena was dead as well. He only knew about his dead father, and what Erena had told him about what his father had been doing to keep a hold of the original masterpieces he had said he had been burning all along. So he's sitting there, alone, with that tape of his father talking to his lawyer about ending his present life and starting over somewhere else.

"And that's when the idea hit him.

"I can almost see him, sitting there, looking at that tape and knowing that there were millions of dollars worth of pictures hidden in his mother's house. All the secrecy and sneaking around associated with Erena and the Russians was pointless now. All that mattered was the vault.

"And then he thought of me. He knew his mother had come to me to handle the funeral because she had left him a message on his answering machine to meet her at my funeral home later in the morning. Eddie had read about me in the newspaper. I'm a snoop, remember. An amateur detective, according to all accounts. If he could entice me into working for him, all I'd have to do is expose the picture-forging plan . . . which, if I was too stupid to handle on my own, he could always make sure I did by dropping me the right clues along the way. Everybody involved would take the fall, except him. All he was, was a boyfriend. He could even deny knowing what was going on, if it ever came to that. His father's scheme would be exposed in the press, Uri and the Russians would be deported, John Gilbert would go to jail, and he would be left with his father's amazing collection . . . all safe and sound at home.

"So he edited the end off the tape he had on his home stereo system, making it sound like a rather vague suicide threat, and then he manipulated me into sticking my nose in the business. If he'd known that the pictures were really worthless, he wouldn't have done it. But he was already rich in his mind. When they arrested him for Erena's murder, it was all the better. I was already working the case, and he was innocent. The more publicity everything got, the more he liked it. He, like his father's secret paintings, was sitting safe and secure, and it was all only a matter of time until he was free . . . really free, financially, forever."

"I should never have hired you," Eddie hissed, looking at me as if he were wishing he could tear out my eyes.

I looked back at him, sighed, and said, "You didn't hire me, Eddie. I never formally took on your case. Your mother hired me to prove that you hadn't killed your father, or Erena Batilovna. And that's exactly what I did. As far as I'm concerned, my job's done. The rest is up to Sheriff Paulson."

With that, I put my arm gently around my wife's shoulder and we left the vault. There were a number of voices behind me, trying to call me back, but I ignored them. I was tired. And I didn't have anything more to say. . . .

Until I got home.

Upstairs in our apartment's living room, I picked up the phone and made a quick call. Aggie O'Toole answered on the second ring.

"Hi, Aggie," I said. "Bill Hawley. Remember my promise about filling you in on the details of my case? Well, have you got a pencil?"

Nat was looking at me with a furrowed brow as I spoke. I smiled at her reassuringly.

"Ready, Aggie?" I said when Aggie announced that she was set. "Well then, here's your story. . . ."

EPILOGUE

■■■■■■■■■■■■■■■

THE PLAIN DEALER ran Agatha O'Toole's account of what they called the "Kane affair" under the banner, "Funeral Director Cracks Case." Nat read it aloud to me the next morning, sitting in an aqua-blue easy chair I've got next to my desk in the office with Quincy on her lap. Looking up when she'd finished, she said, "It's got everything in it. Every detail. You really gave her a scoop."

I nodded, adjusting my tie in the mirror over the coffee bar and combing my hair. "Yup," I said. "That I did."

"How did you know that none of the paintings were real?" she asked, laying the paper down on the desk.

"Uri never would have let Kane burn them if they were," I replied. "Why should he? It sounds like a great idea on the surface, but just think about actually putting a match to something that's worth a million dollars. I don't think I could do it, no matter what I was up to. And I'm sure Uri couldn't. He was too much of a wheeler-dealer. It just didn't make sense."

"And what about the carpet fibers from Edward Kane's Porsche that were found on Erena's coat?"

"Uri sprinkled them there because he knew it's one of the first things the police would look for. After all, he had his investments to protect."

"What investments?"

"He owned the apartment building where he lived and three more on the block."

"And why was Alexander Kane going out to Logan's Town that night?"

"That," I said, kissing her on the forehead, "I don't know. And, in the end, I don't think I even care. See you when I get back from the bank."

The air that morning was cool, but the sun was warm, so I dropped the top on the Miata and took the long way down, driving slowly and enjoying the ride. I was on the way to cash the check Sheriff Paulson had given me to pay off our bet. "A bet's a bet," he'd said. And I agreed.

The skin sample taken from the rope used to strangle Erena Batilovna—which is how I still think of her since we'll probably never know her real name—matched Vaslov Liski's blood type. And he, and his father, are facing all sorts of charges . . . including murder. Uri's in deep shit, too, for his part in trying to pin the girl's death on Edward Kane. Leopold Chimmings, Alexander Kane's lawyer, and Mrs. Kane have come to a mutually acceptable understanding, which isn't hard to believe since Chimmings is the one who knows where Alex Kane hid all his money in preparation for his impending divorce. Although I don't know the details of their agreement, Mrs. Kane's word as to its equitability is good enough for me. Aggie O'Toole loves me now. And in Cleveland, at least for the time being, I'm big news. A household word.

Edward Kane hasn't spoken so much as a single word to me since that afternoon in his mother's house. I think to him I represent the loss of seventy million bucks. He doesn't seem to realize that I saved his ass. But he's young. I figure that by the time he's thirty or so he'll understand just how lucky he was. Until then, I'll probably remain an asshole in his eyes. So fuck him.

In my suit coat pocket I was carrying a letter I had received by overnight mail from the Ohio Organization of Funeral Professionals. They want me to report to Columbus, our state's capital, next week for a hearing on the status of my funeral director's license. I've decided to fight it, though I don't know what good it'll do. With my license on the line, I've really got my back to the wall. We'll just have to wait and see what happens. As far as I can tell, I may be looking for another job soon . . . and maybe that would be just as well.

The telephone call I was expecting came within fifteen minutes of my arrival back at the funeral home. Nat was upstairs in the hot tub, soaking her bruises, and waiting for me to come up and rub her back. I was just hanging up my jacket when the phone rang, and I answered it to hear a very upset John Gilbert shout, "Hawley, you son of a bitch! This is like a death warrant! Do you understand what you've done to me? You might as well have taken a gun and put a bullet in my head! Do you understand what you did?"

"Yes, Mr. Gilbert," I replied, and hung up before he could continue.

I knew exactly what he was talking about: it was the article in the *Plain Dealer*. I know who the people he sold those forged pictures to are. Maybe not by name, but I'm sure I know the type, and they won't appreciate finding out how they were deceived. John Gilbert's name is sure to get back to them, especially since I made sure that Aggie O'Toole described the phony picture scam in detail. Somewhere in this country there are a bunch of pissed-off big shots with connections. Somebody will be looking for Mr. Gilbert, and it won't take long before they find him. Even if Sheriff Paulson decides not to charge him with anything, his life isn't worth a plugged nickel . . . and it's all my fault.

Good.

It serves him right, because I know damn well that Richard Hickle didn't take it into his head to hurt my wife on his own. Someone sent him. He specifically said, "I'm supposed to hurt ya, lady." It was his job. I know that Deputy King told John Gilbert that Nat and I had come to Logan's Town that morning asking questions. And with Uri back in Cleveland, it had to have been Gilbert, that dirty bastard, who sent Hickle to warn me away. But instead of going after me, he went after a woman and a man in a wheelchair. Larry Fizner might have taken care of Hickle, but I took care of Gilbert.

The phone started ringing again as soon as I hung up, and I let it. Calling into Jerry's apartment, I told him that I'd be busy for the next couple of hours, and he shouted back, "Okay. I'll keep an eye on things."

"Yeah." I smiled, closing the door. "I know you will."

With the memory in my mind of him lying on the floor next to his overturned wheelchair, one arm protectively over Nat's shoulder, I nodded, realizing that the three of us, Nat, Jerry, and I, are now, and forever, a team. Come what may with the review board in Columbus, or with the business taking hold in a new town, or the article establishing me as a local celebrity, I know now that for as long as the three of us stick together, we'll always be all right.

Then I went upstairs and washed my wife's hair.